THE MENAGERIE

DOCTOR WHO – THE MISSING ADVENTURES

Also available:

GOTH OPERA by Paul Cornell

EVOLUTION by John Peel

VENUSIAN LULLABY by Paul Leonard

THE CRYSTAL BUCEPHALUS by Craig Hinton

STATE OF CHANGE by Christopher Bulis

THE ROMANCE OF CRIME by Gareth Roberts

THE GHOSTS OF N-SPACE by Barry Letts

TIME OF YOUR LIFE by Steve Lyons

DANCING THE CODE by Paul Leonard

THE MENAGERIE

Martin Day

First published in Great Britain in 1995 by
Doctor Who Books
an imprint of Virgin Publishing Ltd
332 Ladbroke Grove
London W10 5AH

ISBN 0 426 20449 2

Cover illustration by Paul Campbell

Typeset by Galleon Typesetting, Ipswich
Printed and bound in Great Britain by
Cox & Wyman Ltd, Reading, Berks

In memory of Brian Hayles (reading *The Ice Warriors* during a wet holiday in Wales got me into all this) and Ian Marter (for postcards from around the world). Thanks to Steve Bowkett and Eric Pringle, for encouragement; to my agent, John McLaughlin, for help beyond the call of duty; and to all those who commented on the text, especially Ian Abrahams, Ian Atkins and my partners-in-crime Paul Cornell and Keith Topping. A final acknowledgement is due to Umberto Eco, for names (*Foucault's Pendulum*, p. 539) and inspiration. Did we make it? Good night.

Dedicated, at last, to Helen.

Prologue

When Jenn Alforge was young she had built elaborate mazes for a group of white mice. Her father had given her the creatures, but they were gifts given in embarrassment rather than pleasure. It wasn't difficult to see why.

The mice had been genetically manipulated as part of a programme to develop antibodies to the second great space plague. These specimens were on the verge of viability: one had only three legs, another a tail that ended with three blunt prongs.

But they were hers. Jenn treasured them with an ignorance of disability that transcended normal human responses. The mazes that she diligently constructed from spare sheets of plastiglass were very different from the cruel experimental machinery of her father. The mice enjoy running down these corridors looking for cheese, she remembered thinking, as much as I enjoy building the mazes.

Her little subjects became more and more astute, getting to know the various doors and short-cuts, rejoicing in the rule of a benign, thoughtful monarch. She had looked down on the mazes like a child-god.

She was older now, and the nature of the maze she observed brought disregarded tears to the edges of her eyes.

In front of Jenn there were a number of projectors, throwing up 3D presentations in garish, flickering colours. Taken together they showed a computer-generated cityscape reduced to a table-sized maze, populated by toy soldiers.

She passed her hands over a number of sensors, and the scale changed. The toys expanded in size and became men – only their unblinking stares reminded her that they were androids – and the walls almost seemed real. But the accuracy of the cityscaping was not the point of the exercise, and neither was the technical sophistication of the androids.

'I'm recording now,' she announced into a small communications device. 'Release the creatures at will.'

Despite the guns they carried, despite their gigabytes of military training, the android troopers were mere mice in a maze. And now their pursuers were being set free, released into random areas of the synthetic city.

Jenn soon saw the true objects of her study in action. A soldier was patrolling a gunmetal-grey corridor, his features rigidly impassive. He rounded a corner and came face to face with a creature. Instantly he released three rounds at point-blank range and – the animal's arms powered forward – reached with his free hand for his comm unit. His hands found space where his right shoulder and upper chest should have been.

The bloodless arm clattered to the floor, spasmodic mechanics flexing the hand and drumming against the grip of the rifle.

The android pitched forwards, the pink lips babbling with grotesque disinterest. 'Human death would have occurred approximately two seconds ago as a result of massive haemorrhage to the shoulder and –'

'Save the reports for later,' snapped Jenn. 'Increase realism for all other androids to maximum: turn off automatic cauterisation, take emotional simulation up to maximum.'

The sound of laser fire soon brought others running. With the enhanced programming the men and women looked tense. Beads of desalinated sweat clung to their brows.

The creature seemed to have vanished. The 'dead' android was motionless.

'Can't have gone far,' said the leader of the group, looking about him. 'We've not been passed, and with this length of corridor . . .' He trailed off, and looked upwards, gun raised at the tall roof.

There were only shadows.

'Thank God for that,' he muttered. 'I thought that –'

A man at the end of the group exploded in a shower of red. A creature, cool and dripping, stood in his place.

A volley of blaster fire ripped into the monster, but not before it had effortlessly torn two women to pieces, their choking screams swamped by the noise of the guns.

The leader raised his weapon, but he was furthest from the monster and unable to fire without risking hitting the other troopers.

He had a few seconds to admire the creature. Although humanoid, four massive arms extended from its shoulders and chest, the lower two bent back on themselves like the claws of a mantis. Its entire body appeared to lack a covering of skin, strong silver muscle and sinew rippling as it moved. Genetically bred to prioritize its own survival above all other considerations, it wasted no time bellowing at the pain it felt as one arm was torn from its body by the laser fire. It ran forward on triple-jointed legs. The leader noticed for the first time a rough hole in the floor near the ruptured feet of the second dead man, and a similar half-concealed hole near the corner. The creature had tunnelled under the floor, and simply forced its way up again, through the soldier that stood there.

The creature reached out for a trooper with an arm as powerful as an industrial piston. Its clawed hand plunged into the chest of the soldier, moving effortlessly through the synthetic tissue. The claws withdrew and the man fell silently to the floor. The other arms lunged forwards. A trooper threw herself towards the ground and away from the outstretched talons.

There was a gap now, through which the leader could aim. Instantly he added his fire to that of his companions, and the stench of burning meat filled his nostrils. The creature was collapsing at last, its huge claws flailing blindly. One trooper got too close to the animal's death throes and lost most of his lower leg.

Soon all that remained of their attacker was a single grey leg and part of an arm, blackened and twisted. Traces of the lower face could be seen, awash with blood that was not its own.

The leader tapped his comm unit as the remaining soldiers fanned out from the broiling haze surrounding the corpse. 'Trooper twelve to Centre. One test subject destroyed. Four troopers lost, one severely injured and unlikely to survive.' The man nearest to the burning creature was whinnying deep down in his throat, holding on to what was left of his leg.

'You'll never play the piano again,' said a woman, looking down at the injured man callously.

'They were less impressive in a city scenario,' reported Jenn soullessly, pausing the 3D replay. 'As you saw there, the creatures tried to use their normal tactics when attacking multiple targets – tunnelling, stealth, and so on – but were impaired by the non-organic nature of the location.'

'And the kill ratio?' queried one of the men towards the end of the darkened table.

Jenn consulted the tabular information on a recessed screen in front of her. 'Just over six point five to one.'

'Again,' came another voice, 'you have to remember that the test involved unarmed creatures taking on combat-ready troops. A civilian ratio would be much higher.'

'Those creatures would simply tear the non-military population of a city apart,' said Jenn.

There was a pause, and eyes began to turn to the large man at the far end of the table. His fingers drummed slowly against each other for a few moments as he stared at the final freeze-frame, deep in thought. Then he smiled.

'A most exciting presentation, Dr Alforge,' he announced. 'Quite the most chilling thing I've seen in a long while. I think my colleagues and I will be able to draft an encouraging report.' He took a few sips from a small tumbler of water. 'Yes, I do believe that Project Mecrim could have a crucial effect on the war. Do my learned colleagues agree?' His eyes scanned the lower end of the table in a way which hinted that he expected no dissension.

'Thank you for visiting our establishment,' said Jenn, trying to avoid the man's eyes. 'We are pleased to know that you esteem our work so highly.'

The man's eyes twinkled as he rose, but he said nothing more. The observers and scientists slowly filed out, leaving Jenn alone. She tried to imagine the monsters let loose in cities swarming with Draconian women and children, but could only see the Head Observer's gloating face as he watched the half-real carnage.

Jenn ran to a hand basin, wanting to be sick, but nothing came.

– she was running through a cardboard tunnel something was so close behind her she couldn't turn around to see just felt its breath on her neck and the sound of its feet something huge she was crying out suspecting something deep within but unable to break through just kept running dead end suddenly huge glaring eyes eyes that accused her shocked her to her very core something someone she once recognized but no longer knew betrayed betrayed betrayed –

The comm unit buzzed again. Jenn groaned. Her fingers skimmed the control as she fell back into the bed. It was only –

'Half five, yeah, I know,' said the voice, anticipating her thoughts as usual.

The dream had faded sufficiently for Jenn to realize that there was tension in the voice. She reached for the first nicotinesub of the day. 'What's the matter, Nik?'

'Routine testing has turned up something non-routine. I think that you should come down.'

'Okay.' She switched the unit off without asking whether Nik had been working late or had started early.

She hoped that the shower would settle her but, as she stood under the stream of water, she became more and more aware of a pain in her lower stomach. It felt different from the nervous tension that had surged through her body over the last couple of days as she had waited for the arrival of the observers. She tried to massage the ache away but it didn't budge.

It would have to wait. She reached for another nicotinesub as she pulled on her clothes, still puzzling over the pain. Maybe she'd be the first woman to discover that 'sub was carcinogenic, too. That really would be a terrible way to start the week.

Confidential Memorandum

From:	Dr J. Alforge Pr. Mecrim	**To:**	C. Y. Dugied Control 429
Date:	2417,0706,22:30 (WST)		
Subject:	Mecrim gut microbe 23D (see memos 0405, 2805, 0406)		

Ciaran –

Must insist that your reply 0606 simply isn't good enough. I don't believe that we can wait that long. Nikolas has done some more tests; appended to this memo. I'm sure that you now appreciate the nature of the problem that we face. Two dead already.

I request immediate evacuation.

'We who have no history have made our history a thing of pain. We have always been, and will never cease to be. There is no beginning, no end, just a terrible, cyclical now.

'Yet, for the purposes of writing, it is helpful to analyse the slight changes, the slight shifts in the now *that gives us our life – our* sense *of life. For, without progress, we are mere animals – but progress, it must be remembered, is a mere fading change in the* now, *not something we make of our own volition.*

'The heretic might say: "Does not the light of the sun and the darkness of its absence enable us to assign names to our lives and to the development of our people?"

'But they do not understand, my children. Each one of us carries with him a sense of awesome wonder, a sense of the long existence of our race – a long existence because of, not in spite of, our absence of progress. How can this be? How can this be when each generation passes on less than nothing to the next?

'Progress is an illusion. We have always been, will always remain here – and our "history" (which might best be defined as our irrational sense of the slight movement within the cyclical now*) is a phantom. A phantom no less real for being exposed.*

'What then shall we say to the heretic? That changelessness is a virtue, an attitude, a moral imperative to be grasped? Of course, but such words cannot convince the evil-thinker. Our words fall down on their heads like rain from the skies but are barely a hindrance. Their souls *must change to find the true* now, *the ongoing is-ness of life that death merely ripples. We must pray that the sinners change, and, if they do not change, we have no option but to encourage them to enter into a new stage of being.*

'This fills them with fear. It is so difficult, my children, to tell them that to truly attain that most beautiful sense of the undeviating constant involves the casting-down of our fear, of our conception of beginning and end, of dawn and dusk.

'Yet it seems self-evident to me that the nature of our life, as I hinted previously, does indeed lead to the illusion of change, of progression. We lack history, and yet we know of the concept of

"history": we lack true change, and yet we acknowledge that it could exist.

'But what could exist is mere fancy in the face of our undying nature. The heretics have their ideas, and try to read them into the world. Much better to do as generations have done, as generations will do, as generations are now still doing, and look first to the constant, the immutable. To do otherwise is to talk to a mirror or gesture to a blind man – the ultimate in folly.

'We are alone. We are all. We have no beginning and no end. We will pass on nothing, and will inherit nothing.

'These words write themselves: I commit them not to any sense of time (thankfulness to the "past" or a legacy to the "future") but to now. *These words have always been written, and they were never even dreamt of – never, even in our most diffuse dreams of change.'*

> Extract from the introduction to *Systematic Approaches to the Thoughts of the Kuabris*, written by Grand Knight Magisuan. Subsequently banned and destroyed by order of Grand Knight Uscolda.

One

Over the years the city had developed in a rain-soaked valley, banked with fog. Even on those days when the clouds receded the damp buildings and blunt green spires looked like an ancient conurbation discovered beneath the lapping waves of a great ocean.

The smaller buildings shrank back from the strident winds and thunderous rain clouds. The narrow passages between the overhanging houses were flickering with activity, as men and women pulled on furs and woollen garments and went about their business. They no longer noticed the constant background patter of the drizzle, but, heads bowed, shoved their feet forwards through the grime and sodden refuse that sat in putrid layers over the cobbled streets. Their downcast eyes avoided the watching black castle, the largest of the handful of buildings tall enough to split the low-lying fog. Three large towers were set into the broken rocks of one hillside, surrounded by bulbous turrets and buildings and a double skin of thick concrete walling. Occasional windows glowed through the myopic fog.

The other massive building was known as the Furnace. It was some distance away from the castle and seemed to avert its face from the fortress, retreating into the dark hillside as if too heavy and bloated with water to support itself. It was a squat edifice of dull brown brick topped with blackened chimneys, from which flowed a constant breathing cloud of steam that merged with the fog, occasionally giving it a poisonous tang. Groups of black-coated men wearing simple cotton masks walked the area, leading huge horses tugging at sledges containing wood and coal. Inside the main building cavernous furnaces were fed, flames occasionally leaping out of the boilers with a spit of soot and flame. Steam hissed and escaped as huge turbines moved in groaning agony, smaller pistons pounding with fragmentary bursts of power.

In the city itself even the shuddering percussion of the engines was lost to the constant wash of the rain.

Defrabax emerged from his darkened house, extinguishing a candle in the window, and cursed the incessant downpour. Squashing a floppy hat over his thinning grey hair, he stared at the twin extremes of the city – the Furnace to his left and the castle to his right – and seemed to snarl at them both, before setting his course and moving out into the streets.

The houses he passed were clumsy wooden constructions, leaning at crazy angles and seemingly close to collapse. The last great storm had thrown odd tiles down into the street; young boys had combed the refuse, and were already attempting to sell them back to the populace.

'Lovely roofin' slates, perfect for your storm-damaged 'ome.' A group sat in the gutter, laughing and joking with the passers-by. One lad ran in front of Defrabax, carrying an example of his wares, his face full of desperate pleading. Defrabax stopped, his eyes gripping the boy as surely as a strong pair of hands.

'Do you not know who I am, lad?' The man's voice was like the whisper of ancient pages turned by an inquisitive hand.

The boy began to shiver, but was just able to force a shrugging signal of ignorance. His friends looked on in silence.

'I thought not. If you knew who I was you would not dare to trouble me with such pilfered garbage!' His left hand passed twice below his gnarled chin, fingers flexing in arcane gestures, and then both hands came together, squeezing gently.

The boy, freed from his terrible paralysis, ran into the shadows, choking and unable to scream. The slate dropped just in front of Defrabax's boots, and shattered into a hundred pointed shards of grey. The other boys ran silently from the roadside, taking the piles of slate with them.

'Superstitious apes,' breathed Defrabax.

Moments later he passed an infamous local inn, and seemed drawn to its bright windows. Square bulbs of light hung from the ceiling, spinning gently. He peered in, and saw rows of tables and bottles of drink. The room was crowded, oaths and arguments providing the unintelligible lyrics to the surging apocalyptic tune played by the man in the corner. The musician was oblivious to what was going on around him, his sightless eyes staring through men in earnest conversation who drank and threw knuckle bones. The state of the musician's soul was communicated only through the dexterity of his fingers as he played the instrument in his lap, holding down strings, creating strident chords from a looping bass rhythm, then collapsing into stuttering, chasing individual notes of sadness.

A puzzled look crossed the blind man's face – one sometimes didn't need eyes to see Defrabax – and the old man moved on, past the beggar with one leg and the sleeping drunk slumped against each other in the doorway.

Defrabax smiled as he spied a group of women standing at the corner. They immediately covered their immodest red dresses with shawls as they saw him approach, and shrank from his path.

Defrabax doffed his hat to them. 'I could have use for you all on a night like this, but I'm afraid I have business to attend to. Some other night, perhaps?'

'Clear off!' shouted one woman, a doll-like white mask cracking into a grimace. 'We'd trust you this far,' she said, spitting towards his feet.

Defrabax replaced his hat. 'Times must be good for you, ladies. When I was young, whores were not so choosy.' He turned his eyes from them, and continued his walk towards the castle.

Cosmae pushed open the keyhole-shaped door and pressed a crude switch. The room was instantly bathed with a yellowish glow, and his companion gasped in surprise.

'Come in,' said Cosmae proudly.

The girl followed him with some degree of hesitancy. Only when she was safely within the main room of the shabby little house did she liberate her long brown hair from the rough confines of the grey hood. She looked around. 'Electrical lighting . . .' she said in wonder.

'Only in this room,' admitted Cosmae. 'And only for special occasions, or when my master wishes to read late into the night.'

'Your master is richer than any mystic I have known,' commented the girl.

'Well, he is cleverer than the others, that I'll grant you.' A broad, uninhibited smile broke across the young man's features. 'I might never be as wise as my master, but I am twice as devious.'

'And you are sure he will not return for some time?'

Cosmae pulled curtains across the room's few windows. 'Have you ever heard of the Knights of Kuabris dismissing someone in minutes?'

The girl shivered. 'He has been summoned to the knights?'

Cosmae nodded, feigning nonchalance. 'So he said.'

'Then he might not return at all,' stated the girl slowly.

'Well, that'll give us more time together, eh?' The boy's eyes glistened.

The girl, still clinging tightly to her hooded robe, strode up and down the room, inspecting its contents slowly. The bowed walls were dotted with cheaply-framed etchings and esoteric charts. She saw that some were of the pathways of the celestial bodies, and some seemed to detail the inner workings of creatures. What furniture there was – a thin table, ample chairs of frayed leather, a couple of footstools – was covered with dirty plates, strange objects and sheaves of old paper.

The pale light in the ceiling coloured everything with a gentle, hazy luminescence. A moth circled the lamp at dizzying speed. A strange smell hung in the air. It reminded her of the smell of the men that came to take her father's corpse away. It was a falsely-clean smell, a pungent attempt to cover something up.

She tried to suppress another shiver as she turned back to the young man. She'd learnt long ago not to let anything bother her.

'I'm glad you sought me again,' she said. Her full lips glistened in the dappled light, and Cosmae's gaze was drawn to them like a doomed insect.

'I'm pleased you remembered me,' he heard himself saying as if from afar.

'You're gentle,' said the girl simply. 'I always remember that in a man.'

Cosmae sank into one of the grandly-comfortable chairs, still watching the woman closely. 'I've not been able to get you out of my mind,' he suddenly blurted out.

The girl, staring at a complex diagram of interlaced lines and irregular boxes, snorted in derision, but then caught a glimpse of the boy's pale, intense face and regretted her scorn. She stared down at the table while she spoke. ' 'Twould be better for you to forget. And there are plenty more like me. My sister fared no better after my father's death.'

'I haven't been with anyone since my first night with you.'

The girl blinked, and a forced rigidity bound her face. 'Scant money?' she asked as cruelly as she could.

'No!' exclaimed Cosmae angrily. 'I've been looking for you.'

'I've been busy,' she said, turning the pages of a small book.

'I want to –'

She turned round and fixed his flushed face with a resolute stare. 'Listen to me,' she said firmly. 'Just for a moment. I do not care what you think of me. You have some money, and I need it. That's all I want from you.'

The young man looked so crestfallen that for a moment she thought she had been too harsh. As he stared at his feet he reminded her of a schoolboy on the verge of tears.

He sniffed and returned her gaze. 'I'll pay you. Whatever you want. Just get this disease out of my head.'

'I cannot promise that.' Her voice carried a hint of genuine regret.

'I know,' said Cosmae. He reached into his tunic, pulled out a bag, and shook a couple of coins into his hand. He held them out to her as a weak supplication.

The girl smiled sadly. 'Oh,' she said, her voice fragile with regrets and broken promises, 'let's make the best of this light, then.' She let the heavy cloak and the robes underneath drop to the floor.

Defrabax tried to cover his fear by bellowing at the young soldiers who stood to attention in the main gateway. 'I'm here to see Grand Knight Himesor,' he said in a gruff voice. 'I am Defrabax, the great mystic. Let your leader know that I have arrived, and be quick about it. I don't want to stand here in this rain any longer than I have to.'

The soldiers ushered him into a small partly covered courtyard of dark stone while one of their number hurried through the rain towards the main tower. A fitful fire spluttered in the centre of the yard, and around it clustered a number of bedraggled women and children. Their robes were torn masses of wool and frayed leather. The children had no shoes, but continued to play in the puddles with a stunted puppy. The soldiers and the women watched them with hopeless eyes.

A pot of foul-smelling broth simmered over the fire, but it was enough to make Defrabax feel hungry. He massaged his stomach. Surely this wasn't nerves? Defrabax, the great mystic, scared of the knights?

By Ukkazaal, he *was* nervous, but he knew that if he were to succeed he had to continue to play the part of the confident, fearless mage. He stared up at the numerous lit windows of the castle's towers, glimpsing occasional figures moving along the corridors or pacing in the rooms.

A door opened in the base of the main tower, and a knight stood illuminated in its glow. Unlike the soldiers – mere peasants with halberds and axes – the knight looked impressive. The silver armour glinted in the light, a plumed helm carried firmly under one arm. Over the armour and chain mail was a blue silk robe. A long sword hung from the belt. The knight indicated that Defrabax should come across the main courtyard towards him. Defrabax smiled confidently back at the soldiers at the gatehouse, and walked towards the tower.

'I am Commander Zaitabor, assistant to Grand Knight Himesor,' said the knight once Defrabax was within range. 'The Knights of Kuabris have many things to ask you. Please follow me.' The knight turned sharply, and walked stiffly down the long corridor.

Defrabax followed the knight at a slight distance, marvelling at the large glass windows set into the walls and the plush carpet that extended the entire length of the corridor. Ornate stems of brass held electric lights at equal distances along the walls. They almost seemed to dim reverentially as Zaitabor's long azure cloak flicked by them. His leather boots, covered with mail, beat out a steady rhythm as they walked.

They eventually came to a halt outside an imposing wooden door the colour of fresh blood. Zaitabor rapped on the door, and then opened it.

Defrabax peered in at a large, ornate room. The walls were of marble panels set into carved golden frames, the floor of the same polished wood as the door. The roof was a gentle dome, and was painted with stars and moons. A fire crackled in a grate set into one wall.

The room was dominated by a huge table which, at one end, formed a virtual throne of precious stones and polished metals. There sat Grand Knight Himesor, surrounded by documents and a number of advisors bent double with age. Himesor seemed much older than Defrabax had expected, as if the weighty mantle of responsibility that had descended across his shoulders at the inauguration ceremony some years ago had month by month sapped him of life. His face was deeply lined, his hair was greying and receding, but his eyes were intense. They pierced Defrabax the moment he entered, and did not release their grip for quite some time.

'Welcome,' said the Grand Knight at last, rising to his feet. He too wore the full regalia of the knights, his helmet and his sword set to one side of the table. He waved the advisors away impatiently. Zaitabor closed the large door behind them and stood at Himesor's side.

Defrabax nodded curtly, not wanting his words to betray anything.

'Please, come sit at this end of the table.' Himesor indicated some high-backed chairs with the flick of a once-powerful hand. 'Now, let us talk for a little while. I have been told that you are not a man that cares much for social pleasantries,' observed the Grand Knight. 'I can respect that. Let me then come straight to the point: we have a need for your homunculus.'

Defrabax fought to control his surprise. He forced a quizzical look across his features. 'Homunculus, my lord?'

'Indeed. Do not think that the idle chatterings of the directionless scum that live down there in the city do not reach us here.' Himesor wiped his mouth as if the mere mention of the filthy city brought forth an acrid stench. 'Tell us about the homunculus you have created.'

'My lord, I . . . I don't know what you mean.'

'You deny that you have, by your various and diverse magics, called forth such a creature?' Himesor's voice was gentle, the words alone carrying enough threat.

'My lord, I have tried, but the nature of such a process . . .' Defrabax sighed. 'It is beyond even my powers.'

Himesor shuffled a few papers in front of him, averting his eyes for a moment. 'And yet you brag of your creature: when you lower your guard, drink a little too much in a tavern, think that no one of any importance is listening . . . Remember always that our ears are everywhere, beholding the evil and the good.'

'My lord,' said Defrabax, 'I beseech you not to pay too much attention to an old man's foolishness. Please believe me. There is no creature.'

Himesor rubbed his chin in thought for a few moments. 'I have no way – yet – of proving that you lie. But, please, entertain me for just a little longer. If you had a genuine need for such a creature, how would you go about creating it?'

Defrabax smiled confidently. 'I would consult the standard works on the subject. Despite some contradictions, the authorities seem to be united in their belief that the most important factor –'

Himesor coughed impatiently. 'The precise details of your arcane arts are of no interest to me.'

Zaitabor took up the questioning, his voice and unblinking eyes having none of Himesor's mock friendliness. 'You admit, then, a familiarity with these works?'

'Why of course,' said Defrabax. 'Any mage worth their pennies could tell you –'

'But you have made it your *special* interest.'

'No, no, no,' said Defrabax. 'I dabbled in my youth, under the little known mystic Qaxaop, but our greatest moment was the brief reanimation of a brown bug.'

'Then what are you currently working on?' asked Zaitabor.

'The use of pyramidal structures to accelerate the harvest, potions that can mould the memory . . . I do the work that I am asked to and paid for.'

'If we asked you,' said Himesor, 'do you think that you could construct a homunculus?'

Defrabax rubbed his chin. 'I am less than sure. I have never succeeded in the past. I would have to consult the texts and . . . But we're going round in circles.'

'If you were approached to create such a man-creature, or had your own reasons for wanting such a thing to do your bidding,' asked Zaitabor with a smug smile on his face, 'do you feel that science would have something to offer you?' The way Zaitabor spat out the word 'science' hinted at terrible heresies.

'Of course not,' said Defrabax instantly. 'I am quite aware of the evil of science, of the penalties that face the unlicensed scientist, of the majesty of the knight's teachings and –'

'But we feel that the temptation might be there,' said

Himesor gravely. 'If we find any evidence that you have been dabbling where you should not . . . I think you know what will happen.'

'Indeed, my lord,' said Defrabax, fidgeting slightly.

'On the other hand,' continued Himesor, 'if you come to the conclusion that the Knights of Kuabris might have a use for the homunculus, then you will always be guaranteed a sympathetic ear.'

'There is no homunculus,' said Defrabax, almost through gritted teeth.

Himesor laughed. 'Oh yes, I forgot. I was only imagining what might happen, were you to have brought forth such a creature from the ground. Please forgive my rudeness.' His smile animated his face for a moment longer, and then he was cold and hard again. The discussion was over. 'Take him away,' said Himesor brusquely.

This time, as Zaitabor led Defrabax from the room, his metal-gloved fist rested firmly on the old man's shoulder.

Cosmae and the young woman slept in each other's arms, her face resting in the crook of his elbow. The girl's hair flowed in glorious disarray over Cosmae's outstretched arm, catching the light from a single candle that flickered by the bed. Their legs were entwined under a rough woollen sheet. The young man snored gently.

Cosmae's room was small and bare, but had all the intimacy that the main room, with its electric lighting, lacked. Even the young girl, who had trained herself to always look for the potential worst in people, felt content here. Sleep had come to them both easily, adult games giving way to the tiredness of young genderless children.

The girl's eyelids fluttered slightly, her hand half-consciously reaching behind her to rub a purple bruise on her lower back. That had been her reward for the last time she had been taken in: abused, yes, but with not even a penny to show for it. The coins Cosmae had given her were clenched in her other hand.

The dull nagging from the bruise eventually woke her. She turned her head slowly, staring at the ceiling for a few moments, thinking, and then slipped from the bed.

Cosmae muttered something, rolling onto his side. The girl reached across to pull the sheet over his exposed back and buttocks, and then stood up. Time to go.

Seeking her clothes she gingerly made her way towards he stairs. The house was silent, and dark but for the cant illumination from Cosmae's room. Her hands out-tretched, she followed a damp wall until she found the irst wooden stair. It creaked as she stood on it, and in the ilence it was like a crack of thunder.

Better get out before the mage returns.

She walked down the stairs as quickly as she could, her knuckles almost visibly pale as they gripped the rough wooden poles of the makeshift bannister.

She found a candle in the hallway, and lit it carefully. The main room was just before her, but she didn't want o risk the electric light. Her clothes were a puddle of material near the table. She stepped over to them, and pulled a white blouse across her shoulders.

Her attention was distracted by the charts on the walls. n this light it was almost impossible to read the writing, but the pictures were clear enough: a tree with a man's ace, armoured creatures with bulky hands that belched ire, a complex annotated pentangle, a box containing various levers, a troop of huge ape-like animals. She ecognized nothing as her eyes scanned the walls: these lustrations might be of the inhabitants and magics of abulous lands, or were perhaps from only a city or two way, but they were still as distant to the girl as the stars.

As her shadow passed across the table she noticed cube of what looked like glass, threaded through with a string of tight leather, glinting in the wavering

candlelight. She reached for it, and was surprised by it
lightness and its warmth. Whatever it was, it certainl
wasn't glass. Within it were small gems of varyin
colours, linked by lines of burnished gold, that blinked o
and off with a light of their own. She could not imagin
how it had been constructed, and what invocations mus
have been chanted over it to imbue power, but she like
the way that it warmed her cold fingertips. It must be
talisman, and perhaps she should . . .

It was stealing, but it might bring a change in he
fortunes. And the room, like most of the house that sh
had seen, was so untidy that it wouldn't be missed fo
days, until long after she had gone. And Cosmae's maste
could surely make another.

She pulled the loop of leather around her neck, and le
the glassy box hang between her breasts. As she move
the talisman glittered like a jewel, and she felt its powe
spreading through her body.

She pulled on her rough brown skirt, and was jus
tightening her belt when she heard a noise from toward
the back of the house. Instinctively, her hands went to th
knot behind her neck, but it had already become to
tight. Still only half-dressed she ran towards the door, fea
pounding through her body like the great pistons in th
Furnace. She tried pulling the talisman over her head, bu
the string caught in her hair.

There was another noise, and she stopped strugglin
against the glass charm. She walked towards the corrido
tightening her belt. It sounded as though someone ha
come into the house through a back entrance. Her ea
strained to hear the footsteps, but she was only aware of
shuffling sound, like the wind through autumn leaves.
was much too dark in here: far better to confront th
returning mystic in the light. She pulled a thin dagg
from its place on the belt, and held the finger-long silv
spike tightly.

Still attempting to button her blouse over the talisman, she stepped into the corridor.

Facing her was a creature taller and broader than any man. Its dull grey robes seemed to merge straight into its green face and hands. Bright points of orange light stared down at her from either side of a squashed nose. The rest of the face was featureless, lacking ears and hair, a terrible approximation of humanity.

The creature stank of corpses and clay.

The girl screamed.

Two

The Doctor fussed at the console, searching for the switch which raised the shutter from the TARDIS scanner. He wasn't looking at what he was doing, but instead fixed Zoe and Jamie with his most affable, charming gaze. 'After all that to-ing and fro-ing in space,' he said, 'it's time for a little stability.'

'Aye,' said Jamie, 'I'm glad to see the back of the LIZ. I swear I'll never criticize the TARDIS again.'

'I'll remind you of that,' said Zoe.

'I know you can't stand the TARDIS food machine, Jamie, so I thought we'd have a little bite to eat here.' The Doctor scratched his head distantly. 'Wherever here is . . .'

The scanner opened to reveal a drizzling grey landscape of flattened brick buildings. Jamie's face fell, but he said nothing.

Zoe couldn't hide her disappointment. 'What a terrible place,' she announced.

'Oh, I don't know,' said the Doctor. 'There's always something to engage the brain, stimulate the imagination, fan the fires of artistic yearning.'

'It's a bit primitive,' continued Zoe, sniffily.

'That may be true,' said the Doctor, 'but I've always felt that great learning should make us feel privileged rather than smug. Don't you agree?'

'But what can I possibly learn from *that*?' asked Zoe, indicating the windswept scene.

'Tell me, Zoe, what do you know of . . . What was the fellow's name . . .? Hoddrigg . . . Heddreiger . . .'

'Heddeigé?' suggested Zoe helpfully. 'Best known for his anthropological approach to the discrete development of non-contiguous equivalent cultures?'

The Doctor's eyes sparkled. 'Quite right. Oh, Zoe, you would make any tutor proud.'

'I appreciate what you're trying to do, Doctor,' Zoe said, as graciously as she could. 'I'm sure I could learn a lot from that culture. But does it all have to be so *wet?*'

Jamie snorted. 'Looks fine to me. You've never seen the Highlands, have you, Zoe?'

'I must say, I think it looks rather . . .' The Doctor struggled for words.

'Grim? Foreboding? Spectral?' Zoe showed no such hesitation.

'Bracing,' said Jamie firmly.

'Bracing,' agreed the Doctor. 'With a hint of the resilience of the human spirit.'

'So what did this man say?' asked Jamie.

'Refresh my memory, please, Zoe,' said the Doctor.

Zoe smiled confidently. 'Heddeigé postulated that two identical societies would evolve along completely different lines.' She smiled sweetly, and Jamie quickly nodded. 'Specifically, the elements will appear from the same set of possibilities – the deep resource bank – but in different orders, at different times, and the interreaction between these deep possibilities will prompt a whole new continuum of subsets. His theories were a radical expansion of Grotski's second law of cultural retrenchment and . . .'

Jamie sighed with a deep, confident honesty. 'Stop,' he said. 'I think I understood the first bit. All you're saying is that one . . . . clan . . . will be different from a clan on another planet.'

'Or even during a different age or in another region,'

said the Doctor. 'Yes, you're quite right.'

'And this wee man became a professor or something for that?' Jamie looked to the Doctor for encouragement. 'That's nonsense.'

'I agree his basic conclusions are common sense,' expanded the Doctor. 'But a great mind will amplify, clarify, investigate . . .'

'I'm happy with common sense,' stated Jamie firmly.

'Well,' said the Doctor, refusing to let go of the point he was pushing. 'Just think of how it affects common-sense individuals like yourself. Imagine that you had never seen a wheel, but that your father was an engineer specializing in long-distance communication.'

'So?'

'Well, think, Jamie. How would you look at the world?'

Jamie rubbed his chin. 'Well, wheels help you to move around easily. Without them – and maybe without horses – you'd never see beyond your village.'

The Doctor nodded. 'And?'

'I've seen machines that allow you to talk to people hundreds and hundreds of miles away. So . . . You'd see or hear things from the other side of the world, but maybe you'd never go to the town further down the valley.'

'Well done, Jamie! You – a common-sense individual – would have a whole host of attitudes based on a knowledge of far-off places, but no *practical* experience of the way of life mere miles away.'

'But could that happen?' asked Jamie. 'To have such talking-devices without something as simple as a wheel?'

'Well,' said Zoe, 'the Aztecs were a tremendously advanced culture, but they never perfected the wheel.'

'A good example,' said the Doctor. 'But that's just head-knowledge.' He smiled again. 'I feel a certain affinity towards common-sense people like Jamie. So . . .'

He operated the door control. 'Let's go and see for ourselves.

Grand Knight Himesor massaged his greying temples. 'Do you believe that wizard?' he asked in a quiet voice.

'Grand Knight,' said Zaitabor, standing to attention at his side, 'the man is lying. I could see it in his eyes, in the nervousness of his fingers. He does have a homunculus.'

'I agree,' said Himesor, reaching for a bundle of documents from the table in front of him. His fingers toyed with the thick ribbon before finally releasing the knot. Folded sheets of parchment spilled down onto the table in disarray. Commander Zaitabor noticed a number of seals of blue wax, the personal stamp of the Grand Knights. 'The obvious course of action is to observe Defrabax's house.'

'I'll assign Araboam to it straight away.'

'Araboam?'

'One of my youngest knights. A subtle character. He is outstripping many of his peers in terms of learning, spirituality, temperament.'

'I leave the details to you,' nodded Himesor, crushing a seal between his gauntlet-clad hands. 'I believe that the foolish Captain Oiquaquil has sought an audience with me?'

'More civilian complaints no doubt. A tedious man. I sometimes doubt his commitment to the Knights of Kuabris.'

'Deal with him as before.'

'My Lord.' Zaitabor bowed, and then marched from the room.

Himesor read the letter once he was alone, a dark frown drawn across his features. He closed his eyes for a moment, and then crushed the sheet of paper into a tight ball. He hurled it into the fire, where the dry parchment burnt fiercely.

His fingers, made clumsy by the gauntlets, reached for another letter.

'Cosmae? Cosmae?' Defrabax closed the front door of his home, and peered up the dark stairs. He shrugged off his cloak and hat, and shuffled into the main room, flicking on the electric light. The bulb flashed and then glowed brightly.

The grey creature stood motionless in the room, its orange eyes ranging towards the old man.

'You shouldn't wait for me here,' snapped Defrabax. 'Go to the back room.' The homunculus turned, and walked into the corridor, its arms hanging at its sides. 'You can report then.'

'Understood,' intoned the creature in a flat voice, its slit-like lips barely moving.

'Cosmae!' shouted Defrabax, rooting around with the documents on the main table. 'Where in Ukkazaal's name is that boy?' One of the young apprentice's roles was to keep the old man's home in some semblance of order, but it had soon dawned on Defrabax that Cosmae was even untidier than he was. Still, Cosmae really ought to have made the effort: what else was there to occupy his attention on such a grim evening?

Defrabax's eyes caught sight of an extra element amongst the clutter, lying in the centre of the floor. He walked over to it, and bent down. A cloak, of passable quality, smelling slightly of cheap perfume. Defrabax straightened, tutting under his breath.

Cosmae finally appeared in the doorway, yawning and running a hand through his tousled hair. He had pulled his garments around him very hastily. 'I, uh . . . I . . .'

Defrabax threw the cloak towards the young man, who caught it clumsily. 'Do I pay you so much, Cosmae,' said Defrabax, with mock criticism in his voice, 'that you have enough to spare on the local sluts?'

'She's not a –'

'I assume that your dissipation of desire involved some sort of financial transaction?' interrupted Defrabax, walking towards the young man.

'Well, I –'

'So I obviously *am* paying you too much. Believe it or not, I remember being a young man. But, really, that scant pay of yours should go to the pursuit of the spiritual rather than the carnal. The spiritual is eternal. The carnal is . . . fleeting.'

Cosmae looked a little sheepish.

'Come now, lad,' said Defrabax abruptly, clapping the boy on the shoulder. 'Let's question the homunculus.'

In a single glance Oiquaquil saw that Commander Zaitabor had the arrogant insecurity common in one who has risen quickly through the ranks. Intrinsic to Zaitabor's reputation as a man able to accomplish any task entrusted to him was a grim suspicion of anyone and everything. The people of the city didn't have a word for paranoia, but if they had Zaitabor's mannerisms would have formed part of the definition.

Oiquaquil, the civilian Captain of the City Guard, continued to watch the Commander closely. Zaitabor was like a wild beast made dangerous by its injury and was likely to lash out at anything, if the mood took him, whereas Grand Knight Himesor was sure of himself and confident in the loyalty and ability of the other knights. Oiquaquil had sought an audience with Himesor, but he had ended up in Zaitabor's chamber, reminding himself that he must say what he had planned to say, whether to Himesor or to his brash deputy. The people deserved nothing less.

Zaitabor stood at his desk, rooting through some books and stray parchments on the table with one hand while removing his plumed helm with another. 'Captain

Oiquaquil, Grand Knight Himesor extends his deepest apologies. Certain matters call for his immediate attention. He hopes that I might be able to relay your message to him, and perhaps also that I might be able to allay any of your general concerns.' Zaitabor's voice was crisp with exact recollection, the pitch lowering as he slipped into his own words. 'Now, Captain, what's the problem?'

Oiquaquil took a deep breath, puffing up his little chest beneath the shabby armour. 'I am most grateful for your time, Commander Zaitabor. I wish to talk to you about the attacks from the sewers.'

'One of the areas that Himesor, I can assure you, is looking into as a matter of great priority,' commented Zaitabor.

'I am grateful for the involvement of the knights. My own men are a poorly equipped rabble,' said Oiquaquil, who couldn't help but glance at Zaitabor's engraved breastplate and clean mail tunic. 'It is sometimes all I can do to issue simple commands. Their weapons are poor, their morale low. And these terrible creatures . . .'

Zaitabor sat down and brought his fingertips together in front of his face. 'I have always advocated that the City Guard should be introduced to our techniques of training and discipline.' He extended a broad palm towards the Captain, before bringing his fingers together in a tight fist. 'Give me a boy for a few weeks, and I'll show you the man within.'

'The knights are rightly feared throughout the city.'

'Feared? No, "respected" is surely a better word,' smiled Zaitabor with grey contempt. 'But you did not come here to discuss training.'

'Indeed,' agreed Oiquaquil. 'I would, however, request that the knights aid us wherever possible.'

'Of course,' smiled Zaitabor. 'Although this assumes that the creatures will emerge again.'

'You believe that they will not?' asked Oiquaquil.

'Who can say?' replied Zaitabor. 'But the retribution of the knights will soon be obvious to all.' His voice lowered to a conspiratorial whisper. 'Better, of course, to take our swords to the creatures than stand idly waiting for their next attack. The creatures are dumb brutes, mere vermin. We will obliterate them. We will be held in even greater *respect* than before.'

'The populace believe that these creatures are merely the first that we should expect from the Menagerie of Ukkazaal,' said Oiquaquil in a quavering voice.

'Expect?' asked Zaitabor, his voice becoming harder. 'What do you mean, Captain?'

'The legends . . . The legends are clear.'

'The legends should not concern us. They are a phantom of so-called history. We have no need for legends.'

'But the stories are . . .'

'The stories are not to be trusted! Whatever may have prompted the tales cannot affect us now.'

'But the prophecies clearly state that scientific research shall be punished by the creatures from the Menagerie –'

'You brazen fool!' Zaitabor rose as if to strike Oiquaquil. 'You sound like one of the Brotherhood of Rexulon!'

Oiquaquil's face blanched at the words. 'Commander, I . . . I assure you I have no sympathy for the brothers and their terrible aims. The knights must remain immutable if our city is to survive and –'

'The brotherhood must be rooted out and destroyed,' interjected Zaitabor. 'They have encouraged these macabre tales.'

'Indeed, Commander,' nodded Oiquaquil hastily.

Zaitabor walked to the window, and stared down into the city. From the great Kuabris towers it looked like a smoking refuse heap, damped down by drizzle. Zaitabor pointed across to the buildings and chimneys of the Furnace, the red bricks blackened by soot, the walkways clogged by slag-heaps, tumbling piles of coal and forests of chopped timber. 'The Furnace and the buildings like it in other cities are the only exceptions to our opposition to disgraced, fiendish science. Rest assured that other projects, any unlicensed scientists, all dissent – all will be crushed by the knights.' He turned back to the Captain, and fixed him with a level gaze. 'And remember, too, that the brotherhood, and its sympathizers, will be annihilated. Their wives, their children – they too will be purged.' He smiled. 'There is no other way.'

The Captain rose to his feet, and reached for his cape. 'Please be assured that my men will hunt down the brotherhood, and will continue to seek the faithless scientists.'

'I am grateful for your continued dedication,' smiled Zaitabor. 'Your concerns have been noted. I will inform you when we have made progress against the creatures from the sewers.'

'Thank you, noble Commander. I have taken quite enough of your time. I too have matters to attend to.' Oiquaquil shuffled towards the door, half-bowing before the Commander, who seemed distracted once more.

'Goodbye,' said Zaitabor, staring out of the window once more at the fluttering electric lights.

As Oiquaquil closed the door he heard the Commander spit the words 'Spineless fool' after him. He quickly returned to his untidy consignment of frightened men.

'It's very backward,' said Zoe, pulling a long-sleeved jacket around her shoulders.

'Well, Zoe,' said the Doctor, 'we've been to many advanced worlds recently. Perhaps it's time for a change.'

The TARDIS had come to rest in a tiny alleyway,

almost completely blocking it. The walls of the buildings curved upwards, the upper storeys virtually touching their opposite number, and were composed either of rough wood or crude brown brick. There were windows filled with glass, while others were open to the air, but all were internally obscured by shutters or drab curtains. Jamie peered down at his feet, and noticed with distaste the refuse that obscured the rough cobbled surface.

'This should be a home-from-home for Jamie,' noted Zoe wickedly.

'There's no need to be rude,' said the Doctor. 'Let's take a brisk walk, keeping an eye open for a shop or something to sell us some food. And on the way we can see how Heddeigé's theories work out in reality.'

'It would be nice to meet some normal people,' said Jamie firmly, beginning to walk carefully down the alley. 'Folk that I can talk to. Not scientists and professors from the future.'

'If this were Earth,' said Zoe, 'I'd say the architecture was almost Elizabethan.'

The Doctor nodded. 'Except?'

'The design is a little more advanced. And there seems to be evidence of some sort of concrete.'

'Good,' the Doctor said as they emerged into the street. The rain had ceased for the moment, and occasional street lamps forced spears of light down into the low-lying fog. People hurried by the three time-travellers with scarcely a glance.

'Clothing?' asked the Doctor.

'Primitive,' said Jamie proudly. 'Very primitive.'

'Lighting?'

'These street lights seem to be crude electric units, utilizing some form of inert gas,' pronounced Zoe.

'And the source of this electricity?' asked the Doctor, indicating the furnaces just visible on the edge of the city.

'Well,' said Zoe, following the dark clouds as they

plotted a viscous course across the sky, 'it's certainly not environmentally friendly.'

Araboam watched Defrabax's house from a partly concealed position in a doorway, trying to turn his discomfort and boredom into some sort of spiritual discipline. Commander Zaitabor had issued strict instructions for him to stay out of sight, and to look for a non-human creature leaving or entering the wizard's house. Araboam had no idea what the creature was, or how dangerous it might prove, but he was a novice knight, and he remained absolutely convinced of the strength and invincibility of the way of Kuabris. He followed orders, knowing that it was important for him to impress Commander Zaitabor. He knew that Zaitabor and the Grand Knight were collaborating on some important scheme, a series of plans that affected the safety of the entire city, but the details simply didn't bother Araboam.

Araboam concentrated on watching the house.

All the curtains and shutters were drawn, but the young knight could see that the only illumination came from downstairs and towards the back. It was unlikely that the creature would turn up banging on the front door, so Araboam began to move around to the rear, to see if there was a secondary entrance into the building.

He emerged from the shadows, pulling a long, dark cloak more tightly around him to obscure his bright knight's armour. His feet ground across the street, making a single intrusion into the silence. This was clearly a residential area, and the pavements were deserted. There were very few street lights here, and Araboam was soon back in the darkness, flattened against the rough wall of the house next to Defrabax's. Both houses had simple slit windows on the sides, and the knight, sure that he could not be seen, strode quickly towards the rear of the buildings.

The square area formed between the backs of the houses and a few small shops was piled high with refuse and wooden crates of old fruit. Diminutive scavenging owls picked amongst the rubbish and flapped up the mountains of crude wooden boxes. The smell of rotting vegetables ate into his nostrils, and Araboam coughed into his fist.

There was a back door into Defrabax's house, a small wooden thing held together by strips of bronze. There was also an open window set close to it, and light burned in some back room. Araboam looked about him, and saw no one. He walked quickly towards the window.

There was a scream and the sound of sudden confusion from some distance away. Araboam paused in thought for a moment, but he knew that his allegiance to the people of the city was stronger than his temporary orders from Commander Zaitabor. He ran towards the back of the shop before the noise attracted Defrabax's attention.

The shop was one of a number on a tiny street on the edge of the commercial area. It wasn't difficult to see where the noise was coming from. The metal cover of a drain set towards the centre of the road had been thrown aside, and huge creatures were spilling up from it. They were bipedal apes, larger and much bulkier than most men, and consequently they struggled to pull themselves from the narrow constriction of the sewer tunnels. Their arms were long and strong, and their heads extended straight from their broad shoulders. Their thick fur ran in rough and irregular stripes over their entire bodies, alternating with exposed patches of tough brownish-red skin.

They ran towards the shops and a group of frightened onlookers, chattering and howling like monkeys. Araboam dropped the cloak from his shoulders, and drew his broadsword. He ran forwards, his chain-mail leggings ringing against the moaning shouts of the beasts. A number of scruffy City Guards stood towards the front of the terrified knot of people, but their eyes too were full of fear.

'You men!' shouted Araboam in a voice of confident authority. 'Draw your weapons and repel those creatures!'

The guards – more frightened of the knight striding over to take charge than of the hideous animals – fumbled for their pikes and short swords, and swung them towards the apes. The beasts stopped in their tracks, eyeing the weapons flashing towards them, and bared their long teeth in what could almost have been grins. There was a quick grunt from one of the apes, and they scattered away from the humans, running towards the shops, picking up rocks from the road and hurling them at the buildings. Windows shattered and doors and painted signs were torn away by the apes' great hands.

Araboam ran towards the creature that was closest to him – the ape was looking the other way, concentrating on ripping off the shutters that closed over a butcher's window – and without warning sliced the blade of his sword through the air and into the thick muscle of the beast's neck and shoulder.

The creature cried out and staggered, one hand immediately attempting to staunch the blood from the wound. It turned, and made as if to lunge at Araboam, but its mind, such as it was, visibly struggled against its instincts. Instead of attacking the ape growled and backed away, moving towards the sewers.

Araboam risked a glance across the street, and saw a similar chain of events there. Having caused a little damage to property, the creatures were retreating back towards the drain, some of them even knuckling across the ground at great speed.

A few of the guards were now gaining confidence and, with great affectation, made swings at the brutes, joking with the city folk who were near them. Araboam was sensible enough to realize that he was facing a foe much stronger than himself, and he recognized that the apes were retreating of their own volition. But the guards were ignorant fools, enjoying a brief moment of infamy, trying to impress the women.

Araboam felt a sad contempt for them.

The apes were scuttling back down into the sewers, chattering in what could almost have been delight. Araboam shouted a word of encouragement to the guards as the last of the creatures disappeared below the surface of the road.

Araboam indicated one of the guards. 'You – get these people dispersed.' He pointed to another, fear fixing hold of features that moments before had been chuckling in egotistical abandon. 'You – check on the damage caused, and report back.' The other guards he waved away impatiently.

Araboam knelt down at the drain hole, and stared into the darkness. The noxious fumes were intense, and he almost retched. Hand over mouth and nose, he leant down into the drain, rested his fingers on the top rung of a rusted ladder, but, as he expected, he could go no further.

Eyes fixed on the dark hole, he pushed the metal-latticed cover back into position.

The Doctor returned to the corner table where Zoe and Jamie sat. 'Now then, Jamie,' he beamed, 'I think I've found something to tickle the fancy of a jaded Scot. And some food will follow shortly.'

The Doctor placed three drinks on the table top, and settled down on to a rough wooden stool.

The drinking establishment was very primitive but had a certain charm. The beverages were served by a man and a woman, who shouted orders through a hatch in the wall as in a cheap Terran restaurant. The rest of the floor space was filled with tables and stools, mostly occupied by drinking men. Zoe had received some strange looks when she first walked through the door, but the people had quickly returned to their own conversations.

Electric lights hung from the roof. A wide stairway ran up to an upper walkway studded with doors. There was a steady trickle of men and women into and out of the rooms. As certain men walked up the stairs loud cheers rang out.

'What's that?' asked Jamie, warming his hands over a brazier suspended from the roof.

'Fruit juice,' replied the Doctor. 'Being drunk in charge of a time vessel is a very serious offence. I remember one fellow who went off to celebrate a series of extensive repairs and came back a little the worse for wear. He atomized his TARDIS. Tremendous mess. All because he hadn't brought the mercury links on line.'

Zoe, as ever, didn't know whether to take the Doctor seriously or not. 'I rather fancied having what Jamie's . . .'

The Doctor tutted under his breath. 'You're much too young and much too pretty.'

'How did you pay?' asked Jamie, eyeing the small earthenware tumbler with suspicion. The fluid within smelt like burnt peat.

'Ah,' said the Doctor. 'A little secret. If you really concentrate, you can make someone think that you've paid even when you've not a bean on you. I don't suppose they'll accept the well known trans-galactic cards for another few centuries. You see –'

'You *stole* these drinks?' interrupted Jamie.

'Well, not as such, no,' replied the Doctor quickly. 'It's more, er . . . Well, Jamie, think of it as advance payment. After all, one day I might come back to this world, save them from the Daleks or some other great menace. They'll be only too pleased to thank me then, showering me with gifts, and I'll say, "No, I'm quite content with the drinks that my friends and I had some time ago." In fact, I might have been here already. Perhaps without me this city would have been destroyed by the Quarks or . . .'

'Where *are* we?' asked Zoe, sipping her drink gingerly.

'Ah,' said the Doctor. 'The computer didn't give me a name. Just a number. This planet really isn't very important. Everyone just leaves it alone. The people here are clearly not about to discover space flight, so . . .'

'So, we're going to have a quiet drink, and then go somewhere exciting?' suggested Zoe.

'Sometimes,' said the Doctor, 'I despair of you, Zoe, I really do.'

'That man's looking at me,' said Jamie suddenly, pointing towards someone at an adjoining table.

'Well,' said the Doctor, 'they've ignored us very decently so far.'

'If he's looking for a fight then –'

'Oh Jamie, Jamie, Jamie,' said the Doctor. 'Calm down. Despite my understated and elegant dress sense, even I occasionally draw attention to myself.'

'Speaking of which,' said Zoe, 'I think we're all going to be the subject of some scrutiny.' She pointed towards the door. 'That man wasn't looking at Jamie at all.'

In the main doorway stood a small number of dirty-looking soldiers, dressed in similar rough garb to the city dwellers. They wore sashes as some mark of authority and tiny conical helmets. A selection of swords and converted agricultural implements were clutched in their dark leather gloves.

At their head stood two knights in brightly polished, almost ceremonial armour. Unlike the soldiers, they reminded Zoe of 3D representations of medieval Terran knights that she had seen, all polished and ornate and almost clumsy. Their breast plates were intricately carved and inset with gold leaf. The rest of their armour, which took the form of mail or leather strips covered with plate metal, was equally clean and shy of real battle. They carried full-face helms under their arms and elaborate swords at their belts.

Zoe noticed the entire room had become quiet and motionless. All eyes were on the knights.

One of the knights held up his hand. 'This establishment is not acceptable to the Knights of Kuabris. It is unlicensed. You will all be taken away for questioning.'

Three

Cosmae watched the grey figure walk out through the door and into the darkness of the yard beyond. Defrabax placed a fatherly hand on the young man's shoulders. 'Your girl must have been frightened out of her mind,' he commented.

'Her name's Kaquaan,' said Cosmae in a quiet voice. He pushed the door closed, and turned to look at Defrabax. The mage suddenly seemed very old, despite his strong arms and darting eyes. His encounter with the knights appeared to have sapped even his limitless energy. Cosmae shuddered. 'You think there was a knight watching the house?'

'I'm sure of it. It's my business to know these things,' Defrabax announced grandly, returning to the main room. Spurning the electric light, he bustled towards the table with a candle.

'Then the attack of the brutes from the sewers was most fortunate.'

'Fortunate?' queried Defrabax, rooting through the papers on the table for something.

'You mean you planned that? You know these creatures?'

Defrabax smiled. 'I tell you little, so that if things go wrong, you will not find the knights pursuing *you*. It is best that you don't know.'

'But you've done so much for me,' said Cosmae. 'I feel that I ought to be involved and –'

'Now you're sounding like a child again. Do hush a moment. I'm looking for something.' Defrabax almost threw the parchments and books to the floor in increasing exasperation.

'What?'

'A key. The homunculus needs access to a special room.'

'Why?'

Defrabax ignored him. 'Where is that key?' he muttered angrily. 'Cosmae, I can peer into the mists of the not yet, I can feel the temperature of minds in a locked room, I can even animate creatures from the clay of graveyard soil – but I cannot find this accursed key!'

'Why did you let the homunculus go without the key?'

Defrabax sighed. 'Because, my young friend,' he said with irritation, 'the knights could be back at any moment. I have just told them that I know nothing of the homunculus. If they found the creature here . . . Well, the knights can't abide liars.' Defrabax abandoned the table, and walked around the room, peering up at shelves and scratching his head.

'What does this key look like?'

'Now, that's the first sensible question you've asked in many minutes.' Defrabax eased himself down into a chair in resignation. 'It's not what you would think of as a key. It looks like a glass square inset with coloured filaments.'

'I don't think it's here,' announced Cosmae after a while.

'I last saw it on that table. And unless you've taken it . . .'

'I have not!'

'Then that whore of yours must have walked off with it,' said Defrabax darkly.

Cosmae's face went pale.

'Therefore, you will go and get it back.'

* * *

To his immense irritation, the Doctor had been separated almost at once from Jamie and Zoe. A group of soldiers had marched them promptly from the drinking house to a large building not too far away. This, the Doctor had learned, was the headquarters of the City Guard. Its rotten and dark interior indicated eloquently that the real authority in the city did not rest with its occupants.

Herded into a large, bare room with about twenty other men, the Doctor tried his best to remain patient, but without his recorder he had nothing to occupy his mind. Besides, his friends were in trouble as well.

Moments later the Doctor found himself marching to the front of the queue of prisoners waiting to be questioned. He extended his hand to the guard who seemed to be temporarily in charge.

'I'm delighted to meet you. I'm the Doctor. I'm very worried about my friends, and would be grateful if you could –'

The soldier, taking notes at a desk, barely looked up. 'Return to the back of the queue,' he ordered.

'Your superiors will be most annoyed if I am not handed over to them without delay.'

'Really?'

'Well, that tends to be the normal pattern of things,' noted the Doctor sadly.

The soldier placed his quill on the table, and looked at the Doctor closely.

It was at times like these that the Doctor really longed for his previous body: tall, striking, with severe hair the colour of silver moonlight. Back then he could stop a charging bull in its tracks just by clearing his throat. Now? He was sure to stand out from the overweight drunks behind him, but his little body lacked the imposing authority that would have been so useful. Still. He drew himself up to his full height, such as it was, and smiled disarmingly.

'So,' said the guard, 'you don't want to be fined and sent home?'

'I have already paid my fine,' said the Doctor in a forceful voice.

The guard stared back at his unblinking eyes for a moment, and then scratched his head, coughing. 'No you haven't,' he said, with a querulous uncertainty in his voice. 'I've only just started talking to you.'

'If you say so,' said the Doctor sadly. He was clearly very out of practice.

'I assume from your clothes,' said the man, indicating the Doctor's dark frock coat and check-patterned trousers, 'that you are from one of the neighbouring cities.'

The Doctor nodded.

'Ignorance is no excuse,' said the soldier. 'We allow others into our city for up to two days as a concession, not so that they can cavort around the disreputable bars of –'

'I wasn't cavorting,' said the Doctor levelly. 'That's not my style.'

The guard snorted, and reached for another sheet of parchment. 'What is your name?'

'As I said, I am usually called the Doctor.'

The soldier frowned. 'That word means nothing to me. Is it a rank or a mark of peerage?'

'Neither, really,' said the Doctor, watching the man scribble notes across the page.

'Your business here?'

'I don't know,' replied the Doctor. 'I haven't found it yet. Can we fill that bit in later?'

The guard rose to his feet and with a gloved hand took hold of the Doctor's throat. 'Your city might cherish such impertinence. Ours does not.'

The Doctor pulled himself away. 'Well, of all the confounded stupidity!' He looked around him, desperately. 'I'm simply trying to make your job easier!' He began to shout. 'Somebody, somewhere, I am sure, will find me very interesting indeed!'

'What's all the noise?' came a voice from the far side of the room.

The soldier crashed to attention. 'It's this man, sir. He fails to heed the authority of the City Guard and –'

'Well, he's hardly the first to do that,' said the newcomer, walking across the room towards the Doctor. 'I am Oiquaquil, Captain of the City Guard. You are?'

'The Doctor. I'm a visitor. My friends and I were interested in examining Heddeigé's theories at first hand. I've not sampled a culture such as your own for quite some time.'

Oiquaquil turned to the guard. 'Do these words make sense to you?' The soldier shook his head. Oiquaquil returned his gaze to the small, energetic man. 'Are you a magician, sir? Your words are mere sounds in my ear.'

'Most certainly not!' spluttered the Doctor. 'I am a philosopher, an explorer, a scientist of some renown –'

The room had been almost silent from the moment that Oiquaquil had entered. Now it was quieter still. A sinking feeling in the Doctor's stomach indicated that he had made his first mistake of the day.

'A scientist, eh?' said Oiquaquil. The small Captain rubbed his hands with delight. 'You are either very ignorant of our city, or very brazen. You'd better come with me.' He flashed the Doctor a brief smile lacking teeth and warmth. 'I think you're right. I think the knights will find you very interesting indeed.'

Cosmae could not get Kaquaan's face out of his mind. He saw her beguiling eyes, her full lips, her pale cheeks notched with tiny nicks of scar tissue. He remembered her hair, tumbling around her shoulders, and in his mind he reached out to caress her.

The fact that it was her face that ebbed and waned impossibly in his vision troubled Cosmae. He'd known many beautiful women, and quite a few charming whores. Defrabax had said that, as Kaquaan was one of many, she'd soon be gone from Cosmae's mind, and that he lusted after her rather than loved her. After all, Cosmae had first seen her mere weeks ago, and he hardly knew her at all. He only knew her name because she'd let that slip when they had talked in bed earlier that evening.

And yet he wanted so much to know her better, to have a role on the stage of her life. If his passions had been inflamed by nothing more than lust, he postulated, his diseased mind would be taunted by images of her legs, her breasts, by the sounds of their lovemaking – but no, it was her face, her laugh, her eyes, her eyes, her eyes . . .

He saw her eyes everywhere, but still he hadn't tracked her down. He had returned quickly to the street where he had most often seen her, but she was nowhere to be found. Women with painted faces and dark robes paraded up and down, but she was not among them.

Cosmae sensed an extra tang in the air, and it was a deep fear, an amplification of the usual unease that was normal for any area where the Knights of Kuabris held sway. The creatures from the sewers, whatever they were, and whatever sort of connection Defrabax had with them, had upset what little calm existed in the city.

Up ahead there seemed to be a cluster of people, gathered around some central point, making excited, sighing exclamations of surprise and fear. Perhaps someone had been killed by the sewer creatures.

Cosmae ran towards the group, and heard a voice he recognized. He pushed his way through the mass of people, ignoring their scornful looks and their curses, until he was just close enough to see what was going on.

It was Kaquaan, and she was talking to a young knight.

The nature of her story ensured that the people's usual fear of the knights had for the moment waned. The entire crowd hung on her every word as if she were a master storyteller.

'It was a terrible grey thing of the graveyards,' she was saying. 'The creature didn't move – I didn't give it the chance. I just ran out of the door.'

Cosmae watched the young knight stand in thought for a few moments before he turned to one of a number of guards who stood behind him. 'Take her to Grand Knight Himesor at the castle,' he ordered. 'He will doubtless wish to question this strumpet at his leisure. And make sure you mention that it was Araboam who found her.' The knight could barely resist a self-satisfied smile.

Cosmae watched the girl being led away. The guard had a fistful of hair and yanked her head regularly. Somewhere Kaquaan had lost a shoe, and one foot was swollen and bloody. She hobbled to keep up with the guard.

Cosmae swallowed down his desire to smash the guard's face on the pavement, and slipped away from the crowd, following them towards the Castle of Kuabris at a discreet distance. At one point the girl seemed to look behind her and recognize his face amongst all the milling people, but the guard cursed and dragged her forwards again, half on her knees.

Imagination or not, Cosmae saw tears like jewels about her cheeks.

The creature sat in darkness, staring at the points of light just above its head. Through the metal drain cover it could see people's feet as they scurried about like over-developed insects. The clanging rhythm provided basic accompaniment to its whirling thoughts.

'Soon,' it said, its voice flowing down into the sewers

like a sigh. 'Soon.' We leave here. We go up. Dark to light.' Its fingers stretched out to stroke the undersurface of the grating as tenderly as if stroking a child.

'Soon,' it said again, and then disappeared back into the darkness.

Zoe sat with her head in her hands, staring at the floor, trying studiously to avoid visual contact with any of the others in her cell.

The guards had herded the women into one small group at the rear of the ale house and then bundled them into a square horse-drawn waggon. There had barely been room to stand, but only Zoe seemed perturbed. The other women, including those that had sold drinks and a large number from the upstairs rooms, were stoic in the face of discomfort and possible imprisonment. They had skittered one into another like wooden pins with barely a sound, their faces blank and resigned.

Zoe had been pulled from the back of the waggon and then kicked by a guard as she lay on the floor, her head spinning. She had tried to protest, but before she could another guard had interceded and helped her to her feet. The women had been directed with shouts and oaths into a cramped cell the mere smell of which made Zoe's stomach churn. There had been a squabble for what few benches there were – it was like watching primitive animals assert their position in some awful pecking order – but Zoe made straight for the darkest corner, hoping to be ignored.

Some minutes had passed in silence, but she didn't dare look up. Perhaps if she concentrated hard enough she'd just vanish. Perhaps if she were patient enough the Doctor or Jamie would whisper to her that they were about to rescue her, like they always did, and then the great metal-latticed door would come crumbling inwards. Perhaps . . .

There was a gentle hand on her shoulder. 'No, my cloud, don't fall asleep.'

Zoe looked up, her vision swimming. 'I was just – I was . . .'

'Shh,' advised the woman, who was now coming into focus. 'I saw your head nodding. It's not a good idea to fall asleep in the company of loose women.'

Zoe found that she was almost embarrassed to look at the woman – the dress she was wearing was so immodest, so blatant – but she smiled weakly in thanks. The woman had tried hard to obscure her age, but Zoe noticed even in the poor light of the cell dark lines around her eyes, the first swelling of fat under her chin. Her long hair, although dirty and matted now, had a lustrous hint that obviously enabled her to compete with the dominant young women who sprawled on the benches. There was a kindly, strong beauty about her. Her lower lip was swollen around a tiny purple cut. Zoe watched her lips for a moment before realizing that she was speaking again.

'Sorry?'

'I said, you're clearly not part of this game . . .'

Zoe shook her head firmly.

'You see, fall asleep in here, and you'll awake with no money to pay your fine. And then . . .' The woman paused at Zoe's expression. 'You do have some money?'

Zoe shook her head sadly.

'Nothing? Oh dear, oh dear. You see, the guards are only interested in a nominal warning. We'll be here for a few hours, I suppose, and then we'll be fined and released. All good women,' she almost spat the phrase, 'carry a few coins about their person.'

'But I haven't got –'

'Shh,' said the woman with a warning finger to her lips. 'Don't let the guards hear you say that. If they can't get their coins then they'll look for . . . payment in other forms.' The woman's fingers brushed across Zoe's cheek. 'You're pretty enough, my girl, but I think you'll bruise too easily.'

'But I couldn't –'

'I'll see what I can do for you.' The woman delved down into her substantial cleavage and pulled out a leather pouch, which she raised to her failing eyes, pretending to cough. A moment later a few tiny coins were being pressed into Zoe's damp palm. 'That should be enough.'

'Thank you,' stuttered Zoe. 'How shall I get the money back to you?'

The woman laughed, rearranging her dress. 'You're obviously not from this city, and you're clearly too naive to be involved in this sordid game. Just take the coins, my cloud, with the compliments of the Knights of Kuabris.' The woman spat on the floor. 'It's their rules, you see. They order the raids. It's so difficult to earn a living with people like that around!'

There was a movement towards the door. A number of guards appeared, and pulled open the heavy door of the cell. One by one the women filed out, placing coins in a series of outstretched palms. The young women went first, laughing crudely with the guards.

The old woman had bustled towards the front of the queue, cuffing about the head another who was about to protest. Zoe joined the end of the queue, swaying unsteadily on her feet. She watched as one woman tried to reason with the guards, explaining that she had no money, but they were having none of it. She was dragged away, screaming.

Zoe nervously extended her fist of coins towards the line of guards. The one at the front looked down at them closely, and then started to laugh. 'Foreign currency!' he shouted. The other soldiers started to chuckle. 'Good woman,' the man said to Zoe, 'you do surely know that trade in foreign currency is illegal here? You were very foolish to accept payment in this form, but perhaps the black market in currency is springing up once more.'

Zoe stared at him in uncomprehending silence. The guard took the coins anyway.

'There is a strict fining system for such crimes,' said another guard. 'But it appears you have no money for that, either.'

'But I'm a traveller here,' blurted out Zoe. 'I've got nothing to do with those women –'

'I believe you,' interrupted the first guard. 'I might have asked you to accompany me for the evening, but there's not enough meat on you.' He smiled icily. 'So don't worry, you'll be away from this city by tomorrow morning.'

Zoe felt the second guard pull her arms up sharply behind her back. The first guard shouted after her as she was marched away. 'You'll be sold at the slave market in an hour's time.'

Four

Defrabax was translating an ancient text on deadly gemstones when he heard the unmistakable sound of his door being kicked down.

Quickly pushing his papers into a drawer, he darted towards the front of the house. Commander Zaitabor stood in the centre of a mound of sharp splinters, imperiously instructing his men in their search. His harsh features passed from darkness to light and back again as a suspended lamp twisted above his head. He pretended not to see Defrabax for a moment.

Defrabax snorted and spluttered indignantly, rubbing his eyes for effect. 'What is the meaning of this? I was asleep in the back room and –'

'Defrabax,' said Zaitabor, his eyes colder than the moon-kissed air. 'What a pleasant surprise to find you up at this hour. What mystical designs can so occupy your mind, I wonder?'

'The curfew only applies out there,' said Defrabax, wincing as he heard an axe being applied to a locked box.

A chill wind floated through the doorway, briefly tugging at Zaitabor's cloak. He nodded to the two knights who stood on either side of Defrabax. One pulled Defrabax's shoulders behind him, the other held a slim dagger to his throat. 'You of all people,' said Zaitabor, 'could tell me what would happen if the knife were to slip and graze your throat.'

Defrabax swallowed against the cold metal point. 'What are you looking for?'

Zaitabor made a show of examining the sketches on the wall closely. 'I'm not sure. This is just a routine search, of course. Even good citizens can expect an occasional visitation from the knights.' He tapped a yellow-framed illustration of a nesting rat hawk. 'This is very good.'

'My ward, Cosmae,' said Defrabax. 'He is very talented.'

'Indeed.' Zaitabor looked up as Araboam reported to him.

'No trace of the homunculus, my lord.'

'As is to be expected,' said Zaitabor, returning his gaze to Defrabax once more. 'After all, you do claim not to have one.' He nodded at the two knights. 'Let us return to the castle.'

The knights let go of the old man and pushed him to the floor. Defrabax landed awkwardly and moaned with pain. Drizzle fell onto his upturned face through the doorway as he watched the knights leave.

Jamie felt a perplexing contentment as he stood in a doorway watching the headquarters of the guards. Although he knew that his prospects of ever going home again rested entirely with the Doctor, for once the expectation of trying to liberate his friends did not fill him with fear. There were no monsters, no guns, no baffling invisible doors. Just people he understood and buildings made of stone and windows with metal bars.

It was like real life, and even his flight from the guards had brought back memories of Redcoats. The soldier had fallen for a ruse so simple that even an Englishman would have seen through it. 'Look over there!' Jamie had exclaimed, pointing, as the guard came towards him with manacles – and the old man fell for it! They were very primitive people.

Jamie had followed the cortège of soldiers and criminals to the dark building at the centre of town. He had walked around the building twice, ascertaining that there were two main doors and a number of smaller hatches down into the cells. The squat building covered a surprising area, and there was no way that he could observe all the entrances. He settled down into the bricked-up doorway of a facing tenement to observe what seemed to be the main entrance, brushing some dirt from his kilt. As he did so he caught a flash of motion further down the broad cobbled street. The movements were furtive, as befitted one moving after the curfew, but Jamie's keen eyes could track the figure as it moved from shadow to shadow.

It seemed to be a young lad whose eyes were so locked on to the guards' building that he failed to notice Jamie mere yards away. After a pause the boy ran across the street and skidded to a halt in a large puddle just beneath one of the barred windows. Jamie watched the boy looking about him nervously. Seeing no one, he craned his head into the window. Immediately the lad ducked down. Someone was there.

Jamie decided that the one thing that he needed now was a friend. It was time to give the boy a hand, whoever he was. Jamie only hoped he'd be appreciated.

Jamie stood up and coughed loudly. The boy immediately sank back into the shadows. Jamie could see the spreading stain of water creep up the boy's legs. Pretending not to have seen him, Jamie walked casually across the street, for all the world a gentleman out on a brisk midnight stroll. He whistled tunelessly to fortify his confidence.

There seemed to be a single candle burning inside the main door. The archway was of strong grey stone, and gave way to a number of shallow steps leading downwards. The roof was so low that Jamie had to crouch slightly in order to get in.

The small room at the bottom of the stairs was bare and smelt of stale alcohol. A desk of wood and slate sat in the centre of the room, one leg, a good three inches shorter than the others, supported by an empty scabbard. A man sat slumped at the desk, his arms extending over the length of the table, his face on the cold surface, snoring loudly.

'I've just come from an illegal drinking house,' said Jamie loudly, remembering the words of the knight when they were arrested. The man barely stirred. 'I said, I've just come from an illegal drinking house.' He shook the man by the shoulder. 'So I think you'd better come and arrest me.'

The man snorted and grabbed for a nonexistent weapon. 'You . . . It's after curfew . . . You shouldn't . . .' He got to his feet, swaying slightly, big balls of fist rubbing his rheumy eyes. An empty bottle rolled across the desk and on to the floor. It bounced and then split in two at Jamie's feet. 'What are you doing here?' the man finally exclaimed.

'Looking for a friend,' said Jamie, edging towards the door. 'I think I'll come back later.' With that, he ran back up the steps and on to the street.

The man roared and came after him, sword in hand.

As they ran down the street Jamie risked a glance over his shoulder, and saw that the soldier was puffing already, gesticulating wildly. The young man crept into the building.

Jamie turned his head and concentrated on running, which was made difficult by the damp, uneven surface of the road. He glanced at the buildings as he passed, hoping to avoid getting lost.

His keen ears soon lost the sound of pursuit. He slowed, and a few minutes later he turned the corner that would eventually take him back to the guards' building.

Walking towards him from the building was the young man. He was clearly downcast, his body language seeming to indicate that he was resigned even to capture.

Jamie stopped and looked at the lad. He was about Jamie's age, slim and slightly gangling, with unkempt hair the colour of dirty straw. The boy smiled eventually, a grin of such warmth that Jamie was very much put at ease by the stranger.

'I have heard that fashions in the other cities are unusual,' said the young man at last, 'but never did I expect to see a man in a woman's skirt.'

Araboam and Zaitabor stood to attention as Himesor examined the papers they had brought. 'The first proof, Grand Knight,' said Zaitabor. 'Proof that Defrabax has a homunculus.'

Himesor stared down at the pages in front of him. 'Meaningless words,' he said. 'And this sketch?' The drawing showed a cadaverous, slab-faced creature with unnaturally long arms.

'Drawn by the wizard's boy,' explained Araboam. 'He invited the whore into their house. She saw the creature.'

'I will question the girl later,' said Himesor, nodding to himself. Almost without thinking he found himself smudging the charcoal, blending the sharp lines into subtle suggestions of sinew and bone. He sucked the blackened end of his thumb. 'I was an artist before I was a knight,' he said, looking up at Zaitabor, seeking whatever passion lay beyond his cold features. 'Where once I dedicated my works to the Higher, now I chase golems and apes from the sewers. I think I lost something a very long time ago, and I know not how to get it back.'

'And this man?' asked Zaitabor impatiently, indicating the small figure who stood silently towards the back of the room.

Himesor turned, observing the stranger. He wore a

dark coat, beneath which was a hint of azure, and square-patterned trousers. He blew his nose into a large handkerchief as if to imply that he wasn't listening to their conversation, but his eyes were intense.

'A scientist from another city. Oiquaquil brought him here. It seems that the night, though not yet spent, has many surprises for us.'

'He should be executed,' said Zaitabor instinctively.

Himesor shook his head. 'No. While I might oppose his beliefs with all my strength, I can at least offer him the common courtesy of politeness. Better to win an enemy round than to destroy him.'

Zaitabor opened his mouth as if to disagree, but then paused. He nodded curtly. 'My lord.'

'I am tired,' announced Himesor. 'I will talk with this scientist for a few moments before I rest. Araboam, you have done well today. Please wait outside this chamber for the prisoner. You will escort him to the cells when we have completed our business. You will then be dismissed until I next call for you. Do not neglect your meditations.' Himesor turned to Zaitabor. 'Thank you, my friend. We do seem to be making progress. Keep an eye on Defrabax. Soon his creature will come out into the open. Good night, Commander.'

The two knights bowed, and turned for the door. When they were gone, Himesor stood, sipping from a glass of water. 'Your name?'

'I am the Doctor,' said the little man, stepping around to the front of the Grand Knight's immense table.

' "Doctor".' Himesor turned the term over in his mind. 'The word refers to a scientist who is wise in matters of health and the destruction of disease, does it not?'

'That is one of its meanings.'

'Then that is what you do?'

'In a manner of speaking. I tend to be more interested

in . . .' The Doctor paused. 'Did I hear you discuss golems?'

Himesor laughed. 'You did.'

'Golems of great evil,' said the Doctor, his eyes the grey of battlefield smoke. 'I think of *them* as a disease to be destroyed.'

'Noble sentiments. I once believed the world to be black and white. Since becoming Grand Knight I've been less sure.'

Uninvited, the Doctor sat down at the table. He nodded sadly. 'I know.'

Himesor looked out of the window. Dawn was not too far off, but the shroud of sleep felt far from his body now. 'Of course, I still believe in the ultimate evil and the ultimate good. But we people are made grey by our struggles towards the light and the ropes that bind us to the dark.'

'I once had a friend,' said the Doctor, his own eyes far away. 'We had everything in common – everything. But he enjoyed being scared of the dark a little too much. It swallowed him. I doubt that I shall ever see him again.' The Doctor stared at the sketch of the homunculus. 'I keep reminding myself that we're still the same man. We took different roads from the same junction, that's all.'

'Ultimately we gain nothing from the past,' stated Himesor dogmatically. 'I must rid these phantoms from my mind. My dedication is unchanging.' He returned to the table. 'You recognize this creature?'

'No,' said the Doctor. 'I've seen something similar in an old work of fiction, but –'

'I assume that you are in our city to investigate the Menagerie of Ukkazaal?'

The Doctor shook his head. 'I tend to wander without knowledge of my destination. But please tell me about it.'

'I do not place any faith in legends,' said Himesor with

a note of steel in his voice. 'But it is said by some that this city rests over the great menagerie. Men who felt tempted to meddle in science were cursed and turned into beasts. A warning hangs over our heads: if we also meddle, the beasts will emerge to slay us.'

'I must say,' observed the Doctor, 'that from what I have seen your people seem in little danger of that. Science is feared, reviled. I can't help but think of the chains that await me in my cell.'

'It is right that the evils of science are opposed,' said Himesor. 'It is science that leads us into thinking about the problems of yesterday and the improvements that can be reached tomorrow. It is a fickle fantasy!'

'And yet I see that you have some sort of power station on the far side of the city.'

'The Furnace is a solitary exception!' spat Himesor. 'With the authority that rests in my status as Grand Knight I sanctioned limited experimentation. Scientists from various cities collaborated for a brief period. To my shame such stations now exist in the cities beyond our influence.'

'Shame?'

'I regret my decision.'

'Then why –'

'Our people were crying out for relief from their drudgery. I had to act. But now they have seen a glimpse of the seeming glory of science they will thirst for more.' Himesor closed his eyes for a moment. 'My time is short.'

'I must say,' said the Doctor, 'I was expecting torture and inquisitions. I wasn't expecting such honesty and –'

'It does not matter,' said Himesor flatly. 'My admissions will not go beyond these walls. You will help us penetrate the Menagerie of Ukkazaal. And, if I have betrayed faith to science, then we will all die at the hands of the beasts that wait there.'

* * *

The man soon found Xaelobran's fish stall. Without coming too close he attracted the stallholder's attention.

Xaelobran nodded quickly, and said something to the boy at his side. A few moments later the two men shook hands warmly, their voices almost lost under the noise of the crowds.

'Argaabil!' exclaimed the stallholder. 'Good to see you away from the Furnace for once.'

The fat man brushed some soot from his overalls. 'Always a pleasure to breath good air,' he said. 'Now, I seem to remember a friend of yours being interested in esoteric and unusual creatures.'

'I'm expecting him any day now,' said Xaelobran. 'What have you got?'

'A dead animal in a case has come into my possession. I don't suppose I should have accepted it, but it seemed a fair stake at the time.'

'No one with any sense would gamble with you,' said Xaelobran. 'What's this beast look like?'

'It's like a huge insect,' came the reply. 'I can't say where it came from. It's in a casket, the like of which I've –'

'The creature. My friend is only interested in the creature.'

The fat man scratched his chin. 'Four huge arms, claws, some sort of vicious snout, long legs. The casket is frosted-over. I think the animal is grey or silver. Looks like its skin's been flayed off.'

'And it's genuine?'

Argaabil nodded. 'As far as I can tell.'

'I'll tell my friend. Anything else?'

'No. But I'm very glad the thing is dead.'

The Doctor lay quietly in his cell, listening to the drip of water and the insistent whispers of fear. Not for the first time he wondered where Jamie and Zoe were.

Perhaps he should look within himself for some of the peace of Det-Sen. If he liberated his mind from its earthly confines he would be better prepared to face whatever evil lay within the menagerie. Although the Doctor did not greatly believe in the veracity of mere feelings he knew that something deadly rested beneath the city. He caught a sense of the evil from time to time, not from the source itself, which seemed dormant, but from the fears of the humans. The terror must have derived, perhaps over the centuries, from something very tangible indeed.

He let his mind wander still further. He allowed phrases and images from the recent past to reform into something new. 'Bloodthirsty . . . I cannot agree to that request . . . Outside is . . . Nothing . . . No one believed . . . A war they cannot win . . . Immediate results . . . If you kill me . . . Want to return . . . The Doctor's going . . . Evacuate the area . . .' Faces, images he had not even seen – all began to blur in his mind, forming a pattern, an image, a sensation. And –

Someone shouted from a cell further down the corridor. A guard clanged on the door until the noise subsided.

Sighing after the interruption, the Doctor struggled to remember his mind's composition. When he relaxed it returned to him once more. It was an image and a phrase, from so far in the past the Doctor could not count on its accuracy.

It was a woman's face, talking earnestly into a computer recording device. Her face was grey with worry. Her words repeated over and over in the Doctor's mind.

'I request immediate evacuation.'

Five

Diseaeda had seen countless marvels on his travels. On this trip alone he had explored a towering city of glass, crossed a lake of fire, and examined at first hand what was claimed to be the claw of some huge reptile. He was privileged enough to have been the first outsider to smoke the legendary urparfel plant in the company of the elders of Tebrain, after which they took him to see the famed backwards-running river at the top of the mountain. However, by then his vision was so distorted he wasn't sure what he was supposed to be looking at.

All these things he had seen, and more. And yet nothing amazed him more than the excruciatingly slow pace of his horse. The animal was well fed and excessively pampered, and she repaid her master with a slow, resolute pace. Extremes of terrain and temperature did not affect the animal in the slightest. Plod plod plod. Diseaeda's horse was about as accurate as the ticking clocks of Hacoruin.

As the nameless city of the Knights of Kuabris began to creep into sight down in the valley, spreading like a grey mould, Diseaeda jabbed with his spurs, to no avail. He didn't like visiting the city. He was always keen to pass through as quickly as possible. As a man whose mind had been expanded by travel the awful insularity of the knights cast a dark chill over him. He was not a superstitious man, but he made a few signs in front of himself, accurately copied from the preparations of his acrobats. He wasn't sure what they meant, but he needed all the help he could get. The city had turned up many an interesting exhibit or act in the past, and he couldn't afford to skip it, but on occasions he woke up with a nightmarish vision of the Knights of Kuabris still fresh in his mind.

Just get in, he reminded himself, check with Xaelobran at the market, and get out again. Avoid trouble with the knights. Travel light.

He'd sent the fruits of this most recent exploration ahead of him, to the show. Now it was just him, and that damn horse.

He could see the chimneys of the power station known as the Furnace, and the Castle of Kuabris gripping the hillside like the crystalline skeleton of a hunting beetle. A light wind was beginning to blow the clouds and fog away, leaving only the fumes from the Furnace behind. He'd never been to the city and avoided the rain before. Perhaps it was an omen.

Diseaeda reached down into one of the leather bags slung to the side of the saddle, and unfolded a wide-brimmed hat. The sun was already making his neck itchy, although the wet noise of the horse's hooves as they sank into drenched grass reminded him that such a state of affairs was purely temporary. From the other saddle bag he produced a small bottle of ointment. He splashed a little into his weathered palm, and then slapped some on his neck. He made sure that the bottle was well concealed before the gatehouse came into view.

Avoid trouble. Travel light.

As usual it was the rather pathetic City Guard who manned the gate. There were four of them there, and the youngest, barely out of school, was booted into the sunlight to examine Diseaeda's papers. The others continued with their furtive gambling. Now Diseaeda knew a trick or two. When he had owned nothing but his own stall and the clothes he stood in he'd relied on such conjuring. But he fancied he'd get little from the guards. Best to keep quiet. Concentrate on the boy.

'You got papers?' asked the boy.

Diseaeda looked down from his horse. 'Of course.' He produced a sheaf of parchments from his pocket. The folds had become tears, and the boy had great difficulty extracting the required authorization. A tiny stream of sand poured on to the guard's boots as he fumbled with the papers. 'Aren't you a little young to be carrying a sword?' asked Diseaeda without thinking.

'Still your lips,' said the boy, giving Diseaeda's letters of authorization back. 'My ma's a great lover of roast tongue, and she ain't too partial where it comes from.'

'Apologies,' said Diseaeda, cursing his joking that would one day surely be the death of him. He nudged his horse forwards as the gate squealed open, and made straight for the market.

A horse was doubtless a rare sight in the city, and Diseaeda was well aware of the looks he was receiving. Despite his fear, it did wonders for his ego. He fanned himself regally with his papers before stuffing them away again.

A woman rushed up to him, gabbling something about her dead husband. Diseaeda smiled, but didn't stop.

He dismounted at the edge of the market, and looked around for Xaelobran. It didn't take him long to spot the man, making a show of juggling some small yellow fruit whilst bellowing that his produce was the best, the cheapest, and the most wholesome.

'Xaelobran, you old dog!' shouted Diseaeda, causing the trader to fumble.

Xaelobran turned, his feet now stained yellow, and started to laugh. 'I thought the stink in the air was a blocked chimney. I should have known better!' A woman took over Xaelobran's position at the front of the stall as the two men embraced. 'Not seen your face for a long while.'

Diseaeda nodded. 'Been busy with the show.'

'Successful?'

'There are good months and bad months. Yourself?'

'Wouldn't like to say.'

'The knights can't stop you having memories,' said Diseaeda, suddenly lowering his voice.

Xaelobran nodded, his eyes defensively examining the faces in the crowd. 'Aye,' he said. 'But they keep on trying.'

'Madness,' said Diseaeda. 'A city built on the principles of madness.'

'And the influence of the blessed knights extends day by day,' hissed Xaelobran. He turned to pat his friend's horse. 'A fine creature. I'll get my son to water her and keep her safe.'

'Thank you.'

'So, what are you looking for this time?'

'Difficult to say until I've seen it. Heard anything?'

'Two things we must do before you leave. I've just been told about something that might interest you. Some sort of dead animal in a metal box.'

'Sounds like a passable side exhibit. And?'

'There's an auction this afternoon. We might find you some deformed creature . . . Or perhaps some cheap whore who's not paid her fines.'

'Well, you dirty old dog,' said Diseaeda. 'We all live in hope.'

'We'll make a good team, Cosmae,' announced Jamie, pushing his plate across the table. The young man had brought Jamie to a lodging house, saying that he dared not return to his master.

Cosmae held his head in his hands. 'Maybe.'

'Come on, man,' said Jamie, shaking the boy by the

shoulders. 'We got around that guard, didn't we?'

'But the girl I'm looking for wasn't there. Defrabax will kill me if I don't get that key back.'

'Where do you think she is?'

'In the castle. I had hoped that they'd finished questioning her and sent her back to the guards.'

'I'm sure that's where the Doctor will be as well,' said Jamie.

'But we'll never get in there,' said Cosmae.

'Why?'

'Because it's the castle of the Knights of Kuabris. What more do you need to know?'

'I'm a traveller,' said Jamie. 'Tell me more about the knights.'

Cosmae couldn't take his eyes off the castle, framed through the stone window. 'They protect us,' said Cosmae. 'At least, that's what they claim. They uphold our laws, intercede for us in prayer, and wrestle with problems of justice and morality.' There was a slight mocking lilt to his voice.

'Presbyters with claymores,' said Jamie, but Cosmae didn't hear him.

'They are only interested in the present, the here and now. For them the past is gone, and the future is unknown. We are to seek the Higher as best we can from moment to moment.'

'Is that why you fear them?'

'Of course not,' snorted Cosmae. 'Religious twaddle. At least, that's what my master says, and I've no reason to doubt him.'

'Then why?'

'Something happens when you become a knight. You see men – kind and gentle men – initiated into the ways of Kuabris, and they are never the same again.'

'The Doctor would call that brainwashing,' said Jamie.

Cosmae stared blankly for a moment, and then

continued. 'Day by day they simply surrender to their worst instincts. It is only to be expected, I suppose.'

'So far,' noted Jamie, 'you've described nothing more than evil men with swords. If you saw some of the things that the Doctor has come up against –'

'But it's the potential power of the knights that frightens me,' interrupted Cosmae. 'They have centuries of learning, which they vigorously destroy. They have dark secrets and powers far beyond even my master. By their destruction of knowledge and their consumption of the secret workings of the world, they become stronger and stronger.' Cosmae looked Jamie straight in the eye, his pupils dilated. 'It is the souls of the knights that I most fear.'

Zoe awoke with a sinking feeling in her stomach that was becoming all too familiar. Where once the sounds of her own city coming to life had woken her, today she came to because she could no longer block out the stink of the cell and the harsh pressure on her neck and spine. Her travels with the Doctor made her long for comfortable beds and people who were actually pleased to see her. She'd finally nagged the Doctor into installing some sort of orthopedic bed in her room in the TARDIS, but just at the moment she'd settle for a pillow. And some air freshener.

The weak light filtering into the room reminded her that the soldier had said she'd be sold at a market in an hour. And that was about five hours ago. Since she'd been moved to this smaller cell she hadn't heard a single voice.

'Peasants!' she finally exclaimed, her voice ringing against the walls of rock. 'Primitive peasants!' Such an emotional response would have been frowned upon by her tutors at the Earth School of Parapsychology, but to hell with them. The logic of this particular situation was inescapable: place one young woman in some benighted, centuries-old gaol, give her zero items to help her with any escape plan that she might formulate, and the end result was a very angry, impotent prisoner.

'Doctor, Jamie,' she muttered to herself. 'Now would be a good time to come to the rescue. A very, very good time.'

Himesor thumped the table in exasperation. 'What do you mean, she's vanished?'

'She isn't there,' said Zaitabor flatly. 'I've double-checked all the cells myself.'

'I'd have expected more of the *guards*!' spat Himesor. 'A vital prisoner, one who can tell us about the old wizard's homunculus – and she just vanishes from before our eyes.'

'The little man is waiting outside,' said Zaitabor.

'Good to know we haven't lost him yet,' said Himesor.

'Well, you might have done,' announced a sing-song voice from the door. 'But my curiosity demands that I stay.' The two knights turned in surprise. 'Sorry to barge in, but I was getting a bit cold out there in the corridor. And these chains are so very tight . . .' The short man indicated the manacles that locked his wrists together.

'Release the Doctor,' said Himesor.

Zaitabor walked across the room. 'Araboam was supposed to be guarding you!' he said as he turned a small key in the lock on the Doctor's wrist.

'And so he was. But I felt a bit thirsty, and he very kindly went to get me a drink. Maybe that's what happened to that poor girl. Perhaps she just crumbled to dust in one of your cells.'

'You overheard our conversation?' asked Himesor quietly.

'As it turns out, I did,' smiled the Doctor. 'I do have rather good hearing.' The Doctor coughed into his hand as he sat at the great table, and made a show of examining the scrolls that covered its surface. Himesor glared at the man, and pulled them away from him. 'Anyway,' continued the Doctor, 'the girl's disappearance is hardly a secret. All the knights are talking about her.' He suddenly looked up, his eyes fixing on Himesor. 'Some say the Brotherhood of Rexulon took her. After all, she has been contaminated by contact with science.'

'What do you know of the Brotherhood of Rexulon?' exploded Himesor. 'Everywhere I turn there is talk of the brotherhood. Day by day it seems that the power and influence of the knights is being sucked into the black, bottomless pit that is that cursed, unnatural fellowship! How I long for the whispers of their existence to cease.'

'Tell me about them,' said the Doctor quietly.

'Mere superstitious nonsense.'

'Even so,' said the Doctor. 'Tell me. You were most forthcoming last night. The legends of the Menagerie of Ukkazaal sound most fascinating.'

Himesor's reply seemed as much addressed to Zaitabor as the Doctor. 'The talk of a tired old man late at night.'

'Then you don't want me to help you penetrate the sewers and the menagerie beyond?'

Himesor turned to address Zaitabor. 'Go and find the girl.'

'My Lord.'

The Grand Knight watched Zaitabor as he marched through the door. Just before it slammed there was the sound of shouting. Himesor recognized Araboam's voice, made weak with apology.

'I am intrigued, Doctor,' said Himesor when the noise had subsided. 'You say that you could have escaped from our cells?'

'Oh, I expect so,' said the Doctor casually. 'I'm used to a better standard of straw-filled mattress, if you catch my drift.'

'But you didn't?'

'No. As you will have already realized, I am not a superstitious man. But there *is* something wrong here, isn't there?'

'Perhaps. Perhaps there is always something wrong here.'

'No, I'm talking about an unusual feeling of fear. I feel as if I'm camped out on the battlefield with an untrained army, waiting to be strafed by an attack plane.'

'Your words are meaningless to me, Doctor.'

'Perhaps. But I think you know what I mean. And that is why I have stayed.'

'Do you know where the girl is?'

'Gracious me, no. But is it possible that one of your own knights could have contrived her "disappearance"?'

'No Kuabris would ever betray the wishes of the Grand Knight.'

The Doctor stared at Himesor. 'I want to help you. I would rather help you from something approaching a position of trust.'

'You are a most unusual prisoner, Doctor.'

The Doctor smiled warmly.

Himesor relented, and spread out his hands in a sign of honesty. 'For your information, Doctor, the Brotherhood of Rexulon are a fanatical sect. They oppose science, as we do, but have no morality, no justice, no breath of the Higher. And believe me, Doctor, for all our faults, we knights do strive to ensure that the majority of the populace are as content as possible.'

'Thus the power stations.'

'Indeed. But the brotherhood are ruthless, subversive. I have every reason to believe that they are behind these stories of the menagerie. It is in their interest to make the populace believe that we are all being punished for the brief period of scientific experimentation that I sanctioned. That is why we must penetrate the sewers and find out what is down there, to reassure the people, to destroy any beasts that we find.'

'And creatures are emerging from the sewers, aren't they?'

'That is true.'

'Do you know who the brotherhood are?'

'I am not yet convinced that they exist. Only once has a man admitted to my face that he was a brother – and then only seconds before he hurled himself into the flames of the Furnace.'

'I believe that there is something below this city,' said the Doctor. 'I think that you and I and some of your most trusted men should explore the sewers and beyond, just as you indicated last night.'

'Without the homunculus, how are we to do that?'

'Well, a few moments ago I spoke of trust,' said the Doctor. 'I'm told you have some sacred artefacts, accoutrements of your religion that only the knights have ever gazed upon.' The Doctor smiled his most winning smile. 'I want you to show them to me.'

Diseaeda wiped his brow in the heat, and stared at the motley collection of people shuffling into position on the raised stone dais. The slave market was, as usual, late in starting.

Xaelobran eased himself further back into the folding chair. 'Not long now,' he said. 'Still, I'm in no hurry. Gets me away from the stall for a while.'

'You looking for something?' asked Diseaeda, watching the other buyers move into position.

'Well, ideally I could do with another pair of hands to help out. But it'll depend on the price.'

'Do you remember the last time I was here? Ended up buying Reisaz and Raitak.'

Xaelobran shuddered. 'Those two women, joined at the waist? It isn't natural.'

'That's my trade. Don't suppose I'll see their like here today.'

'Oh, I don't know. If one of my daughters was deformed I'd send her down here as quickly as possible.'

'Compassion and kindness flow from you like juice from a fruit,' observed Diseaeda.

'Well,' said Xaelobran, 'the way I look at it is this: there's no point eating plants when you're surrounded by carnivores.'

'I have no idea what you're talking about,' said Diseaeda. 'Anyway, the show's about to start.'

A man strode out onto the stage, his clothes formed from interlocking loops of grey leather. A little wooden baton was clenched in one fist, a fat cigar held in the other. His eyes glittered like discovered gold. 'Good people, good people, welcome to the auction. I can promise you the usual selection of waifs and strays, and dutiful servants for the very rich. All the people for sale here have been sanctioned by the guards, who will of course be delighted to assist you, should your purchases prove unreliable.'

'I just chain 'em to the floor!' shouted one man from the little crowd, to much general amusement.

'Now then, good people, without any further inaugural, introductory or dedicatory remarks, let's examine the first item.'

There was something approaching laboured applause from the audience. Diseaeda watched as the man nodded to one of the guards who stood behind the row of people on display. A few words and a prod from a sword encouraged a young boy towards the front of the stage. He looked no more than about eight years old, and it was impossible to tell where his dirty skin ended and his ripped clothes began. His eyes were as wide as plates, unblinking against the sun.

'This young thing,' said the man, 'has been released to

the guards for disposal by the generosity of the Knights of Kuabris. He is a persistent criminal, even when well fed and cared for. You'll have to keep an eye on him, I'll admit, but when he's under your gaze he'll work as hard as anyone. We're not asking much for him. Will anyone pay seven coins?'

'It would take seven coins just to add extra locks to your 'ouse to stop him escaping,' whispered Xaelobran.

'I'll give you four and a half,' came a voice from the crowd.

'You couldn't buy a dog for under five,' said the slave trader.

'Granted,' came the reply. 'But four and a half's my offer.'

'I'll give you five and a half,' said someone behind Diseaeda, who yawned in boredom. He scanned the men and women waiting to come forward. It pained him to look out for deformities, to almost expect revulsion, but, as he had said, that was his job. They all seemed quite unremarkable, impressively free of even the slightest disfiguring disease.

His attention was drawn to a young woman who stood to one end of the line. She wouldn't have seemed more out of place if she'd been levitating. Although her fingers were blackened and she looked tired, she was otherwise clean, healthy and clearly not of this city. Underneath the anguish Diseaeda saw a bright, open face, surrounded by a smooth cut of shortish, dark hair. Her nose twitched whenever the man waved his arms too vigorously and the cigar smoke came near.

She had a good figure, although her girlishness was in marked contrast to the huge woman who stood next to her, glowering at the crowd. The young girl wore what appeared to be a pair of short trousers and a colourful, long-sleeved top. The fabric alone was enough to fascinate Diseaeda: its colours glowed like gemstones, yet the material seemed light and flexible.

'Some might consider her skinny,' said Xaelobran, noting the direction of his friend's gaze. 'Nice face, though.'

'I could do with another helper,' said Diseaeda.

'Call it what you like,' said Xaelobran.

'She looks very lost. She's obviously not from around here.'

Xaelobran grunted. 'Looks like she's next.'

The man on the stage paused to light another cigar before pushing the young girl forward. 'What am I bid for this little creature?' he asked.

The Most Holy Place was deep in the bowels of the rock on which the castle sat. The Doctor fancied that he could almost hear the towers above them sonorously grinding down into the dark stone. Certainly the sounds of conversation, the clink of armour, the background hum of chanted meditation, had subsided. Even Himesor had fallen silent, doubtless still wondering if he had made the right decision.

These tunnels had been carved out of rock and elaborately engraved. Despite their impressive structure a soft wind scurried around their feet and up into the vaulted ceiling. Electric lights had been placed in the ornate holders that had presumably once held burning torches.

The warren of tunnels baffled the Doctor. The carved patterns were in a regular sequence and therefore could not also function as direction or location markers. And yet at each junction Himesor barely paused before pressing on.

A few moments later the Doctor realized what the secret was. At each intersection, Himesor took the tunnel that led down. The Most Holy Place seemed to be as deep under the castle as was possible.

'I'm sorry that no trace can be found of either of your friends,' said Himesor suddenly.

'Perhaps they've already escaped,' said the Doctor. 'They're very resourceful. Anyway, I am grateful to you for trying.'

'I quickly understood, Doctor, that I would get more from you if I asked than if I ordered.'

'Few men in authority have such sense.' The Doctor paused for a moment to examine another impressively constructed junction. 'Tell me about these tunnels,' he said, his voice ringing in the chill air.

'There are hundreds of tunnels under the castle towers and down into a natural cave system,' said Himesor. 'Most of them are part of the library.'

'I don't see any books.'

'No,' said Himesor, finally coming to a halt before a huge set of doors. 'I wouldn't expect you to.' He turned to the Doctor. 'We're here.'

The Doctor looked up at the doors, fully two storeys tall. Slabs of polished marble sat within perfect frames of iron. The Doctor ran his fingers over the surface. It was entirely smooth and precise. The doors had been constructed with pinpoint accuracy.

Himesor pulled gently on a large loop of brass. The door swung outwards without a sound. 'Enter, Doctor.'

'Thank you.' The Doctor followed the tall knight into the room.

Inside the expanse was so huge that even the Doctor's eyes could barely perceive its outermost limits. Electric lamps glowed high up in the roof like stars, casting pools of light in a narrow line through the centre of the room. On either side of the road of lights were glass cabinets, framed with gold. Some were about as high as a man, others were on their sides like huge treasure chests. Within each was a velvet cushion or a silver frame to hold up some object for inspection. The Doctor scurried along the cabinets like a child in a toyshop, glancing at crowns, books, swords, jewellery. Himesor followed at a more respectful pace.

'What do you know of the holy relics?' asked the Doctor.

'A little,' said Himesor. 'They are devices that tell of the knights' knowledge of and dependence on the Higher. In themselves they are worthless trinkets, but they are symbols that point elsewhere.'

'How old are they?'

'I cannot answer that.'

'Were they brought here from somewhere else?'

'They are here now. That is all I know.'

The Doctor stopped by one case, drumming a finger against his lips. 'Worthless trinkets, you say?' He pointed into the case at a small group of shiny purple spheres. 'They look more like advanced powerpacks to me.'

'Powerpacks?'

The Doctor scratched his head. 'Small objects that hold as much energy as, well, I'd say not far short of what one of your power stations produces in a month.'

'You cannot destroy my faith so easily, Doctor. I have always suspected that the holy relics are mundane objects made glorious by knowledge of the Higher.'

'My intention is not to destroy your beliefs,' said the Doctor quickly. 'Long ago you made a choice, the results of which you still live with. As did I. I'm here to find a way to . . . Aha! What have we here?' The Doctor scuttled off to a row of identical cases, each containing glowing white costumes on rough wooden manakins.

'The ceremonial armour of Kuabris,' said Himesor.

'Indeed,' said the Doctor. 'It has another use as well. You have said that the poisonous gases are the only thing standing in the way of your exploration of the sewers and the menagerie beyond. Yes?'

Himesor nodded.

'Note the cord that links the helm with the breastplate. It's a hollow tube. And the breastplate is actually a self-contained air supply. The armour would not just protect you against swords, but against germ warfare and dumdum bullets.' The Doctor turned excitedly to Himesor. 'You might think that I'm talking gibberish, but these suits are exactly what we're looking for!'

Outside the great doors two figures stood, straining after the sound of the Doctor's voice.

Commander Zaitabor ground his teeth in anger, and set off back up the tunnels. Araboam followed, disbelief rather than aggression clouding his features. 'Why, lord? Why let an outsider stare upon the holy relics?'

'Himesor says he has his reasons,' growled Zaitabor. 'But you and I both know that only death can follow such a violation. May that charlatan "Doctor" be cursed!' He thumped his fists together in outrage. 'We have much work to do,' he said in a quieter voice. 'We shall at least be able to dream of the Doctor's certain death while we do so.'

Zoe had never felt so humiliated and abused. The aches of her body, the clamouring emptiness of her stomach, the dirt under her nails and in her hair – all these things she would get over in time. But to be sold in a market like a piece of livestock – it was entirely beyond her comprehension.

When the man with the cigar had prodded her and laughed with the crowd she could almost have believed that she was having a nightmare.

But now the sun had turned to rain, the crowd had gone, and she was alone with her 'master'. 'Come with me,' he said, as though she had a choice in the matter. Her wrists were bound together with leather that bit tightly, and a rope led to the man's broad hands. 'I've bought some food, for when we get home. I'm afraid we must be leaving now. I can't stand this place.'

'I can't leave,' said Zoe. 'My friends are here. We're travellers, you see. I didn't want to get involved with any of this. If they leave without me –'

'The law is the law,' said the man. 'Especially here.' He paused in thought for a few moments. 'Here's what I'll do,' he said. 'I'll have my friend make some enquiries. If your companions are willing to come to me and make me an offer, then we shall see.'

'Where are we going?'

'Not too far. The next town. Trouble is, my horse is not the fastest creature that the sun has blessed, and with two of us on it . . .'

'Two of us, on one horse?' Zoe's mind filled with a confused rush of domesticated mammals that she had learnt about, and for the moment she couldn't remember which one was a horse. But whichever it was, surely it wouldn't be big enough.

'I'm afraid so,' said the man, leading Zoe through the crowd of the market. 'I also purchased an interesting casket, which is being sent ahead separately. I'm afraid I cannot do the same with you.'

'Oh,' said Zoe. She really didn't know what to say.

'Don't worry,' said the man, finally coming to a halt by a huge, pale, four-legged thing with flowing hair and large teeth. 'We'll be as gentle and as quick as we can.'

And without another word he reached down to bind Zoe's ankles together, and flung her over the back of the creature. Moments later they were off and beyond the city walls.

'It has been put to me that, by striving to exist beyond the harsh strictures of time, the Kuabris effectively have no meaning.

'Nothing could be further from the truth.

'As we have seen, it is the definition of science that begins to give it substance. Opposition needs to stem from knowledge, from definitions, from a pinning-down of the moth that is meaning. As impossible as it sounds, we must know what science has been, and what forms it could take in the future. We use the words of our enemies to condemn them.

'Therefore, we gain our existence as a contrast to the existence of something else. The Kuabris take on form to combat science: without science, we have no meaning. When we truly succeed in overthrowing science and the rational beast that lies dormant in all our minds, then – and at that very moment – the Kuabris will cease to exist, will take on some new and distant form.

'As with science, as with time. It is in the casting down of our knowledge of time that the Kuabris have meaning. Our secret knowledge points always in this direction. And when time stops, the Kuabris will take on a new form, a new pattern. For the moment, we exist because our battle exists.

'The further the evil man wanders from the Higher, the more he thinks in terms of legends. It could almost be argued that legends and stories from the past are in themselves meaningless, that they have no essential power. They are mere phantoms, voices without motivation.

'Some might claim that the legends that exist beyond the Kuabris are similar to our own noble secrets. However, the nature of the secrets and legends is paramount: this gives them a hint of divinity or the stink of evil. The common legends of the masses point to the past and insinuate an effect upon the ongoing now. *The Higher secrets of the Knights of Kuabris instead have no meaning beyond their very existence. There was never a time when they did not exist. They encourage us to travel onwards* now. *Mere legends point to the past and struggle to engineer an influence.*

'Our legends, our great artefacts, are made great by our

resolute strivings to attain the changeless now. *Just as science tugs and tempts, so tales "from the past" are birthed in evil. Science and depraved legend are strange bedfellows, but when they are allowed to combine their grotesque effect is enormous.*

'We must split them asunder, taking our meaning only from the now, *from our great secrets and all that we have, and destroy science* and *legend.*

'Recognition of legend pulling to the past is not difficult to those who have sought the Higher in praise and prayer. True recognition of science is more complex, and its pulls to "past" and "future" will be examined in more detail during the course of this book.'

> Extract from *Towards a Definition of Science*, written by Grand Knight Uscolda. Subsequently banned and destroyed by order of Grand Knight Zipreus.

Six

The brightly coloured tents and ox-pulled caravans were scattered over an area of flat ground at the edge of the town. The main tent had been erected first and was already surrounded by sideshows and exhibits. Lurid poster boards were being touched up with gleaming paint. Growls emanated from within portable huts as animals were fed and watered. A group of women scuttled from tent to tent, cleaning the mud from the unfurled canvas.

The workers were now constructing a light fence around the site, with a tall kiosk taking shape like a castle gatehouse. The hum of the wind on the ropes was lost to the intermittent chugging as the portable generator was coaxed into life. A miasma of smoke drifted across the field.

Even Zoe could feel the apprehension in the air. Mere hours from the first show there was still much to do, but the men and women seemed happy to have completed their latest journey.

As, indeed, was Zoe. Her back ached, and her face felt numb from the wind. Although the rope had long been removed from her wrists they still throbbed from their recent ill-treatment.

Despite the discomfort of the journey Zoe had felt a gathering lightness of spirit as they left the dark, rain-drenched city behind. The countryside had become lighter and more open, well-managed copses breaking into view over tumbling fields of grass and corn. It was as if the soil around the city was so thick and dark that it gave up few of its nutrients to the plant roots that burrowed down into it. A few miles beyond the stifling walls and the land seemed richer and more accommodating. Zoe remembered watching farmers and labourers waving from the fields, although perhaps it had been too much to expect any of them to rescue her.

The town was a carefree clutter of thatched roofs warming under the intermittent golden sun. She noticed a power station similar to the one in the city, but here its unrefined nature was more bucolic than overbearing. White clouds hung quietly in the air over its chimneys and then dissipated.

Although the larger houses on the far side of the town were dark and smugly impressive, in the main the place was a collage of painted stone and wood. The gaudy circus did not seem out of place against so colourful a backdrop.

'Diseaeda's Travelling Freak Show,' announced the man at her side. 'I'm sorry the journey was rough, but I think you'll agree that it's quite a sight.'

'I've never seen anything like this before,' said Zoe. A small troupe of jacket-wearing monkeys danced by, cartwheeling and chattering, their trainer in hot pursuit. 'There are animals here, and yet the purpose is clearly to provide entertainment and not to facilitate zoological research.'

'Entertainment is exactly it,' said Diseaeda. 'You've got a good head on your shoulders. I'm sure you'll come up with some valuable ideas in future.'

Zoe pondered this for a moment. 'I get the impression that you didn't purchase me because of any business acumen I might have.'

Diseaeda laughed. 'Indeed no. It's much simpler than that. Unlike most of my friends, I bought you because you're pretty and you've got two arms and two legs. I'm expecting you to work hard. But I'll make sure that it's all worth it. I promise.'

Zoe could tell that Diseaeda meant well, but she felt very lonely indeed without the Doctor and Jamie. 'How long will you be staying here?' she asked, trying not to let her fear show in her voice.

'A week, maybe two,' said the man. 'It depends on the crowds. The folk round here are quite generous and, more to the point, they're not easily frightened.'

'So this town is very different from the city we've come from?'

'As different as night and day. The knights wouldn't tolerate a show like mine.'

'So perhaps the knights aren't so bad after all,' said Zoe, more harshly than she'd intended.

It was clearly an argument that Diseaeda was familiar with. 'You think I exploit these poor creatures?' he asked. For a moment Zoe couldn't tell if he meant the animals or the semi-human grotesques. 'Maybe I do. But if it's a choice between death in a gutter or life in a show, I know what I'd choose. Anyway, you'll have plenty of time to ask my "exhibits" at first hand.' He suddenly bellowed to someone behind Zoe. 'Oi! Go and put those tent pegs in properly!' Zoe turned to see a young lad sheepishly return to a job he thought he'd completed.

'So this is your latest acquisition?' came a female voice at Diseaeda's side.

Zoe turned back, and saw two young women standing at Diseaeda's side. Their almost identical faces bore the smiles of delighted imps, and they fidgeted constantly with the buckles of their overalls.

With an almost audible gasp Zoe noticed that the women were joined at the waist, two bodies atop a single pair of legs.

'I'm Raitak,' said one, before Zoe could say a word.
'I'm Reisaz,' said the other.
'Two of my very best friends,' said Diseaeda. 'They'll show you around. By all means ask them what I'm like to work for.'
Reisaz giggled, then fell silent under Raitak's icy stare.
'I'll see you before the first show commences,' said Diseaeda before striding off into the distance.
'Right,' said Raitak. 'Follow me.'
'Us,' said Reisaz.
As if in a nightmare Zoe followed the twins into a nearby tent, struggling all the time to not let the shock that she felt show on her face.

Himesor reverently removed the first of the holy Kuabris robes from the cases. A young knight came forward, eyes averted from the metal and cloth construction being handed to him. His hands trembled as he took hold of the clothing.
The one-piece under-suit was designed to cover the entire body, with the exception of the head. The material was the colour of gold, and it rustled like silk as the young man pulled it on. Obviously surprised by its strength, the man gently poked at the fabric. His face was a picture of disbelieving privilege and extreme bewilderment.
Once the man had pulled strong metal plates on to his shins and forearms, the Doctor helped him with the bulky white chest-piece. It too had the appearance of armour, but the Doctor recognized its true function. He took the end of the transparent tube that ran into the helmet, and plugged it into the top of the air supply on the breastplate. He motioned for the knight to hold the helm under his arm for a moment.
The Doctor turned, and saw that the five other knights, including Himesor, had followed suit. 'Now you, Doctor,' smiled the Grand Knight.

'Yes, of course.' The Doctor struggled into the proffered body-suit. His trousers, trapped within the golden leggings, bulged around his knees. He struggled to put things straight. 'Give me a hand,' he said, flustered. 'There's a good fellow.'

Himesor pulled the suit into position.

The Doctor clapped his hands together. 'Now, you've told your men how these robes work?'

'They are conversant with the secondary properties of the Kuabris armour,' said Himesor carefully. 'I have ordered that a complement of knights accompany us to the entrance to the sewers.'

'Oh, really, there's no need,' said the Doctor. 'I can't stand fuss. Let's just pop down into these sewers of yours and –'

'I am agreed that we need to proceed with some degree of urgency,' said Himesor, turning to face his men. 'We will pray for the success of our mission in this holy place,' he announced in a loud voice. 'Then we shall proceed to the armoury to collect the best of the Kuabris weapons. These shall surely slay the evil creatures below the ground.' He smiled. 'All glory to the Higher!'

'Higher be praised!' responded the knights.

'*Gesundheit*,' said the Doctor solemnly.

Defrabax had once been told that in some distant region men caught and ate creatures of the rivers. He was reminded of this repugnant practice because the men who caught the creatures needed great patience, sitting on the river bank with, he was reliably informed, only a stick and a long piece of thread for comfort.

Defrabax, on the other hand, was not a patient man. His natural disinclination to wait was not helped by the fact that mere feet away a huge stone pipe from the sewers fed directly into the river, and the smell was nauseating. It was raining again, so the effluent was taken away at some speed, but that was scant consolation. Defrabax was not only bored and smelly but wet. Three worse states combined he could not imagine.

He shifted his weight, trying to find some escape from the drizzle under the bare branches of a tree. Without getting to his feet he reached for a stone, and then hurled it into the water. A thick green spray marked its silent passing.

The creatures were late, as usual. Sometimes it amazed him that they could think and walk at the same time. Still, their stupidity meant that they were unlikely to question his motives. Until their tiny little brains worked out exactly what was going on, they'd follow him blindly.

At least, that was the idea.

There was a sound from deep within the pipe, just audible above the sound of the water. A few moments later the first creature emerged, followed by another two. They swung themselves up on to the top of the pipe with their strong arms, and then dropped down to the grassy bank. They made a great show of wiping their feet before coming across to Defrabax.

Defrabax rose to his feet. 'I'm pleased to see you –'

'We are tired,' snapped the leader of the ape-like creatures, his already heavy brow furrowed in concentration. 'Long ago you say we have part of bright world. Defrabax still in bright world and Rocarbies still in dark.'

'Don't worry, my friends,' said Defrabax. 'Everything is working out for the good of your people.'

'Defrabax promise part of bright world if we help. We help. Do not have part of bright world.'

Defrabax smiled. 'Just a little longer. I still need to overthrow the knights.'

'We do not care about the knights.'

'No,' said Defrabax, more firmly this time. 'You must listen to me. Unless we proceed carefully the knights will destroy your race. When the new governing authorities are in place, however, I am sure that they would be delighted to receive a delegation from your people.'

'Rocarbies restless. Now we have seen the bright. New leaders not come, not let us up soon. We come and take this bright world!'

'There will be no need for that. Your attacks are already causing great confusion and uncertainty. The knights are powerless, their influence is waning. My homunculus has reported that almost everything has been prepared below ground. New leaders will soon be required – no, demanded – by the people.'

'Knights come to dark world.' Typically of Rocarby speech patterns, the question sounded like a statement, Defrabax puzzling over the meaning of the words for a moment.

'The knights cannot come down into your world,' said Defrabax firmly. 'They don't know how to. You and the other underground races are perfectly safe.'

'Good. Do well for us, Defrabax.' With that the ape creatures turned away from the old man.

Defrabax adjusted his hat against the rain and started to walk back to the city.

The Doctor and Himesor marched through the city at the head of a large group of knights. Most were dressed in ostentatious armour, their cloaks held just above the muddy surface of the streets. A small number were dressed in the golden protection suits. They probably made an impressive sight if the apprehensive glances of the city-dwellers were anything to go by. A hushed silence fell over the city as they walked.

The Doctor felt faintly embarrassed in his much-too-large suit, trotting to stay at Himesor's side. The Grand Knight stared impassively ahead, and for the moment the Doctor could read nothing in his face.

Not for the first time the Doctor hoped that the

centuries-old protective outfits would still function. Even more worrying was the fate of Jamie and Zoe, neither of whom he had heard word of since their arrest the previous night. He hated it when they were separated, but would have to trust in their own intuition and ability for a while longer.

He allowed something of the excitement of exploration to wash over him as they approached the drain covering set in the centre of the street. Despite the ignominious entrance, the Doctor trusted that the subterranean world would reveal sufficient secrets for Himesor to release him to find his friends. If in the process the Doctor established the nature and demise of the previous civilization – the same civilization that produced the protective suits and many of the items in the Kuabris Most Holy Place – then so much the better.

Not, as the Doctor reminded himself, that he had much choice in the matter. The Doctor would help Himesor in every way possible, or face execution as a scientist. At least you know where you stand with Himesor, he thought.

The Doctor fanned his face when the knights came to a halt before the grating. He was relieved to note that the crowds that had followed their progress from the castle had quickly dispersed. None, it seemed, wanted to stand around while the knights violated the Menagerie of Ukkazaal.

'What next, Doctor?' asked the Grand Knight.

The Doctor nudged the grill with his foot, sniffing the air sourly. 'We go down, Grand Knight.'

'We'll never get into the Castle of Kuabris,' moaned Cosmae.

'Och, quit your blathering,' said Jamie. 'We're nearly there now.'

'And how do you propose to get past the knights?'

Cosmae pointed upwards at the dark towers. 'You might be able to trick the guards, but the Knights of Kuabris will not prove so stupid.'

'We'll think of something,' said Jamie. But he paused in the shadows of the castle, his face upturned to catch signs of life in the numerous windows. In that moment something cold and electric gripped his spine. It was not that he was frightened. But already he could feel the evil within striving to impress as well as repulse him.

Jamie collected his thoughts. 'It's perfectly simple,' he said. 'The Doctor and your girl are in there. So, somehow, that's where we need to be, too.'

'You have a very clear mind, Jamie.'

'Few'd give me that credit.' He reached down to check his concealed dirk for the hundredth time. 'But with this wee beauty folk have always seen my point.'

'There's a patrol coming,' said Cosmae. The two young men pressed themselves into the shadows and watched as a handful of knights walked the distance between the last few stunted houses and the massive gatehouse. There was no door or portcullis to impede their march. The shadows swallowed them up as they proceeded across the castle courtyard, although the sound of their armour rattling could be heard on the still air for a while longer. 'The one thing we have in our favour,' said Cosmae as he stood up, 'is the fear that the knights have generated over the years. As a result, the castle is barely defended. My master said that there were only a handful of guards stationed at the gatehouse, but many knights within the castle.'

'So the gatehouse should prove easy,' commented Jamie. 'Pretend you've apprehended me. That you're under-cover for –'

'Under-cover?'

Jamie sighed. There were times when his ever-increasing vocabulary was little but a hindrance. 'Pretend that you're a knight or a guard but that you've been tracking me in disguise. If you act like you know what you're doing, they'll believe you.'

'Are you sure?'

'Aye, the Doctor does this all the time.' Jamie handed Cosmae his dirk. It shone like a lamp even in the morning's gloom. 'Hold this to my throat. Not too close, mind.'

Cosmae nodded. They were just within sight of the guards who milled around the open doorway. 'Here we go,' said Cosmae softly, before bundling Jamie forwards.

Reisaz and Raitak pulled back a heavy grey curtain and ushered Zoe into the hut. 'You'll like this,' said Reisaz. 'Diseaeda's collection of dead things.'

'*So* exploitative,' said Raitak, smiling at Zoe.

The Siamese twins had given Zoe a tour of the entire site. They quickly surmised her interests, marvelling at her degrees and her range of knowledge, even though Zoe was sure that most of what she said meant less than nothing to them. They had taken her to the primitive generator that powered the lights strung like dew-covered webs over the expanse of the circus. Without thinking Zoe called it a museum piece. Raitak snapped that it had cost Diseaeda half of his profits for one year, that it had come from the edge of the world and was, in fact, a scientific marvel. Reisaz whispered conspiratorially that the Knights of Kuabris didn't know about the machine, and that their licensed 'research' had done little more than develop what was already common knowledge in other regions. Zoe questioned the man in charge of the machine, but it was clear that he didn't even know what principles the machine worked on. For him, it was magic that it worked at all, and a miracle when it didn't break down.

There were many freaks like the twins. She caught

glimpses of the tallest man she had ever seen, always edgily on the move, checking light bulbs and the overhead cables. There was a man with no eyes, his cheeks rising smoothly to meet a furrowed brow of concentration. A rather short-tempered woman with a beard snapped at her when she bent to examine some slowly cooking stew. And then there were the silent clowns, the strongmen, the acrobats, who spent more time on their hands than their feet, and myriad creatures who grazed on the scrubby tufts of grass or paced angrily in cages.

Her interest in alien morphology had in turn led her to the grandly titled Hall of Grotesques, a large hut of dark wood. Zoe stepped inside, followed by the twins. Raitak held up a lamp, while Reisaz half-turned to secure the curtain with a silken cord. 'Obviously, by evening, the lights in here will be working,' said Raitak.

'It's very cleverly done,' said Reisaz. 'Pools of light, illuminating the dead things just as you turn to the next exhibit.'

'The man who used to look after all this,' said Raitak, 'went mad. Said that the exhibits would move when he wasn't looking.'

Reisaz made a little whizzing sound in her throat and mockingly smacked the side of her head.

'It was very sad,' said Raitak, silencing her sister with a stern glance. 'No one deserves to end up like that.' The twins walked over to the first exhibit. 'Diseaeda ensured that the man was looked after.'

Zoe knew that, as with so many of the twins' comments, the real meaning of the woman's words was simple: Diseaeda is no ghoulish fiend. But Zoe wasn't especially interested in this character reference. Whatever the respect he inspired in the workers and performers, Zoe had been arrested, thrown into a smelly jail, sold at auction, subjected to the most excruciating journey she had ever suffered, and was now working at a glorified freak show. She wasn't in the mood to thank Diseaeda for *anything*. She opened her mouth to speak, but thought better of it. And she promised herself never to complain of space travel again.

'First exhibit: the bones of a dragon,' announced Reisaz. Zoe peered into the glass cabinet and saw on a mock-velvet-covered plinth a humanoid skull and assorted bones. Only a bony ridge on the forehead – probably false? – hinted at anything beyond the strictly human.

'I'm not convinced,' said Zoe quietly.

'The mummified body of a giant insect,' said Raitak, pointing to the next cubicle. 'Found in the icy wastes in the south.'

'Now that's quite impressive,' nodded Zoe. 'The tissue seems hardly damaged.' She saw myriad faces peering back at her from the creature's compound eye. She turned to ask the twins about the probable age of the creature, and caught sight of an exhibit behind them. 'But this is more my field,' she announced, striding across the room to the opposite wall. 'It looks like a cryogenic suspension unit.'

'A woman of fine taste and judgement!' noted Reisaz.

Raitak nodded. 'That's the newest exhibit, my friend. Found in the same city as your good self.'

'Though there,' said Reisaz, 'the similarity ends.'

Zoe unclipped the rope that was held at waist height across the alcove, and dropped on to her knees to inspect the casket. 'It's quite advanced,' she said. 'The principle is simple enough, but the execution is perfect.'

'You're not supposed to touch the exhibits,' said Raitak.

'I wouldn't worry,' said Zoe. 'There's no power left in this thing. The creature will have died centuries ago.'

'Is it a coffin?' asked Reisaz.

'Not really,' said Zoe. 'This will put a creature to sleep.

Decades later, when it's needed, it can be woken up again.'

'And the creature is definitely dead?' asked Reisaz quietly.

Zoe stood up, wiping condensation from the glass that formed the top half of the cabinet. 'Almost certainly.' She stared down at the creature's talon-tipped arms and its rough, muscly hide. 'Some creatures could survive for centuries like this, but –'

There was a brief hum of power, and a 3D display sprang into life, showing a shallow graph of life readings and cryogenic integrity. Before even Zoe's well-ordered mind could take it all in the casket became silent again.

'Ah,' said Zoe, the concern in her voice making the twins instantly look up from the incredible machine. 'There is some energy left in the cells. It comes through in irregular bursts. This unit could have been working until fairly recently.'

'How?' asked Reisaz. 'I see no cables, hear no noise of engines.'

'A battery can hold on to energy and discharge it when required. It's a bit like . . .' Zoe glanced around for an example. 'Like your lamp. Unlike the circus light bulbs it can give off light for long periods of time.'

'I see,' said Reisaz. 'Is the coffin safe?'

'It's not the coffin that ought to worry us,' said Zoe. 'I'm not sure this creature is dead after all.'

Seven

With some difficulty the grating was pulled back. The Doctor squatted and peered down into the darkness. The suit protected him from the stench that for many years had so effectively prevented thorough exploration of the sewers. A glowing lantern – its naked flame covered to minimize the chance of an explosion – was passed to the Doctor. He swung it experimentally back and forth. Silver drips of water twinkled and then faded in the darkness of the concrete shaft. 'There's a metal ladder,' he announced. 'Not much else is visible for the moment. Shall we proceed?'

He turned to the knights, all of whom had now pulled their helmets into position. Only Himesor's height allowed the Doctor to differentiate him from his colleagues.

Himesor nodded, and indicated that he would descend first, the Doctor following close behind.

The Doctor found it difficult to grip the ladder through the thick gauntlets. The rusted metal was slippery with folds of green slime, and he almost fell as he began his descent. Metal flaked away under his grip and fell past Himesor like scarlet shooting stars. Truth be told, the Doctor was glad that he couldn't see where they were going. He wasn't one for heights.

He risked another glance downwards to Himesor, who was already twenty feet below him. The Grand Knight was moving down the ladder with herculean exactitude, the lantern clipped into position on his belt. Above the Doctor, and doubtless impeded by his slow progress, came five more knights, most of whom also carried lanterns.

The Doctor's foot came off a half-broken rung. He wrapped both arms around the ladder while his boots fought for purchase on the ladder. Just as they did so his mind, confused by the darkness, made a sudden cognitive jump, and he seemed to spin dizzily through ninety degrees.

His neck and forehead were cold with sweat. In the terrible black silence gravity seemed no longer to exert a steady influence. One moment the Doctor felt that he was clambering along the underside of a roof; next, the blood seemed to rush to his head as, head-first like a spider, he negotiated a long strand of metal. He couldn't remember if he was going upwards or downwards. Perhaps he should just step away from the ladder and take stock of the situation.

He felt an arm behind his back. The knight above him had descended along the edge of the ladder and was holding the Doctor in position. 'Are you all right?' came the muffled voice through a helmet of frosted glass. The Doctor had decided against telling the knights how to operate the inter-suit communication devices. He wondered for a moment if he had made a wise decision.

The Doctor listened for the regular drip of water, and compared its tempo to that of his blood surging through his body. Very slowly, he turned his head. 'Thank you,' he said, smiling through the darkness at the knight. 'The air here seems a bit thin. The suits don't register any problems, but . . .'

'It's made me feel a bit dizzy, too,' said the knight.

Just at that moment Himesor's voice ascended the deep shaft. 'I'm at the bottom.'

'Come on, then,' said the knight. 'Let's keep on going.'

Breathing heavily, and staring only at his hands as they alternately gripped and released the rough metal rungs, the Doctor resumed his descent.

'I've never seen clothes like that before,' said the old guard, munching on a greasy chicken bone and looking the boy up and down.

'He's a foreigner,' said the lad who claimed to be a knight. He continued to hold the small dagger to the skirt-wearer's throat.

The guard tutted. 'You wait till I tell my good woman when I get back. I scarce can believe my eyes.' He saluted lazily, and then waved the two of them through the gatehouse and across the cobbled courtyard.

Once they were out of earshot, the man turned to one of the other guards, whispering tersely. 'Quickly. Send word to Commander Zaitabor. An outsider, and the mage's ward.'

He watched as the young guard disappeared into a doorway in one of the walls, and then hurled the stripped bone towards the slavering dogs that played around his feet. 'They must think me mighty simple,' he said. Across the yard he saw the main doorway into Castle Kuabris close behind the two young men with an air of grim finality. How many people had the castle swallowed up in this manner, never to be seen again? Perhaps some were still trapped deep below the surface in its icy cells. Or perhaps another fate awaited them.

It was best not to think about such matters. Best just to follow orders.

Diseaeda ran his hands over the casket. They came away covered with condensation. 'You say this thing should always be cold?'

'Yes,' said Zoe. 'It's essential for the proper operation of the device.'

'How does it work?'

'There's no time to explain,' said Zoe impatiently. 'I must reconnect the cryogenic relays and –'

'I'm sorry,' said Diseaeda. 'I can't allow you to indulge in such fancies. Not until after the show, in any case. The gates open in a couple of hours. I'll need you to help sell tickets at the desk. Remember: you've got to be charming and polite. Flirt with the men a little, but don't get –'

'No!' said Zoe firmly. 'That creature could be dangerous. It could still be alive.'

'Well then,' said Diseaeda. 'It'll just have to become a main attraction, that's all. I'll warn the strongmen and the beast tamers to check in here on a regular basis. Now, you must prepare for the fun and games of this evening. We'll leave this magic casket for some other time. Take a wash in the twins' cabin.'

Zoe opened her mouth to argue but was quelled by Diseaeda's implacable gaze. 'I clearly have no choice in the matter,' she said.

Diseaeda nodded. 'Trust me,' he said. 'I've been in this trade since you were a mere bump under your mother's breasts. Everything will be all right.'

Jamie whistled appreciatively as he looked at the polished walls and ornately carved ceiling of the hall. With the main doorway to his back, the corridor extended almost out of sight to his right and left, doors and the bottom of stairs visible in regularly spaced archways. The ceiling lamps flickered erratically, brightening the dull grey wash of light from the huge windows. It had just started to rain again, a light drizzle tapping on the glass.

'Told you it would work,' he said.

Cosmae shrugged, his darting eyes searching for signs of movement. 'I think that old guard knew me.'

'That's as maybe,' said Jamie. 'Now, give me the dirk. Whatever happens, I feel safer with this.'

'Now what do we do?' asked Cosmae.

Jamie was beginning to find the boy's whining just a little irritating. 'Where are the cells?' he asked.

'Somewhere under the castle, I would imagine.'

'Aye,' said Jamie. 'That figures.'

There was a loud creak from the stairway closest to them, and then the sound of footsteps. Jamie grabbed Cosmae by the shoulder, and the two of them ducked through the archway and underneath the steps. Most of the space was taken up by old curtains and sheet, roped together in bundles, but Cosmae and Jamie were just able to squeeze into position. Jamie breathed in a lungful of disturbed dust, and had to hold his nose to stop himself from sneezing.

Moments later Jamie peered around the edge of the stairs and caught a glimpse of a knight in full ceremonial armour. The sky-blue cloak and helmet plumes were a clear indication of senior rank. The huge sword at the man's waist was a reminder of the danger he and Cosmae were in.

The knight paused, a few steps from the bottom. He removed his helmet, his head moving from side to side like a falcon alert for the minutest sounds of prey. The knight's hands were roughly level with Jamie's head. Jamie withdrew as far as he could into the shadows.

Jamie's heart sounded like something being hammered into shape at a forge, his breathing like huge bellows. He was sure to give away their position. He stared at the shadow of the knight on the stairs, expecting sudden movement and capture. He drew in breath as quietly as he could.

After an agonizing silence Jamie heard the man sigh. The knight trotted down the last few steps. He stayed out of sight for a few moments, presumably still searching for something. A few moments later the sound of footsteps moving further down the corridor was music to Jamie's ears.

He turned. Cosmae seemed to have stopped breathing,

his skin an odd blue colour. Jamie nudged him and he drew in a great whooping breath that sounded not dissimilar to badly played bagpipes. 'It's Zaitabor,' Cosmae said when eventually the colour returned to his cheeks. 'Second only to the Grand Knight.'

'Maybe we should follow him,' said Jamie. 'The Doctor's bound to be in some sort of trouble. He's probably being interrogated by the leaders at this very moment.'

Cosmae nodded. 'It's possible if we find this Doctor fellow he'll know where Kaquaan is as well.'

Jamie and Cosmae emerged slowly from their hiding place. When they crept into the corridor they were just in time to see a flash of blue close to a stairway to their left. The stairs of rough, yellowed stone led downwards and into darkness. Even at the top of the staircase they could smell dampness and decay. 'The cells?' asked Jamie.

'Possibly,' said Cosmae.

They walked quickly down the stairway. Jamie descended first, clutching his dirk tightly. Cosmae followed, glancing upwards for movement in the hallway. Both wondered at the quietness of the castle so far – as if the knights were otherwise engaged. A chill gripped them as they moved down the twisted stairway.

As Jamie reached the bottom he saw the knight about twenty yards further down the corridor. In that direction the walls were damp with mould. The doorways which led off from it were of stout, dark wood, with little metal gratings towards the top.

Zaitabor was talking to another knight. Although dressed much like the others, keys jangled from the man's belt, elbows and knees. His dirty helm had a large copper key as some sort of standard in the place of the usual flowing plumes. He held a thick torch of soaked rags and twigs, which provided almost the only illumination in the entire corridor.

Midway between the knights and the bottom of the stairs was a recessed alcove. Thankful for the semi-darkness Jamie edged towards this. Concentrating intently on the conversation ahead of him, Jamie slipped into the alcove. A few moments later Cosmae followed. Jamie could almost feel his fear through the shadows.

Both knights laughed loudly, the noise chasing around the stone columns and buttresses.

'So, has the young lady been apprehended?' The voice – presumably Zaitabor's – was thick with sarcasm, as if the words were intended for public consumption, but the real meaning was altogether different. Jamie felt the hairs on the back of his neck rising.

'No, Commander. The *lady* must have escaped from the castle.'

'What, escaped from Castle Kuabris?' There was a quieter, sniggering laugh. 'That cannot be possible!'

'As jailor, I throw myself on your mercy!'

There was a pregnant pause, and then another storm of laughter.

When it had subsided Zaitabor said, 'It is time.' His voice was cold now, all trace of humour gone.

'Yes, Commander,' said the jailor quietly.

Jamie and Cosmae watched as the two knights marched past their hiding place, oblivious to their presence. A few moments later Jamie set out to follow them. The muffled sound of chattering teeth reminded Jamie that his young friend was not far behind.

The bottom part of the ladder was bolted on to the brick wall of an expansive chamber of echoes and reflecting water. From the far end of the room there came the sound of a constant downpour of water, the source of which the Doctor shuddered to contemplate. The lamplight played weaving strands of silver on to the ceiling, but could not even begin to illuminate the full extent of the chamber. The Doctor estimated from the echoes that the room was roughly circular, and a full hundred feet in diameter.

He turned to Himesor. 'You have the map?'

Himesor nodded. 'Despite the legends of the Menagerie occasional inspections were made in the past, before the fumes became too noxious.' Himesor angled the parchment towards his lamp. The Doctor could see his look of concentration through the helmet.

'You spoke of past events,' said the Doctor. 'A sin for a Knight of Kuabris, surely?'

Himesor ignored him, staring at the parchment. After a moment he nodded. 'Ah, Doctor, I see the reasoning behind the route you propose. I wondered at first what complicated scientific process had so accurately plotted a course through the myriad interconnected tunnels and pipes of the sewer. But now I see. As in the castle, the secrets are always downwards.'

The Doctor nodded, 'Well, it's one possible approach. I don't guarantee that we'll find your Menagerie, but –'

'No matter.' Himesor splashed through the water and towards one of the dark tunnels that led off from the chamber. He could just about fit into it without crouching, but the group would have to move through it in single file. Himesor drew his sword. Scratches along the edge of the keen blade indicated that, unlike much of the Kuabris armour, this weapon had seen battle.

The Doctor heard the other knights draw their weapons. He followed Himesor into the tunnel. It descended quickly and was reasonably dry. The brickwork seemed a few hundred years old, no more. There were occasional signs of more recent repair, of mismatching bricks and bright mortar.

The Doctor was about to comment on this when he heard shouts behind him. Two of the knights were poking about their feet with their swords. One was laughing. There was an animal cry, and a rat-like thing shot down the tunnel and past the Doctor and Himesor.

'No real monsters yet,' the Doctor said as Himesor turned to see what all the fuss was.

'This tunnel doesn't go much further,' said Himesor, trudging onwards. 'Then we should be able to –' The Grand Knight stopped for a moment, and looked around him. 'Doctor. These walls.'

'Hmm?' The Doctor walked up to Himesor, and quickly saw the source of Himesor's concern. The rough brick tunnel came to an untidy conclusion, replaced over a few yards by walls of polished and coloured metal. The Doctor ran his hands over them. 'The metal's as smooth as when this corridor was first constructed.'

'Which was?'

'Hundreds, perhaps thousands, of years ago.' The Doctor smiled at the puzzled Grand Knight. 'It is as I suspected. Your city – perhaps symbolically speaking the cultures of your entire world – is built on the graveyard of a much older civilization.'

Jamie and Cosmae had managed to follow Zaitabor and the jailor for some time without being discovered. On occasions they had been forced to hide from lone knights walking the corridors, but it was clear that they were preoccupied and certainly not expecting infiltrators within the castle.

Despite these interruptions, and Cosmae's anguished expressions of concern that Jamie had quietened, they had not lost track of the two knights. Jamie, used to tracking Redcoats through the heather, had pursued them through the corridors with some skill. It had very quickly dawned on him, however, that the two knights were adopting similarly stealthy tactics. Cosmae had said that Zaitabor was second in command, and presumably the jailor was a knight of some esteem, but both moved like furtive predators. On most occasions they had received the salutes from the other knights that they encountered with dignity, but very occasionally they too had ducked into shadowy alcoves to avoid detection. Jamie was no genius, but he found this very odd.

Jamie and Cosmae turned another corner. The corridor was long and narrow. Jamie estimated that Zaitabor and the jailor should have been no more than halfway down it, but they were nowhere to be seen. There was only one door, at the far end of the corridor.

'I suppose that this is one of the corridors within the walls that link the towers,' whispered Cosmae.

'Aye,' nodded Jamie. 'But where can those two knights have gone?' Jamie tried to think the situation through. Either they had disappeared – which would have surprised him only in as much as his travels with the Doctor tended to indicate that such technology was well in advance of what he had so far seen – or they had used a secret door.

'A what?' asked Cosmae when Jamie explained it to him.

'A secret door, a priest hole, a concealed hiding place or maybe a tunnel that connects two rooms.' Jamie smiled. 'The Doctor is very fond of a game called *Cluedo*. That has two secret passages, leading from the lounge to the conservatory and . . .'

Cosmae looked at Jamie blankly.

'Och, just help me look, will you?'

The walls were made of cold grey stone, covered by a number of floor-length tapestries on both walls. Jamie's eyes twinkled. Surely it couldn't be this simple? Surely real life didn't work like children's fiction?

'Jamie!' Cosmae was standing by a huge tapestry, depicting a forest glade and a virginal woman in long white robes with a sleeping dragon at her feet. Jamie saw the folds of material move as if in a draught.

'What did I tell you?' exclaimed the young Scot in delight. He pulled the tapestry back to reveal a small doorway. The door itself had not been closed properly, and a cold wind ran over Jamie's hand as he opened it further. Narrow stairs went down into the darkness.

Jamie began to descend the steep stairway, anxious not to lose too much time in their pursuit of the two knights. The stairs twisted tightly like a corkscrew. Jamie could see the effects of a flickering light of some sort below him, but of Zaitabor and the jailor there was no trace.

The air became colder as they descended, the stairs leading down from the castle and into the rock on which it sat. The stairs eventually led to a small vestibule of naturally sculpted rock. An iron torch-holder had been unceremoniously forced into position just above the doorway. Just inside the room Jamie could see the stairway continuing downwards.

Jamie stepped into the room, Cosmae following close behind. The chamber contained a large number of wooden racks, pushed roughly against one wall, and a small 'window' where the rock had thinned and then collapsed.

The racks contained a large amount of Kuabris armour and a few robes of red cloth, but Jamie and Cosmae were drawn immediately to the window by a noise from beyond.

The window afforded them an excellent view of the huge cave where, presumably, the carved stairway terminated. The cavern of grey and white rock was hundreds of feet across and roughly rectangular. The floor had clearly been flattened and polished, but most of the rock was untouched, bar the numerous lamps set into the roof. Spindly wooden ladders pushed to one side gave an indication of the time and skill needed to light so unaccommodating a room. The lanterns twinkled in the roof like stars in the night sky.

In the centre stood a large altar of what looked like granite. Its sides were decorated with gold leaf and small jewels, although its once smooth upper surface was deeply scarred and stained with a few patches of what appeared to be dried blood.

To one side of the altar stood three semi-circles of hooded figures, their bodies and down-turned faces entirely obscured by the red robes that matched those few left behind on the wooden racks in the small room. The cavern was filled with random whispers and muffled sobs.

Facing them was a man in brown robes, his face obscured by a huge insect-like mask. Golden mandibles took the place of a mouth, and multi-faceted eyes glittered in the light like huge diamonds. His hands were raised up towards the heavens, revealing arms covered with scars and crude tattoos. He swayed for a few moments, fists clasping and clawing as if battling with something, and then he let out a huge shriek.

The room became silent and the leader lowered his arms. A huge man emerged from the shadows, his arms as thick as most men's thighs. His expansive stomach was hidden by a stained overall. A wooden hammer was gripped in one great hand.

As he approached the altar two acolytes came forward carrying, with some difficulty, an ungainly piece of machinery. Jamie did not recognize it, but could identify individual components: there were cogs, belts, valves and pistons. Even the Doctor would have had difficulty identifying the machine, as the moment it was placed on the altar the huge overall-clad man raised the hammer with both his hands and brought it swiftly downwards. Pieces of metal and spring flew off in all directions. The hooded men pressed closer, excitedly throwing the debris back on to the altar.

The hammer came down again, splitting the device in

two. Slivers of metal cut into the man's hands but he appeared not to notice. The robed men came even closer to the altar, oblivious to the dangers, sighing as the huge mallet came down again.

The man beat out a slow, dull rhythm with the hammer. Soon the altar and the floor around it was covered with mangled metal. At a sign from the leader, he stood to one side, staring down at the floor, breathing heavily.

The debris was taken away. The man with the insect mask spoke for the first time. 'The brotherhood salutes you, oh Higher, Hater of Science, Crusher of Untruth, Purger of Legends Not Our Own!'

'Bow before him!' came the reply, the men's voices sounding like the breathing of the caves.

'Let all who stand on this your world quake and seek you now!'

'No past, no future, no word, no tune, no life, no death.' The cowled figures began to repeat the mantra, some screaming, some whispering. One or two dropped to their knees, whilst others reached upwards, imploring.

'Now!' cried the man in the mask, and there was quiet again. The men reassembled in their orderly rows, their faces cast downwards. 'Now shall we deal with those who oppose the true ways of the Brotherhood of Rexulon! Mindful of the evil that the Higher perceives even in our very midst, let us strive to placate him.' With a curt nod a woman was brought forward from the far end of the room. She was obviously drugged. Two robed men carried her forwards, her bare feet slipping over the floor. She was dressed in a simple black robe, with a white cord around her waist as a belt. Her brown hair had been crudely cut short, gashes in her scalp visible even from Jamie's position. Her eyes occasionally flicked open but her head sagged on to her chest.

As the woman was bundled towards the altar

Jamie heard Cosmae gasp in shock. 'It's Kaquaan!' he exclaimed, so loudly that for a moment Jamie feared that the boy's voice would be heard in the chamber below. Cosmae tried to say something else, but it stayed locked in his throat, his lips moving silently. Deathly pale and transfixed, Cosmae stared through the window.

The girl was pulled up on to the altar surface. Although she offered no resistance her arms were held by the two men.

The insect face nodded curtly and the brotherhood watched silently as the large man returned to the altar. He spat on his hands, and then reached for the handle of the huge hammer.

In deathly silence he raised the hammer over his head and prepared to bring it down.

Eight

Zoe had seen circuses in dramatic reconstructions and on archive film, but never had she expected to join one. She peered out at the audience through a gap in the curtains.

'Is it full?' asked Reisaz.

'Nearly,' said Zoe. She turned to the twins. 'Don't you find it frightening?'

Raitak straightened her jacket, an unusual tension in her movements. 'There are many frightening things in the world. Poverty, illness, hatred. Compared to them, a good crowd is nothing to be feared at all.'

'Mind you,' said Reisaz, 'we both get nervous, if that's what you mean.'

'Some people call it maggots in the stomach,' grimaced Raitak. 'A most unpleasant image.'

'And we're not worried about being called freaks, either,' said Reisaz. 'The whole purpose of our act is to win over the crowd.'

Zoe parted the curtains again and looked through. The huge tent had been assembled with remarkable efficiency, and rows of seating stretched towards the roof. People were making their way to the last remaining seats. Mothers and children barely dressed in rags worked their way towards the benches near the ring as besuited gentlemen with tall, dark hats moved earnestly towards the plusher seats further up. Even higher up, gantries were suspended from the roof, people clambering over them like monkeys and settling into position behind large moveable lamps. The generator that powered them was silent beneath the waves of excited chatter.

All but one lamp flicked off, leaving a single dagger of light to illuminate Diseaeda as he walked smartly into the centre of the ring, dressed in an immaculate blue suit. The crowd immediately became quiet and a hushed expectation filled the air. Even from Zoe's vantage point she could tell that Diseaeda was in his element.

'My friends,' he said grandly, his rich voice ringing out as far as the back seats, 'welcome to the first performance of Diseaeda's Travelling Freak Show and Circus. I hope that you have enjoyed looking around the static displays beyond these walls – if not, then there is plenty of time afterwards to sample our selection of tricks, games and monsters. But for the moment, please enjoy tonight's show, and –'

He broke off as a monkey tugged at his sleeve, seemingly impatient for his attention. A second, smaller light illuminated the little creature.

Diseaeda looked down with annoyance. 'Not now,' he said in a loud whisper, 'I'm trying to greet our guests.' The crowd began to chuckle.

Diseaeda straightened and opened his mouth to speak when the creature tugged his jacket again, even more insistently. The monkey chattered and pointed towards the back of the ring.

Another light snapped on, revealing a figure in yellow and pink clothes suspended head-first from the ceiling by a long rope. The rest of the monkeys ran around in tiny circles, shrieking in alarm. The crowd roared with laughter.

Diseaeda stormed over to the hanging man. 'And just what are you doing there?'

'Oh hello,' said the man in a slurred voice. 'I had a little to drink and then . . . Then these monkeys tied me up and . . . Has the show started yet?'

Diseaeda vainly tried to quieten the crowd. 'You've been drinking! Don't you realize we have children in the audience?'

'That's nice,' said the clown. 'Now I really must get down fro' here and –' He struggled pathetically for a few moments, and then looked pleadingly at Diseaeda. 'I appear to need some assistance,' he noted.

The monkeys pointed to another rope that extended down vertically from the darkness in the roof to a metal hoop set into the ground. The crowd began to cheer.

'Don't worry,' said Diseaeda. 'I'll let you down.' He undid the knot and, taking the strain of the man's weight, began to let the rope slip slowly through his hands.

The man ascended into the roof. Even Zoe was forced to smile at the Newtonian anomaly on display. The more rope Diseaeda released, the higher the clown went.

Diseaeda theatrically scratched his head and let go of the rope. The man disappeared from sight. The crowd hooted with laughter. Experimentally, Diseaeda began pulling on the rope, grimacing at the great weight he was moving.

The clown began to descend, this time tied by his hands and with a monkey hanging head-first from his feet.

'Just what is going on?' shouted Diseaeda over the roaring crowd.

Zoe closed the curtain.

'He's good, isn't he?' said Reisaz.

'A star performer,' agreed Raitak.

'And Diseaeda's not bad, either,' said Reisaz.

In Cosmae's absence Defrabax had taken to talking to himself. He found the habit a worrying one.

He sat at his desk, working through some calculations. A moth fluttered around the lamp before being consumed by the flame. Defrabax blew his nose, and tried the sum again. A different result this time.

After several more attempts he crunched the paper into a ball and hurled it across the room. 'Where is that dratted boy?' he shouted. 'Everything is in place, but I still need that key!'

He'd checked with the house where Cosmae normally stayed when he was annoyed about something and had discovered that he'd been there for breakfast only. It was getting late, and Cosmae had still not returned. Whilst Defrabax had been serious about Cosmae getting the key back, he would never have sent the lad out if he'd known that there was any danger involved.

He got to his feet and paced the room, rubbing his rheumatic knee and muttering darkly. Then he pulled a long cloak around his shoulders and walked to the front door, locking the rear room. 'It's always me who has to pick up the pieces, isn't it?' he grumbled.

He walked out into the street and slammed the door. It was raining again. Damn this rain-sodden place.

A little way up the road he heard the sound of his door being broken down again, but chose to ignore it. 'Someone is forcing my hand,' he said gravely.

He continued his long walk towards the castle.

Cosmae watched as Jamie ran for the stairs which descended into the main cavern, and then quickly followed him. Jamie shouted his battle cry halfway down and, as the brotherhood turned at the unexpected intrusion, he hurled his dirk towards the large man.

The desperately thrown dagger caught the fat man in the shoulder. He dropped the hammer and held his shoulder to staunch the bleeding. Cosmae wondered if Jamie was as expert as he seemed or if he'd just been lucky.

Cosmae and Jamie started to run towards the altar, but

they slowed as it began to dawn on them both that they had no weapons and no plan. The brothers turned to look at them, their faces blank shadows beneath the robes.

'You dare to intrude?' screamed the man in the golden mask. 'You dare to violate a meeting of the Brotherhood of Rexulon?'

Cosmae joined Jamie in backtracking towards the stone stairway. He believed in fighting valiantly for love, but not against such overwhelming odds. He assumed that it was Zaitabor behind the mask, but he couldn't be sure. 'What do we do next?' he whispered urgently.

'I don't know,' said Jamie. 'I get the feeling that we've walked into a trap.'

The man in the insect mask suddenly hurled a grey pellet towards Cosmae and Jamie. As it hit the ground it broke open, releasing clouds of stinking gas.

Cosmae turned to run but was immediately overtaken by the gas. He placed a hand over his mouth and tried to hold his breath but something dry and powerful flooded into his lungs. He struggled for breath, his chest held by a giant fist. Choking, he fell into the sea of grey and found wondrous silence.

They had been trudging through the tunnels for hours. The metal corridor that had so excited the Doctor led only to a room of old bricks and cobwebs. The Doctor was sure that his hypothesis was correct, but as yet they had found no more evidence of the ancient civilization.

The Doctor sat on a boulder and waved for Himesor to stop. 'I must rest for a few moments. I'm very tired.'

'Very well,' agreed Himesor. He motioned for his men to halt.

The Doctor, panting, removed his helmet. He breathed deeply, sniffed the air, and then coughed into his handkerchief.

Himesor looked on, concerned.

The Doctor blew his nose, and then beamed at the Grand Knight. 'As I thought. The air is breatheable now. We don't need to wear the helmets.'

The knights removed their helms and settled down into groups, some talking quietly. Himesor sat next to the Doctor, making notes on the back of the map. 'We're into uncharted tunnels now.'

The Doctor looked about him at the smallish cave in which they had come to rest. The roof was invisible in the shadows, although the tips of stalactites glinted in the torchlight. It appeared to be a natural construction rather than part of the sewers or even the old city. 'I was expecting to have found your menagerie by now, I must admit,' he said. 'Still, let's hope we can get back, eh?'

'That should not be difficult. I've tried to keep a note of the landmarks we pass.'

'We're not alone down here, by the way,' said the Doctor casually. 'I keep glimpsing a humanoid figure moving in the shadows. It's checking on our progress.'

'Are you sure?' asked Himesor. 'I myself have seen nothing, and the knights that we have brought with us are the finest I know.'

'Well, I do have a slight advantage over you all,' said the Doctor. 'I know what I'm looking for.'

'And that is?'

'An android utilizing accepted stealth procedures.'

'A what?'

'A metal man following orders to hide in the shadows.'

Himesor paused for a moment in thought. 'I was about to say that I don't believe you,' he said, rubbing his chin. 'But you were right about these artefacts.'

'Marvellous bits of work, I'm sure you'll agree,' said the Doctor. He fiddled absently with his helmet.

'My interest in their creation is only matched by my

increased awe at the beneficence of the Higher,' stated Himesor before getting to his feet. 'You said that the metal man was following orders. Whose might those be?'

'I have no idea,' the Doctor replied. 'But if Defrabax really does have a homunculus, I would imagine that it's actually an android. And whatever its orders are, it will follow them with immense efficiency.'

Himesor nodded, and then turned to his men. 'Be on your guard for a creature moving through the shadows. The Doctor thinks that –'

Something huge and dark landed on the Grand Knight, knocking him to the floor.

In the blink of an eye the knights were surrounded by a large number of moth-like creatures. As tall as men, their huge bony wings of orange and grey bore them gently to the ground with barely a sound. A number of knights reached for weapons, only to be clubbed to the ground by the creatures' powerful arms.

The Doctor turned to run, but was faced by two glittering compound eyes atop a damp maw of interlocking mandibles. The animal hissed and then lunged at the Doctor. With a single movement it smashed him to the floor. The creature leaned over the Doctor, as if to bite him.

The Doctor slipped into unconsciousness. Far from finding the menagerie, it seemed that some of the creatures had come to find them.

Nine

There was an acrid taste at the back of Cosmae's throat and a suffocating pressure on his lips and nose. So . . . He must have been out drinking and collapsed. That wasn't so bad.

The floor beneath him steadied. He turned his face to one side and breathed deeply as the room continued its travels without him.

Oddly quiet for a tavern, though. Perhaps he'd been taken home and Defrabax had left him to sleep on the floor in punishment. Whatever, it was obviously time to get up. Time to open his eyes.

They remained closed. His eyelids felt as if they'd been glued together. He was lying uncomfortably on one half-numb arm. He moved what he hoped to be his hand into position, and began to rub his eyes.

The blood flowed back into his arm, surging with little pinpricks of pain. He groaned as his eyes fluttered open.

There was a lot of light bouncing into his eyes from the floor. He stared at a whorl in the grain of the wood, observing the dark cracks and fissures and pathways, and then raised his head.

In that moment the memories came flooding back to him.

One of the Knights of Kuabris stood over him, impossibly tall and swaying from side to side. Cosmae blinked, and the image stabilized.

'Welcome back,' said the voice. A hand extended

down towards Cosmae, which he instinctively reached out for.

The young knight hauled Cosmae to his feet. 'Your friends will recover shortly. And then perhaps you can tell me what you're doing in the castle, and how you managed to hide the girl from us for so long.'

Cosmae tried to reply, but his throat felt parched. He licked his lips and tried again. 'Girl?'

'You did well to liberate her from the dungeons. A pity you couldn't escape from the castle.'

'We didn't rescue her.'

'No?'

'Not from the dungeons.'

'Who did?'

'The brotherhood.'

'Say that to Zaitabor,' snapped the knight urgently, 'and he will spill your guts for heresy.'

'Zaitabor is their leader. We followed him and the jailor into a secret chamber beneath the castle.'

'Zaitabor? That's ridiculous.' The knight helped Cosmae to a low leather-covered couch in the corner of the room.

Cosmae noticed for the first time that he was in some kind of office. He saw Jamie and Kaquaan still unconscious on the polished floor, and then closed his eyes until the splashes of colour receded. 'I feel awful,' he said. 'What happened to us?'

'You were found in one of the corridors that connect the towers. Unconscious, in a heap on the floor.'

'A kind of gas affected us. A pellet. The leader of the brotherhood . . .'

'You'd better come up with a better story than that if you ever want to leave the castle.'

'There's a concealed stairway in that corridor. I'll show you. It's behind –'

The knight laughed. 'Do you think the brotherhood

would dare to hold their meetings below Castle Kuabris? How absurd!'

'But it's true!' said Cosmae. Jamie began to stir, groaning loudly. 'He'll tell you. I'm not lying.'

The knight's voice lowered to a conspiratorial whisper. 'I have had certain suspicions about Zaitabor for a while,' he confided. 'I think he senses my unease. He's always sought to demote me or have me expelled. I think perhaps we will take a walk back to this corridor of yours.' He reached out a hand and smiled warmly. 'My name's Araboam, by the way.'

Zaitabor strode grandly into the main chamber of the knights and surveyed the assembled advisers. 'I'm told that the expedition to the sewers has met with failure,' he said.

'A single knight has returned,' said one of the aides, coming forward and bowing. 'He tells of an attack by terrible creatures. He is sure that none of the party will survive.'

'With some regret I find myself in agreement with the knight's conclusion,' said Zaitabor. 'Himesor's death is deplorable. He was a fine and noble leader. We shall of course allow a suitable period of mourning and reflection, but I see no reason why I should not be installed as Grand Knight by the end of the month.'

'Indeed, Commander,' said one of the old men. 'And until that time you are entitled to all the functions and privileges of Grand Knight.'

'I shall accept my new tasks with all due humility and fortitude,' said Zaitabor. 'And although the selection process is complicated, I do have one very faithful lieutenant in mind for the next Commander.'

'My lord,' said another adviser, shuffling forward, 'your direct exaltation to the position of Grand Knight is most irregular.' The man's eyes were downcast and his hands twisted the hem of his long robe nervously. 'Precedent dictates that –'

'I am a Knight of Kuabris! I care nothing for precedent.' Zaitabor took a step towards the frail old figure, half-raising an arm as if to strike.

'My lord is of course quite correct,' said the man hurriedly. ' "Unusual" was the word I was looking for. Each Grand Knight must seek to rule with diligence and in his own manner. Please forgive the words of an old man whose only wish is that he serve you well.'

'I am sure you will,' said Zaitabor with a cold benevolence. He moved over to the throne that rose from the table's end, and ran an appreciative hand over the ornate patterning. 'Your caution would be well advised, however, if you were to suggest that we should not let the people know of Himesor's demise just yet. It is not in our interest to further mythologize the so-called Menagerie of Ukkazaal.'

'Despite the monsters?' asked one of the administrators, rubbing his hands nervously.

'There are strange creatures in caves all over our world. The fate of this misguided expedition does not provide evidence of the Menagerie's existence. Far from it. I shall question the knight myself later to establish the truth of the matter. In any case, the scientist called the Doctor has been punished for his trust in science. Higher be praised!'

There was a loud rap at the door and a moment later a knight strode in. 'Forgive me, Commander, but Defrabax has just delivered a letter to the guards at the gatehouse.'

'What did that damned charlatan want?'

'He did not specify, sir. The letter is addressed to Grand Knight Himesor.'

'Who is dead. Give the letter to me.'

The knight handed the letter to Zaitabor who snapped the seal and unfolded the letter. 'He must have been disturbed by our latest intrusion,' he muttered. He started to read the parchment, and then looked up and examined the faces of his advisers, who were watching him with interest. 'I shall keep no secrets from my learned friends. The mage's letter reads as follows:

' "Sir –

' "When first I was informed of your plans to sanction limited scientific experimentation I was overjoyed. My views on Kuabris suppression and manipulation are well known, and I shall not go into them again here.

' "As your decision seemed at least in part motivated by the poverty of our people, I had hoped that we would soon see the benefits and freedoms being felt by the poorest in our city. The importance of our provision of heat and light to those who have most to gain from it cannot be underestimated.

' "In fact, as I survey our city, I see only that the rich men are now richer. The poor have become increasingly desperate, taunted by phantoms of the quality of life that they could have had.

' "Curse this constant drizzling downpour and curse you, Grand Knight! Your immutable interest in my homunculus, despite the diversion in the shape of the creatures from the sewers, has forced me now to write to you with an ultimatum.

' "Below this city of ours is an older and yet infinitely more advanced dwelling place. My homunculus has informed me that there are power sources down there the like of which you cannot imagine. They could supply all of our city's needs. The technology of our ancient forefathers will allow us to put an end to disease and misery. All our people must reap the benefits of what is down there.

' "I have it within my power to destroy the Furnace. This is not an action I will undertake lightly, but surely you can appreciate the results of this: the people will not allow what little light of science they have to be taken from them.

' "Sanction increased scientific experimentation and let us benefit from the old city! If you do not do this immediately, I will have no option but to destroy the Furnace, and the people will be driven to revolt.

' "Change the ways of Kuabris, or the knights will be swept aside!" '

Zaitabor read the letter again, silently, his face dark with anger. 'Damn that magician!' he cried, flinging the parchment across the room. 'Does he think that science has the answers? Does he really believe the placid folk of the city to be on the verge of rebellion and revolt? Himesor might have fallen for this soft trick, but I will not.'

'What will you do?' asked one of the aides.

Zaitabor sat on the throne and drew his sword. He grabbed a document at random from the table and spat on it, using it as a rag to clean his already immaculate blade. 'Call Araboam and the whole assembly of knights to me. I shall order that the magician be found and executed. If it means every house in this city being ripped apart, then so be it.'

'And then?'

'And then I have something wonderful planned. The way of Kuabris will not be destroyed!'

Jamie pulled the tapestry back with a flourish. Behind it was a blank wall of uninterrupted wooden panelling. He stared at the space where the door should have been in surprise.

'No door,' commented Araboam.

'But it was here,' said Jamie. 'I swear it was.'

Araboam turned to Kaquaan. 'Young lady, can you confirm or deny this tale?'

The girl shook her head. 'No. Last thing I remember was my cell. Then waking up in your room.'

Araboam stared at Jamie and Cosmae. 'Whatever

stunned you,' said Araboam, 'has clearly warped your senses.'

Cosmae stammered an apology. 'It appears we've been wasting your time. I am sorry, Commander.'

'Then I'm afraid the cells await you all with their tender embrace.' The young knight reached out for Kaquaan's face. She flinched at his touch, but did not move away. 'Yet perhaps we can arrange something better for you.' His fingers brushed across her shoulders and neck. 'You're not what you were when first you came to the castle but . . . They say all horses are grey in the dark.'

Araboam's fingers alighted upon the glassy pendant around her neck. He held up the cube to the light. For the first time in many hours Cosmae remembered his ostensible reason for trying to rescue the girl.

'What's this?' Araboam asked. 'An elaborate trinket on so common a girl?'

Kaquaan smiled demurely. 'My lord can have it, if he wishes.'

'No!' said Cosmae. 'You mustn't –'

Araboam turned. 'What's that squeaking I hear? Some mere rodent trying to tell me what I can do?'

Cosmae bowed his head. 'My apologies.' Jamie could tell that his young friend was seething, and wondered how much more provocation he could take.

Araboam turned his attention back to the girl. 'I'm sure a *lady* who so easily spreads her legs must be showered with all sorts of trinkets and –'

Cosmae lunged at the knight, his hands balled into fists. He caught him once, just on the side of the face. Araboam turned and drew his sword with a single graceful movement. Before either Cosmae or Jamie could do anything the silver tip of the sword arced through the air and turned scarlet on Cosmae's chest.

The doors at one end of the corridor opened and a

group of knights marched towards them. Jamie wondered how long they'd been there and what their orders had been.

Cosmae was looking at his bleeding chest with disbelief. His hands were red, his teeth chattering.

'You'll survive,' announced Araboam. 'For the moment.' He turned to the knights. 'This young puppy dares to assault a Knight of Kuabris. Take him to the cells to await execution.'

Whimpering, the young man was led away. Kaquaan stared after him in disbelief.

'Now then, Jamie,' said Araboam as he returned his sword to a scabbard. 'I may call you Jamie? I have found out so much about you since you escaped from those dullards who masquerade as the City Guard. And I'm afraid I have to bring you bad news. It appears almost certain that your friend the Doctor has died.' He paused for a moment to let the words sink in. 'Now, there are certain strange things that you and your friend claim to have seen. I would like to remind you that you have no proof of this meeting of the brotherhood. Is your memory not already beginning to fade? I'm sure it will degenerate further over the coming days. If by some slim chance the Doctor lives and you are reunited – or if in any way you are tempted to act upon your wild claims about the brotherhood – just remember that Cosmae's fate lies in my hands. That of this young strumpet, too. And as you lie on the hard bunk of your rat-infested cell, I want you to think very carefully about what you saw, and what you didn't see.' Araboam began to march Jamie and the girl back down the corridor. 'There's a whole world out there. It would be a shame never to see it again.' He placed a brotherly arm around the girl and slapped Jamie on the back. 'Remind me again what you saw beneath the castle.'

Jamie scratched his head. He could feel things shifting

in his mind, like chunks of ice thawing and crumbling in the sun. And the only image that he could fix on was that of poor Cosmae, being dragged away, feet scraping the stone floor, bleeding. 'I . . . I didn't see anything.'

'Good,' said Araboam. 'You're learning very quickly.'

The cheers from the crowd formed a not unpleasant backdrop to Zoe's chores in the curtained-off section behind the ring. A selection of creatures, clowns and performers moved back and forth. She could just about hear Diseaeda's voice. 'I hope you enjoyed the Tumbling Terrors!' he cried.

Three men, arms and legs held so tight as to become human balls, rolled through the curtain at high speed, and came to rest in the sawdust next to Zoe. They stretched out, panting. 'Not bad,' said one.

'I had to compensate for your slips too many times,' complained another.

The twins walked up to the acrobats. 'Take your arguments somewhere else,' said Raitak.

'The scree beasts are on in a few minutes,' said Reisaz. 'So unless you want your lovely hair covered with scree shit . . .'

Zoe returned to the job at hand, forcing small blue and silver paper strips into the false bottom of one of the clown's buckets. She heard the three men walk out of the tent, still arguing.

'A good little trick that,' commented Raitak, gesturing towards the bucket.

Zoe nodded seriously. 'A good idea, but this hinge isn't ideal. Engineering isn't really my speciality, but I'm sure a micro-switched magnetic seal would be much better.'

'I suppose it would,' said Raitak humourlessly. 'Now I suggest you get that ready or –'

There was a sudden shout from the back of the tent. The twins ran to investigate. One of the strongmen had appeared and was waving his hands, agitated. Zoe had been with the Doctor long enough to recognize the effects of fear on someone's body language. Slowly she got to her feet.

'Zoe!' called the twins earnestly. 'Quick!'

She ran to their side. 'What's the matter?'

'That creature of yours,' said Raitak. 'It's come back to life, broken out of its casket. And now it's on the rampage.'

Ten

The Doctor peered through the haze, fighting back the feelings of nausea. His head thumped painfully but he was determined to remain conscious, to establish where he and the knights were being taken.

He had a faint memory of struggling into semi-consciousness just after the ambush. One of the moth-like creatures had bent down to bite him. The mandibles had opened and a needle-like probe had extended, dripping poison. He remembered the creature's head moving away, its leaf-like antennae quivering, and then everything became dark again.

Some time later the Doctor had recovered consciousness, his neck feeling tender and swollen. The knights appeared to be out cold, each one draped over the shoulder of a moth, carried deep into the darkness.

For the moment the Doctor tried not to think too hard about the creatures, nor what they had planned for their prey. Slowed down by their prisoners, the moth-men trudged along the stone and metal corridors, wings hanging idly at their backs. The Doctor wrinkled his nose at the smell that rose from the creatures' oozing, creaking joints. He twisted his head slightly to one side, keeping his eyes half-closed for fear of discovery, and stared intently at the walls and buildings that they passed.

With an involuntary twitch he realized exactly what his eyes had been telling him for so long. Rough natural caves and crude sewer pipes of stone had been replaced by buildings, thoroughfares, suites and corridors of soft metal alloys and mock wood.

The old city – for that was where they now were – was technologically advanced and well preserved, having idled its time in dusty amber for centuries. The Doctor glimpsed broken street lamps and carefully parked hover-cars, large recreation areas and fortified bunkers surrounded by crumbling razor wire.

So, this was the source of the diverse civilizations that now sprawled across the planet. Once the people had left the city it had been built upon and forgotten, until now its very existence had become the stuff of speculation and legend. The Doctor marvelled at what deceptive progress mankind and nature could achieve over a millennium or three.

And yet the lines of the place, its austere minimalism, worried the Doctor. This was no neglected colony, but neither was it a harsh penal institute or correction centre. Its very form, and the frequency of the bunkers and rusted military vehicles, hinted at a hawkish conformity, balanced by occasional concessions to comfort and the needs of the family.

As this thought passed through the Doctor's mind the spiny foot of the creature that carried him stamped down on a toy ark, upended in a gutter choked with dust and dirt. The wood, made brittle by the passing of time, splintered, spilling out a few plastic animals.

The Doctor had previously thought that the Menagerie of Ukkazaal, if it existed at all, would perhaps be the underground city's zoo. He had expected to find little more than the faintest impression of old corpses, still locked within sorry cages and cracked vivaria. But the very existence of these moth-creatures indicated that large numbers of animals had existed here, enough to found a bestial civilization of their own. And the fact that the city was so clearly a military research area was more worrying still.

What had caused the humans to leave this place? Was it biological warfare, nuclear radiation, or something more mundane? Perhaps a period of galactic contraction had left them stranded without supplies. Perhaps some war had spilled over on to the planet's surface, with most of the population taken away as prisoners or executed and thrown into mass graves.

The Doctor was puzzled by the twilight that gently coloured in the outline of the buildings and streets. Surely, this far below ground, everything should be dark. Either there was some fissure that let in a glint of the surface's dull grey light or . . . The Doctor craned his head around slowly, trying to ascertain the light's source.

Eventually he saw it. A mile or so in the distance was an unremarkable squat building, a few radio masts and chimneys gathered together at its rear. Uniquely among the buildings of the old city its rooms and doorways spilled yellow light, although the Doctor could detect no figures within. Its lights cast little slivers of brightness through the gloom and up towards the artificial sky half a mile or so above his head. Whoever was breathing life back into the machinery and buildings of the city had no idea of the potential dangers.

The moths on the other hand seemed to be quite content in the dark and, indeed, they were moving in a direction that took them far away from the building. The construction shrank slowly into the distance, a single candle slowly snuffed out in a black and stifling Hell.

Araboam locked the door carefully and kicked off his boots. All the while the young woman watched him carefully. She smiled as he turned to her. 'I thought the knights' thoughts were always on the Higher,' said Kaquaan.

'Maybe,' grunted the knight. 'But sometimes we feel the call of our baser instincts. Sometimes I think we are not more civilized than the bulls and cows I watched in the fields when I was young.'

'Situation has meant that I rely on such instincts,' said Kaquaan.

'I'll make sure you're paid,' said Araboam harshly.

'Think of me when you repent and beat the evil out of yourself.'

'I'm sure I will.'

Kaquaan watched as the knight began to pull off his armour, making a neat pile of metal and leather towards the bottom of the small bed. The rest of the room was bare and unremarkable. A few esoteric symbols had been crudely carved into the stone wall, and the roof was covered by a tapestry of the night sky's stars set into a globe and held gently in a pair of great, pale hands. There was little to distract her.

She strode over to the knight, smiling. 'I'm glad my lord does not find my shaven head too ugly.'

'Whoever did this to you had some sense.' Araboam stroked her cheek with his hand. ' 'Tis a suitable punishment for a whore. And it is not your face that I am interested in.' He reached out and squeezed her breasts, smiling appreciatively. 'Not bad,' he said, as if commenting on livestock.

'I'm glad I please my lord,' whispered Kaquaan, averting her gaze. 'I can think of many more ways to bring you pleasure.'

'Good,' breathed the knight, beginning to tug at her coarse blouse.

'And none more exciting than this.' With that, she thrust her knee hard into his unprotected groin. The man collapsed with a shocked moan.

She grappled for the man's huge helmet, and swung it at his head. It took a number of unsuccessful attempts before she managed to club the unresisting knight into unconsciousness. Eventually her hands came away speckled with blood and hair.

She took the knight's sword and keys and carefully unlocked the door. She checked that the corridor beyond the sleeping chamber was deserted, locked the door behind her, and then fled into the shadows.

Diseaeda stood at Zoe's side, tears rolling down his cheeks. 'What can we do?' he whispered.

From their vantage point towards the rear of the tent they could watch the creature in action. It was tremendously strong and quick, darting from group to group, slashing with its four arms, snapping with its gaping maw. It blurred and came straight through tent walls and people, turned on frightened animals and ripped them in two. Its original colouring was lost now under a thick film of brown blood, and it turned its head at every new sound, every scream.

One of the animal trainers, knocked to the ground by a falling caravan, tried to struggle to his feet. The creature swung its head lazily in his direction and, ignoring the monkeys that screamed and dived for cover, extended one arm towards him, secured the man's neck in a serrated vice-like grip, and squeezed.

Zoe swallowed down her bile. 'I'm not sure what we can do,' she said quietly. 'The monster is clearly not killing for food or for any other purpose. Its aim is to kill all living creatures.'

'Can we hide from it?' asked Raitak.

Zoe turned her face away from the carnage. She had just watched a man seeking refuge behind what appeared to be a chess-playing automaton, but the creature stalked over in his direction regardless. It forced a claw straight through the device, and lifted the man to its smooth snout, staring at the creature quizzically through concealed eyes. Zoe hadn't wanted to see the rest. 'It seems to be hunting as much by sound as by sight,' she speculated. 'Unless . . .' She paused in thought. 'Perhaps it's tracking its prey in a different way. Get me a torch.'

'A what?' said Diseaeda. His voice sounded slurred with shock. 'Why do you –'

'Just do it,' she hissed.

Diseaeda slipped into the tent.

The creature paused for a moment, as if to survey its surroundings and to watch the people that streamed away in every direction. When Zoe had first seen the creature fathers had rushed to protect their families and had been torn in two. One of the strongmen, a mountainous figure fully twice Zoe's size, had been battered to the ground and left like a broken toy.

By now, people had recognized what they were up against. This was no game, no part of Diseaeda's freak show. The blood was real, the slaughter enormous, and the thing seemed to be only just getting into its stride. It leapt on to the top of another small tent and forced it to the ground, spilling conjuring tricks and magic boxes. It stared up into the sky and, just for a moment, brayed at the wind. It was a laughing expression of satisfaction.

Diseaeda returned with one of the flaming torches used by the jugglers. Immediately the creature's head turned in their direction.

'Ah,' said Zoe. 'A good experiment, but rather too successful. The creature appears to like the torch.'

The animal clambered down off the wreckage of cloth and wood and stalked towards them, its movements slow and playful.

'So?' asked Reisaz, as they retreated back into the now deserted main tent.

'So,' said Zoe, 'its vision might be biased towards the infrared end of the spectrum. This primitive device gives off more energy in heat than in light.'

'And?' asked Diseaeda as they worked their way through the backstage area.

'And heat is common to all living things, and it's very

difficult to disguise.'

The creature ripped into the tent just as Zoe and the others reached the centre of the circus ring.

'Which means, very simply,' continued Zoe, 'that we can't hide.'

After a grim journey in complete darkness the Doctor sensed that they were now in the creatures' more usual surroundings. Sound was muffled and dull, the air musty, reminding him faintly of an animal house at a zoo.

The Doctor was thrown to the floor. There was great activity around him as he was dragged roughly across the ground. The Doctor tried not to cry out. Something soft but very strong wrapped around his feet. Then his knees were bound together.

With a sudden dizzying rush the Doctor's feet were hauled upwards, his face now swinging above the ground, although he could see nothing.

It was then that he realized that he was being cocooned.

Zoe, Diseaeda and the twins fled across the ring, sawdust flying high into the air. They dared not turn to watch the progress of their pursuer, although the sound of its claws as it paced after them was clear enough.

'We need,' panted Zoe, 'to get somewhere hot. That might interfere with its infrared vision.'

'I can't think of anything,' said Diseaeda, holding his chest and beginning to slow already. 'Perhaps if I sacrifice myself to the creature it'll give you all the chance to escape.'

'Diseaeda,' hissed Raitak. 'Concentrate on running.'

'Leave the thinking to Madam Zoe,' said Reisaz. 'Besides, you'd be barely a mouthful.'

Zoe glanced behind and saw the creature stalking after them, following them down the canvas-covered tunnel that led to the tent's main entrance. It could have caught them by now if it had really wanted to. She could only imagine that it was playing with them, waiting for their exhausted bodies to collapse or trip. She hoped that the creature's enormous, brutal confidence would be its undoing.

'What's the biggest animal in the circus?' she asked.

'The savannah walker,' said Raitak as they ran across the rain-sodden turf of the circus site.

The creature stepped out of the tent and lunged at a terrified horse that ran past. The animal's head blurred as the neck twisted and snapped. Only the horse's momentum carried it forwards but by the time it crashed into the earth in a mass of splayed legs it was very still.

The creature jumped on the horse's back, checking that it was dead, and then set off again after the torchlight.

'I have an idea,' said Zoe. 'Which direction is the savannah walker?'

Diseaeda stabbed a blunt finger towards a collection of temporary animal houses towards the edge of the site. They started to run in that direction, rounding trailers, jumping over tent ropes, all the while screaming warnings to the people that passed them by.

Some of the men and women they watched were almost motionless with shock, their lips quivering, their eyes glazed over at the butchery they had witnessed. Others ran crazily in different directions, senseless with fear and numbed by the desire to survive. Those with slightly cooler heads had gone towards the town, seeking help.

'Let's hope we get there before this thing gets bored with the chase,' said Zoe.

Jamie tried to rest but found that the bunk-like bed in the cell offered little encouragement. His mind turned over and over the fate of his friends, Cosmae and the girl. With every minute that passed his subconscious painted more and more gruesome images behind his closed eyes.

He thumped the bunk in frustration, trying to block out the nightmarish reflections. He had to admit it: despite all his adventures with the Doctor, even in this society he was well out of his depth. Whatever had happened to him previous to waking up in the young knight's office – and his memories were no more clear than a watercolour landscape awash with rain – had left him feeling helpless and unsure. Even now he could feel things moving in his mind. It was as if his memories were items of furniture and a huge hand was dragging them experimentally across floorboards and into new positions.

His head began to pound. He pressed his fingers into his temples, groaning.

The banging got worse, followed by a crash that made him wince.

He pushed himself into a sitting position and saw that the door to his cell had been pushed open. The young woman, Kaquaan, stood framed in its light, jangling a large bunch of keys.

'Come on!' she said, handing Jamie a huge sword. 'The jailor will not sleep for ever.'

'My brave wee lassie!' exclaimed Jamie, jumping to his feet and immediately feeling much better. 'I'm forever in your debt.'

'It was easy,' said the girl. 'In most cases the knights haven't been with a woman for years. I don't care how much you pray to the Higher, there are certain . . . services . . . that I can offer that no man can resist.'

Jamie wiped a sudden trickle of sweat from his brow. 'When I was a bairn I was warned about people like you.'

The girl smiled. 'Put your boots on, and let's go.'

'Aye,' whispered Jamie to himself. 'She's a pawky one, and no mistake.'

* * *

The Doctor had been in more difficult situations, but for the moment he was hard pushed to think of one. His eyes had become fully accustomed to the dark, and the faint natural luminescence of the cave walls indicated the graphic nature of his predicament. He and the other knights, still comatose from the moth-men's poison, were suspended and entrapped in huge woven cocoons, hung from the ceiling on strands of silk as strong as steel cable. Only the Doctor's head was free, allowing him to breath.

The small cave, therefore, was nothing more than a larder, a grotesque pantry of living things. At least, that's what he hoped the cave was. The only other thing he could imagine – that they were all being stored prior to implantation of eggs – was even more grotesque. It was little wonder that he had always found entomology so faintly disquieting.

The Doctor had noted that one of the knights was missing. How had he managed to escape from such powerful creatures? Perhaps he had been allowed to escape, in which case the moths were simply following orders so as to spread terror. But whose orders? The Doctor gloomily concluded that the one knight at liberty would not be able to save the others from the moth-men. He probably wouldn't even know where his fellow knights and the Doctor had been taken.

The Doctor was aware of a slight scuffling sound behind him. He began to rock gently backwards and forwards against the cocoon, inclining his head slightly. A few moments later he had turned sufficiently to allow him a view of the source of the noise. He could just make out a small pair of legs and a slim body, eyes that twinkled in the dark and a long, twitching nose like that of a shrew. Hands on hips and upside down from the Doctor's point of view, the creature stared at him through the darkness.

It scratched its head and sighed. 'I suppose I'd better get you down from there,' it said.

'To conclude, let me draw together the strands of our learning thus far.

'Firstly, the holy artefacts have meanings and functions beyond that which the Higher has so far revealed to us. Secondly, the clear implication is that the Kuabris are not uniquely used by him. We are joined in our struggle for truth by countless unseen brothers. Perhaps when we die we will see them face to face for the first time. Thirdly, one of the robes has been taken, and one must in the first instance suspect human rather than Higher intervention.

'In this annotated catalogue of our treasures I have concentrated on the philosophical and theological ramifications of the first two points. Although my tenure as Grand Knight is drawing to a close and I feel the icy embrace of illness brushing my skin ever more strongly, I do not want to neglect the more practical concerns raised by the missing artefact. I will order a thorough investigation into the stealing of the robe. If a knight is found to have taken the artefact then his body, stripped of clothing, skin and life, shall be cast into the land beyond the city walls. If the thief is a common man – how my heart chills at such a thought – then we are all aware of the terrible punishments that await him and his family.

'It is regrettable that I must end so illuminating and fascinating a study with the threat of death and expulsion from the Higher's presence. My friends, this should not surprise us. Until we attain the Higher there will always be darkness striving for a hold on his light.

'This duality is at the very heart of our definition as people.'

Extract from *Summary of Findings* by Grand Knight Zipreus. Subsequently banned and destroyed by order of Grand Knight Himesor.

Eleven

'I am very grateful to you,' said the Doctor as he followed the shrew-like being through the corridors and streets of the city.

'I am sad that I could not rescue your companions,' he replied. The Doctor had come to think of the creature as male, although there was no evidence to support this. 'The poison proved fatal to the other surface-dwellers: your body must be unusually resistant.' He stopped for a moment, sniffing the air, and then turned into another dark street, his bouncing gait requiring the Doctor to walk briskly to keep up. The Doctor could tell that they were now in the dimly lit residential area. The blazing power station that so troubled the Doctor was a beacon in the distance, casting disturbing shadows on the solid sky overhead.

The little animal looked exactly like some anthropomorphic children's character, a bipedal shrew a couple of feet in height and dressed in a simple uniform the same orange-brown colour as its glossy fur. His paws were hitched casually into a utility belt covered in miniature tools. The Doctor noticed a couple of ostentatious gold rings at the creature's elbows.

'I'm the Doctor, by the way. I'm very pleased to meet you.'

The creature twitched its nose in what seemed to be an expression of amusement. 'I know of this habit you surface-dwellers have, this desire to label everything, including yourselves. It seems more than a little egotistical. I am a Dugraq scout. That describes my position within our society. I am recognizable, and can recognize my friends. We Dugraqs find we have no need for titles.'

'That must make sending Christmas cards rather difficult,' observed the Doctor.

'You talk a great deal,' said the Dugraq. 'Talk is good. Talk is the enemy of fear. Only when reunited with their Queen can the Taculbain communicate properly. That has always been their species' downfall.'

'Taculbain?'

'I have just rescued you from the Taculbain. With their Queen they are a sensible race. Without her they are impressionable and become aggressive because of their fear.'

'What has happened to the Queen?'

'She was taken by a surface-dweller many years ago. He now governs the Taculbain. He doubtless arranged for you to be attacked.'

The Doctor nodded. 'I did sense something more than mere animal savagery at work. What will happen to the dead knights?'

'They will be eaten,' said the Dugraq simply. 'One species consumes another. That's how the planet spins.'

'And who captured the Queen? Was it this magician I've heard so much about?'

The Dugraq made a little clicking noise with his tongue that the Doctor took to be laughter. 'Defrabax? No, Defrabax is in league with the Rocarbies.'

'The Rocarbies?'

'You have much to learn, and ask many questions. Questions are also good.' The creature pushed open a rusted gate and followed the Doctor into what had once been a huge park and recreation area. The plants had died back, and swings and slides sulked sadly in the corner. 'This is where we live. Welcome to the Dugraq camp.'

Jamie stared at the jailor, trying to work out why he looked so familiar. The man was quite the shabbiest knight Jamie had so far seen, his armour painted black and caked with dirt. He sat slumped with his head on the table, snoring, a huge glass of wine still clamped in one fist. His armoured breeches were around his ankles, leaving his legs covered only by grey cotton hose.

'What did you do to him?' asked Jamie.

Kaquaan scanned the other cells but found them to be empty. 'He was drinking long before I got here.'

'Aye,' said Jamie, remembering with startling clarity the guard he had disturbed just before meeting Cosmae. 'There seems to be a lot of that going on.'

'One of the other great forms of escape from a dull life,' pronounced the girl. She turned to Jamie. 'Cosmae's not here.'

'Are there any other cells?'

'You have as much idea as I.'

'Then what shall we do?'

'Get away from our friend the jailor,' said Kaquaan. 'And then . . . I suggest we visit the Furnace.'

'Why?' Jamie was completely nonplussed.

'When you and Cosmae were explaining to Araboam what you had seen you mentioned a huge fat man in overalls who smelt of the Furnace.'

'Did we?'

'Yes. Araboam, for reasons of his own, seemed not to make the connection. But there is a very famous man in our city, a huge hairy great thing. His name is Argaabil, and he works in the Furnace.'

Jamie nodded, carefully testing the sword's blade with

his thumb. 'Let's ask him some questions. Perhaps he knows who's been playing tricks on my mind.'

The savannah walker was an elephant-sized creature, covered with short white fur. Large, timorous eyes dominated its broad face. Its huge legs fidgeted with nervous energy.

Like most of the massive animals it was kept in a rough corral towards the edge of the circus. Horses and a number of creatures that Zoe did not recognize paced about apprehensively.

The twins approached the savannah walker and made soothing noises, stroking its pale cheek and inspecting the saddle-like arrangement still fixed in place just behind the animal's shoulders.

It was quieter now. Most of the people seemed to have dispersed, the circus ground resembling a battle field after the armies have moved on. Zoe watched for their pursuer, trying to see if the deadly creature was still tracking them.

'You're not going to sacrifice this poor animal, are you?' asked Diseaeda, panting from the exertion of the run.

'I have no intention of sacrificing anything,' said Zoe. 'But think for a moment what we know of the creature. It detects its prey by their heat emissions, and kills because it is strong and cunning. It seems to have no concept of technology and intellect. In which case, if its number one priority is self-preservation at the expense of all living things, what would it be most interested in attacking first?'

'The strongest creature in the area?' suggested the circus master.

'And how would it tell that if it can't see in the same way as you and I?'

'I don't know,' said the man without really thinking. 'This is hardly the time for a test.'

'It would hunt down and kill the animal with the largest heat signature, thinking it almost certain also to be the strongest,' continued Zoe, unperturbed.

'Thus the savannah walker.'

'That's right. I suspect that the monster followed us for a while, confused by the torch we were carrying, but now it's probably closing in on this enormous animal.'

'So we'd better get out of here,' suggested Raitak.

As she spoke a group of horses towards the edge of the corral began neighing and flicking their feet in fear. Zoe glimpsed a humanoid figure moving towards the animals. She nodded. 'You're right.'

Diseaeda jumped up on to the walker, gripping its stunted mane in his hands. 'Just about enough room for us all up here.' He reached down and pulled Zoe up on to the beast's broad back. The twins scuttled quickly into position behind her.

Diseaeda snapped the reins and the savannah walker began to move just as their pursuer emerged into the centre of the corral. The horses and other animals scattered, some trying to clear the low fence in their desperation. Behind the monster was the usual collection of twitching, bloody corpses.

'Where to?' shouted Diseaeda as the walker picked up speed.

'I seem to remember that the town has a power station like the city's,' said Zoe.

'Power station?' asked Diseaeda. 'You must mean the generators. They're on the edge of town.'

'Why do you want to go there?' asked Raitak.

'Perhaps the heat from the furnaces will interfere with the thing's vision,' said Zoe.

'And if it doesn't?'

'Then we'll have to ask it very kindly to go away.'

* * *

The Doctor was escorted to the meeting place of the Dugraq council, and he bowed slowly, as he had been instructed. He couldn't resist a smile as he recognized the rusted remains of a roundabout, on which sat eight of the little shrew-creatures. Each one was dressed in ornate robes and held some sort of staff. The Doctor's rescuer had slipped into the crowd that discretely surrounded the Dugraq council.

'Who are you?' asked one of the Dugraq leaders, his grizzled fur clearly a mark of some distinction.

'I am the Doctor.'

'Is that a "name" or a function?'

The Doctor side-stepped the question. 'I "function" as a traveller.'

'Well, Traveller,' said another councillor, 'what brings you to our little world? We are told that you were rescued from the Taculbain, but that the knights were already dead.'

'That's right,' said the Doctor. 'I was forced to help them.'

'The knights persist in looking for the menagerie,' commented a sad figure towards the back.

'Then it exists?'

'In a sense,' said the grey Dugraq. 'Four races live here in the darkness.'

Another creature counted the names out on his claws. 'We Dugraqs are the arbiters of peace. The Taculbain are secretive and normally have no contact with the other races.'

The Doctor nodded. 'Yes, I was told that the Queen has been . . . kidnapped.'

'That's correct.' The Dugraq sighed. 'Oh, there is so much to tell you.' He tutted and then tapped his third finger. 'Then there are the Rocarbies. They are the boisterous children of our land. They cause trouble, but mean well.'

'Are they the ape creatures that have raided the town?'

'Yes. The magician has made some very rash promises.'

'Foolish man!' chorused a high-pitched voice. The Doctor assumed that Dugraq to be female.

'You see,' said the leader, 'for many centuries we were the only race to know of the world of light above our heads. The Taculbain are scared of the light, and never ventured even close to the surface. The Rocarbies worship the Taculbain as gods.' He snorted. 'They live over there.' A finger stretched into the semi-darkness. It wasn't surprising after all this time below ground that the creatures' senses would be keener than the Doctor's. 'In order to access the tunnels that lead to the surface they would have to tread on hallowed ground.'

'And even the Rocarbies have *some* rules,' said the female leader. 'The Taculbain Queen encouraged the superstitions. She was clever enough to realize that if the Rocarbies ever saw the Taculbain as mere mortal creatures – flesh and blood like themselves – then a war could break out. If the Rocarbies were to attack them then sheer weight of numbers might lead to the extinction of the Taculbain.'

'We were also quite happy for the Rocarbies not to discover the surface world,' added another Dugraq.

The Doctor nodded attentively, trying to take it all in.

'But there are so many tunnels,' said the pessimist. 'Sooner or later they were bound to discover a way to the surface that avoided the Taculbain.'

'We became worried,' said the leader. 'The status quo was fragile, but working. If the Rocarbies carried on breeding and expanding in numbers . . .'

'They would either swarm on to the surface or deeper into our world.' The speaker shivered slightly.

'So what did you do?' asked the Doctor.

'We have made occasional forays on to the surface world for as long as our legends are old. We decided to warn the people in the light. Unfortunately, the first person we contacted who claimed to be of any importance was Defrabax.'

'The magician?'

'Defrabax the charlatan,' stated the old Dugraq. 'He has all the supernatural powers of a mange-flea.'

'We were tricked,' continued the leader. 'We released the one operational worker to him.'

'Worker?'

'When this land was the surface – when, according to the fables we tell our children, we were slaves in the zoo of the devil-gods – mechanical workers were used. One remained operational.'

The Doctor smiled. 'So then I was right to think that the homunculus is actually an android.'

The old Dugraq shrugged his shoulders. 'Perhaps. I have heard the term before.'

Another Dugraq continued the story. 'And then Defrabax made contact with the Rocarbies and brought them under his influence.'

'I see,' said the Doctor. 'He asked the Rocarbies to attack the city, presuming that it would be taken as the fulfilment of the legends and prophecies concerning the Menagerie of Ukkazaal.'

'A diversion from his true intentions, which we do not know.'

'And the Taculbain?' asked the Doctor. 'I'm told they too are working for a surface-dweller.'

'We know not who governs their actions,' said the sad Dugraq. 'But recently the Taculbain have discovered that if they emerge on to the surface during dusk or night there is too little light to harm them.'

'There's just one thing I don't understand,' said the Doctor.

The leader chattered in amusement. 'Only one?'

'You said that there were four species. What is the other race down here?'

There was a long pause. The Doctor sensed that it was not that they did not want to tell him, but rather that such matters were never trivialized or made light of. When all the Dugraqs were silently staring at their leader he spoke again.

'Deep in this dark city, in a place that we hope the Rocarbies will never find, there exists the other race. These are the creatures that live at the heart of the Menagerie of Ukkazaal. This race has slept for centuries, and must never be awoken. Our legends say that they are awesome killers, evil personified. They are the source of the surface-dweller's own fears and legends. The fourth race are called Mecrim.'

Jamie and Kaquaan stood at the base of the Furnace, overawed by its huge size and blistering heat. It was an enormous, sprawling building, surrounded by muddy pathways and huge piles of timber and coal-bearing rock. Blackened men with masks and overalls led horses pulling vast wooden sledges. Fuel was taken from the sledges and carried to the furnaces that fed the main generators and turbines, and huge steaming vats of hot ash were rolled away for disposal. Thick cables supported by leaning wooden posts carried the electrical current towards the city.

There was clearly more than one furnace now, but the singular name of the place hinted at the scarlet, boiling haze that passed over the area. It was as if some grim god had set up a forge in which to torture countless souls.

Warm soot speckled down from the chimneys on Jamie and the girl . They almost had to shout to be heard over the sound of the turbines.

'Leaving the castle seemed easy,' said Jamie.

'Good luck,' commented Kaquaan, 'long overdue. Let's find the fat man.'

'How will we –'

'Everyone knows the fat man.'

They walked inside. The multi-level brick building shook with the sound of the pistons. Inside were many more sleighs and carts, the fuel they carried being hurled into the furnaces in a desperate attempt to satisfy their voracious appetite. Huge metal doors swung open at intervals, revealing a bright hot hell of fire that was almost painful to look at.

Jamie noticed that no one was bothered by their presence. Indeed, the young woman seemed familiar to a number of the workers.

They found Argaabil quickly enough. He was truly huge, twice Jamie's width and a foot or two taller. As he turned –

a huge hammer, upraised, over an altar –

an image flicked through Jamie's mind. This was the man. Jamie drew the sword, and shoved its tip none too gently towards the man's throat. 'I don't remember you, but I think maybe I ought to,' said Jamie. He pushed the man into a shadowy corner where their business would go undetected.

The fat man went to reach for some object on the floor but Jamie quickly flicked the sword down at his arm, drawing blood. Jamie noticed little nicks in the man's lower arms –

the hammer coming down, spraying metal –

and glowered at the man. 'This sword is very sharp. Don't try anything stupid.'

The man gulped as the sword returned to his throat. 'I don't – I've never seen you before in my life.'

'I don't believe you,' said the girl. She ran a hand through her badly cropped hair. 'And I'd also like to know who did this to me. Now, you either tell us about your involvement with the Brotherhood of Rexulon, or I let my friend here give your locks a trim, too.'

Jamie moved the sword so that it rested on the fat man's sweating scalp. He was almost blubbering. For all his bulk, thought Jamie, he had a soft heart.

'Please don't tell anyone that I've told you this,' stammered the man. 'They'll kill me.'

'Have no fears,' said Kaquaan. 'We shall be as silent as a cloudless sky.'

'Swear that you won't –'

'You have the word of a McCrimmon,' said Jamie. 'Tell me what you know.'

'Please understand,' said the man. 'My aims in life are simple. Staying alive is one of them.'

'Your interest in esoteric matters is also well known,' said Kaquaan. 'As is your resentment at working here.' She looked around. 'And seeing this place again I can't blame you for that.'

'Tell us about the Brotherhood of Rexulon,' repeated Jamie.

'I was initiated into the brotherhood months ago,' whispered the man. 'I hate these infernal machines. That's what the brotherhood is all about, and that's all I'm interested in.'

'When did you first see me?' asked Jamie.

'I was in the chamber. The lady – dear gods, please forgive me – was on the altar. And my job was to . . .' The man's words were drowned by his sobbing. Jamie couldn't tell if Argaabil was scared of them or frightened of the information he had revealed.

'Who leads the brotherhood?' asked Jamie.

The man shook his head. 'I don't know. Please believe me: I really don't know. But a lot of the knights are involved.'

'How many?' asked the girl.

'About a quarter, I think. A few City Guards, too. And . . .'

'And?'

'I do know that Araboam is involved.'

Jamie nodded. 'I thought he would be. I have a vague memory of following someone through the corridors of the castle. Perhaps it was him.'

'I saw Araboam when Defrabax's homunculus returned to the wizard's house,' remembered Kaquaan. 'He could have drugged me and moved me from my cell. But this still does not tell us where Cosmae is.'

'The brotherhood have their own cells within Castle Kuabris,' offered Argaabil helpfully. 'There are many secret tunnels within the castle.'

Just at that moment Jamie realized that they were not alone in using the shadows of the power plant to conceal furtive activity. A large bipedal figure was shuffling along a wall, half-obscured by the shadows cast by the gantries overhead. Jamie hushed the man, and pointed the figure out to Kaquaan.

From their vantage point they watched an ape-like creature emerge into a better-lit area, sniffing the air nervously. It crouched down, and placed an object on the wall. Satisfied, it bounded back into the shadows and was gone.

Dragging the man behind them, Jamie and Kaquaan ran over to the device. It was a small silver box with a red panel set into its side that flashed numerals. 'It looks like a bomb,' announced Jamie with an authority that he hoped was well placed.

'A what?'

'It'll explode,' said Jamie simply.

'Good,' smiled the fat man. 'Bring this damned place down, perhaps. I wasn't aware that the brotherhood had this planned, but no matter.'

'I don't think this has anything to do with the brotherhood,' said Jamie. He spotted another ape on one of the overhead walkways. It too was quietly affixing a device into position.

Jamie placed the sword back into his belt and turned to look at Argaabil. 'I want you to tell all your friends and fellow-workers to clear the area,' he said calmly. 'I don't greatly care what you think about machines. But if we don't get out of here fast, we could all die in the explosion.'

Twelve

Acting Grand Knight Zaitabor stared down at the dishevelled figure lying prostrate on the floor. He had ordered that Araboam be stripped of his clothing and brought to him under guard. Two knights stood to attention behind the shivering man, staring forward impassively.

'And how did so feeble a creature outwit a Knight of Kuabris?' asked Zaitabor, pushing Araboam's head back towards the floor with his boot when the young man dared to look up.

'I was . . . compromised, my lord.'

'I should have you flogged for that alone,' said Zaitabor. 'Your shameful behaviour has led to the escape of two prisoners. It is perhaps just as well that I ensured that the wizard's boy should be kept elsewhere.'

Araboam risked an upwards glance. 'I am told that the jailor too had –'

'Silence!' Zaitabor kicked the young man in the face, sending him spinning across the room. 'After all that I have done for you, your repayment is most unkind. Do not even say a word in my presence!' Zaitabor paused, trying to remain calm, his fingers drumming on his scabbard. 'The jailor is indeed becoming a liability,' he said quietly. 'Perhaps I should expel him from Castle Kuabris. Perhaps my advisers are right. The loss of a few fingers or a hand might ensure that all people remember the power and authority of the knights.'

'I throw myself upon your mercy, Commander,' exclaimed Araboam.

'Indeed you do,' said Zaitabor. He nodded to the two knights. 'Get him up.'

The knights dragged Araboam to his feet. The young knight stared back at his master. 'My lord?'

'Take a group of knights and track down our prisoners. You said that the boy remembered the fat man. Perhaps they have gone to see Argaabil.'

'And Defrabax?'

'Leave the mage to me,' said Zaitabor. 'In your absence you were unable to lead the knights out in pursuit of that evil man. But I am sure that they will succeed without your help.'

'And Defrabax's ultimatum?'

'Damn his ultimatum! The man has no real power!'

Jamie and Kaquaan watched the explosion from what they hoped would be a safe vantage point. When it came they instinctively ducked down behind a ridge in the hillside. A wave of hot air rushed past them. Moments later bricks and small scraps of metal began to fall from the skies like rain. Jamie protected his head with his arms and winced as he felt fragments cut into his back and legs.

When he raised his head the city was lit up by the flickering flames of the now-destroyed Furnace. The streets and houses of the rich, however, had been plunged into total darkness. He turned to the woman. 'Are you all right?' he asked.

Kaquaan looked up and nodded sourly. 'I thought you said we'd be safe here?'

'How was I supposed to know? I'm no cleverer than you!'

Kaquaan watched the Furnace workers as they darted from place to place trying to extinguish the smaller fires. Even from their distance they could hear Argaabil laughing.

'It looks like the whole place has been destroyed,' commented Jamie.

'So there'll be no electrical power,' said Kaquaan. 'Not that the poor folk will notice the difference.' She got to her feet, and stared at the castle on the far side of the city. Dim lights were now flickering into position at its various windows. 'Perhaps in the confusion we can slip back into the castle.'

'And do what?' said Jamie.

'Araboam is one of the Brothers of Rexulon. He must have Cosmae imprisoned somewhere.' Kaquaan smiled. 'You both came to my rescue. Now it's my turn to help rescue Cosmae.'

The explosion was felt even deep underground in the old city. The Dugraqs looked around in alarm. The Doctor nodded as if he had been half-expecting such a development.

'I assume that you've told me all that you have so that I can help you,' said the Doctor over the nervous squawks of the Dugraq council as the tremors subsided. He smiled modestly. 'I tend to be rather good at this sort of thing. Now, we'll put your fears about the Mecrim to one side for the moment. The thing we must do is take a look at that power station. We must try to find why it has been brought back on line, and how stable it is.'

'And the convulsions we just felt?' asked one of the Dugraqs.

'Probably some little trick of Defrabax's,' said the Doctor. 'I really am looking forward to meeting this man.'

'What can we do to help, Traveller?' asked the leader.

'I'll need a guide,' said the Doctor. 'Someone to ensure I don't get lost. If I can get to the power station and avoid the android then I should have a better idea as to what's going on.'

A Dugraq pulled at the Doctor's sleeve. The Doctor recognized the creature's reddish fur immediately.

'My friend the scout will do the job quite adequately I'm sure,' said the Doctor.

The leader nodded. 'Very well.'

'I must say how nice it is to be trusted for once,' said the Doctor. 'Normally I'm imprisoned, shot at . . .'

'If we Dugraqs have a failing,' said the sad old figure at the back, 'it is that we tend to trust too easily.'

'And look what happened as a result of our trusting Defrabax,' noted the female leader.

'I shall not let you down,' said the Doctor, bowing. He turned to follow the Dugraq scout back across the park.

Despite the savannah walker's surprising turn of speed, the six-limbed killer was slowly gaining ground. Zoe was pleased that her theories about the deadly creature seemed to be correct – that it was prioritizing the destruction of the walker above all other animals – but could only hope that they could get to the town's generators in time. The monster would be upon them soon. Its dark shape, crashing through the undergrowth as it blindly followed its instincts, was getting closer with every passing moment.

Diseaeda urged some more speed from the walker, and shot a worried glance back at Zoe. Zoe smiled back with a confidence she did not feel. Her theory that the massive heat of the furnaces might interfere with its vision was just a hunch. She'd been right about the creature so far, but intuitive speculation was hardly her forte. What if the creature was unaffected by its surroundings? What then?

They had decided to skirt around the town in an effort to minimize contact between the reawakened creature and the townsfolk. So far it had worked perfectly, the animal ignoring all other sounds and movements in its pursuit of the savannah walker. The stunned and fearful shock that had almost palpably descended over the town was perhaps a factor as well. The grim news from the circus had ensured that no one was walking the night-time streets.

Reisaz pointed into the distance. 'There are the generators. Not long now.'

Zoe could see the outline of a series of buildings not far away. The town generators were much cleaner and more efficient than the filthy equivalent she had glimpsed in the distant city, the architecture sharing the playful lines of much of the town. Clouds of white steam settled over the chimneys.

The creature was just a few yards behind the walker, which vaulted a low brick wall effortlessly. It passed through the ornamental gateway into the generating plant just as their pursuer struck.

The creature lunged at the rear legs of the savannah walker, one serrated arm locking into position. The huge horse-like animal crashed to the ground, spilling its riders.

The twins pulled Zoe to her feet, and they ran after Diseaeda towards a small wooden door in the outer wall of one of the ornate buildings. It was locked but the circus owner kicked it down with surprising ease.

By now they could hear the gurgling screams of the savannah walker as it died. Zoe didn't dare look behind her.

'Hide as close to the furnaces as possible,' she said, looking around the orderly generating room. The walls were dotted with large metal doors, with much of the floor space taken up with an enormous turbine.

Zoe knew that self-preservation was the first priority. They had managed to lure the monster away from the freak show but they were clearly no closer to finding a way to kill it. She was determined to ensure that any lives they had saved were not at the cost of their own.

Zoe ducked down behind a metal pipe that stretched up into the ceiling. It was hot to the touch, and she hoped its heat would be enough to distract the creature. The twins flicked open a furnace door and dived for cover. She couldn't even see where Diseaeda had gone.

Despite the hammering of pistons and the roar from the exposed furnace Zoe could still hear the enormous whimperings of the savannah walker. A few moments later there was a squeal, and then nothing.

The creature jumped through the doorway, landing comfortably on its splayed feet. Its seemingly eyeless face scanned the gantries and machinery. After the chase its movements were now slow and methodical. It seemed to know that the small-bodied humans could pose no threat to it.

Zoe crouched down still further, listening to the tap of the beast's claws on the flagstones. She could not tell if it was coming closer or moving further away.

The noises stopped, and the crashing of the machinery became a terrifying silence. Zoe wondered if the creature were standing over her, gloating, its deadly claws gently reaching out for her.

Then the sounds of movement started up again, a few yards to her right. Through eyes half-closed with fear she saw the creature as it came towards the furnace, passing close to her position. It stared at the flames for a while, moving its head from side to side as if weighing up its sensory input.

Then the creature's head turned in Zoe's direction, as if it knew all along where she would be. It trotted towards her and extended its clawed fingers.

As Kaquaan had expected, getting back into the castle had proved ludicrously easy. Despite their other-worldly contemplations it seemed that even the knights were shocked by the sight of the smouldering Furnace. Jamie just hoped that this time he would be reunited with the Doctor and Zoe.

He followed Kaquaan through the quiet corridors as she sought to retrace her steps back to Araboam's quarters. After some time she came to a halt towards the end of a corridor of polished pale-blue stone and pointed to one of the two doors at its end. 'That's the one,' she said. 'That's where Araboam brought me.'

Jamie walked boldly up to the door and banged it with his fist, not really knowing what he'd do if there was a reply. After a few moments he pushed the door open and walked inside. Kaquaan followed, closing the door.

'Let's see if we can find anything of interest,' said the young Scot, opening a small cupboard and rummaging through papers. 'Stand by the door and make sure no one's coming.'

'You can read then?' asked Kaquaan as Jamie scanned a number of frayed parchments.

'Aye, just a little,' said Jamie. 'The Doctor taught me.' Towards the back of the room a full-height wardrobe had been set into the castle wall. Jamie peered in and saw clothing hanging from a rail and wooden racks containing polished armour and boots. The cupboard smelt of cleaning oil and aromatic herbs.

He returned to the paperwork, bundled into little sheaf-like piles. He had hoped to find some indication of concealed cells used only by the brotherhood, but realized quickly that he was most unlikely to find a detailed map giving away such secret locations.

'There's someone coming,' hissed Kaquaan, darting away from the door.

'Quick, get in the cupboard,' said Jamie. There was just enough room for the two of them, and not for the first time Jamie was grateful that he was by no means the tallest of the McCrimmons. He pulled the door closed and held it in position with one hand.

He heard the door to the room creak open and then close again. Footsteps scuffed across the floor.

'Now then, Oiquaquil, there is much that I must attend to,' said a voice that Jamie recognized. 'I have only just returned to my duties. What is it that you want?'

'Rest assured that I would not normally disturb you in the middle of the night but rumour has reached me that Himesor is dead. As Captain of the Guard I am wondering –'

'Confirmation has not yet been received of Grand Knight Himesor's demise,' said Araboam. 'For the moment, Commander Zaitabor has assumed the mantle of Grand Knight.'

'And you are his intended Commander? It seems I am not considered important enough to see the Grand Knight,' the Captain grumbled.

'I am not greatly inclined to believe that I shall be made the next Commander of the Knights,' said Araboam. 'Now, I must ask you again, what is your business with us?'

'It's very simple,' said Oiquaquil. 'This explosion in the Furnace. Do the knights have any information regarding the perpetrators?'

'We have reason to believe that it was caused by Defrabax, who is pursuing a vendetta against is.'

'Defrabax? I always felt that the man was capable of less than half the things he boasted of.'

'He sent us an ultimatum.'

'Then you are sure it's not the brotherhood?'

'Absolutely sure,' replied Araboam. Jamie smiled to himself, knowing the reason for Araboam's confidence. He shifted his weight slightly, straining to catch their words as the men appeared to move towards the door.

'Now, I have important business to attend to,' said Araboam. 'I'll talk with you later, Captain.'

'I notice you have Argaabil under guard.'

'We suspect him of liaising with Defrabax,' explained Araboam hastily.

'That's surely a matter for the City Guard.'

'Not where Defrabax is concerned.'

'Very well. We guards have much to do at the Furnace.'

'Indeed. Good night, Captain.'

The door clicked closed and Jamie could just hear Araboam cursing under his breath. How much longer could he and Kaquaan stay where they were, undetected? Kaquaan was obviously thinking the same thing. In the darkness she reached out to squeeze Jamie's hand.

Despite himself, Jamie smiled.

A moment later Jamie heard Araboam walking across the room towards the wardrobe, the click of his footsteps on the floor growing louder. Jamie tensed, ready to spring, when suddenly there was a crash from the other side of the room.

'Get in there, you drink-sodden scum!' Jamie did not recognize the voice. There was a low thump as something or someone hit the floor, followed by a whimpering sound that was a grotesque parody of human speech.

'Grand Knight Zaitabor,' stammered Araboam. 'As you can see, I was just about to question Argaabil.'

'He's already told me,' replied Zaitabor. 'He's been talking to the Doctor's friend and the whore that you let free. We have to assume that without the correct stimulation and prayer the effects of the herbs will soon wear off. The boy will remember everything that happened.'

'But, my lord, I only told them –' Jamie recognized the voice as that of the fat Furnace worker. There was a cry of pain, and Argaabil lapsed into shivering silence.

'You were an excellent executioner and destroyer,' said Zaitabor. 'But I am sure that I can perform some of your functions with similar efficiency.' There was the metallic hiss of metal as a sword was drawn, and then a choked cry. A pause, and then a shout from Zaitabor, presumably to knights at the door. 'Take this carcass away and feed it to the birds!'

'Grand Knight, was it right to kill him when we still need to preserve some element of –'

'The hiding is over!' exclaimed Zaitabor. 'The brotherhood will no longer skulk in the shadows or work to change people's memories through fear. I am acting Grand Knight. Defrabax has been precipitated into action. The final meeting will go ahead at dawn as planned. It's time for all people to feel the true might of the Brotherhood of Rexulon.'

'And the knights who have resisted the entreaties of the brothers?'

'They shall be destroyed. Only the Brotherhood of Rexulon are capable of governing and interceding with the Higher for the people of this city. Defrabax has done us a favour in destroying the most obvious blight of science upon our land. Although steeped in sin at birth, the Higher has seen fit to use even him.'

'What are my orders, lord?'

'Prepare for the final meeting. I have good news to bring before the brotherhood.' A pause. 'I'll send some brothers along to clear up this offal.'

'My lord is very gracious,' said Araboam.

'The Higher is gracious to all who cling to the true way,' stated Zaitabor. A few moments later the door thumped shut.

Jamie gritted his teeth again. When Araboam opened the wardrobe door for his robes Jamie sprang like a wildcat and clubbed him to the floor. The look of shocked surprise was visible even on his unconscious face.

Jamie helped Kaquaan out of the wardrobe. 'Time to attend our second meeting of the Brotherhood of Rexulon.'

'Your memory?'

'As the man said, it's slowly coming back to me,' said Jamie. 'Let's see if we can learn from the mistakes of last time.'

The Doctor and the Dugraq scout proceeded quickly through the underground city. The light emitted by the power station was such that the Doctor was convinced that he could have plotted the course on his own if he had to.

'What do you know about the android?' asked the Doctor as they walked.

'A little,' said the creature. 'I am led to believe that there were a good many in this city, but this one was the only survivor.'

'Does it always obey commands? Did you ever face any problems with it?'

'I do not think so,' said the Dugraq. 'Once we knew how to operate it we used it to check on the Mecrim and to try to ensure that the Rocarbies did not find a way to the surface. It was the perfect spy, always following its orders exactly and with great efficiency. A few repairs were needed, I believe, but its essential functions were undamaged.'

'Including its limiter preventing it taking human life?'

The Dugraq shook his head. 'It was a military worker. It will simply obey an order. That safeguard would not have proved any help to us even if it had functioned.' The shrew-creature looked the Doctor up and down. 'Don't forget: we aren't human.'

'And you just *gave* the android to Defrabax when he asked for it?'

'We trusted him at that moment. It seemed to be a sensible course of action. As far as I am aware Defrabax took the android away and fashioned it into a passable homunculus. Since then it has functioned as his eyes and ears down here in our city.'

'We all make mistakes,' said the Doctor, smiling. 'Tell me, what do you know of this city?'

'Our legends walk hand-in-hand with our knowledge. I believe it was a large research installation.'

'Working on projects funded by the military?'

'That is correct. We've managed to access some computer terminals, but we tend to leave the main military plant well alone.'

'Because of the Mecrim?'

The scout said nothing, and the Doctor took the silence to be an affirmative.

'And what role did your ancestors have all those years ago?'

The scout paused for a moment at a junction before turning right into what appeared to be a small shopping precinct. 'There were a small number of Dugraq people kept in cages for experimentation. Despite our intelligence, we were kept by the humans because we are genetically very similar to *Homo sapiens*. They thought we were mere animals.' The creature snorted.

'And yet you are clearly a very trusting people,' said the Doctor.

'We greatly prize forgiveness. But we strive to remember and learn from our knowledge of how our race was treated in the past.'

'And the Rocarbies?' asked the Doctor. 'I assume that the Mecrim had a direct military function. What did the original colony want of the Rocarbies?'

'They are manufactured creatures, derived from primates that naturally occur towards the equator of this planet. The files tell us that they were being bred and manipulated as part of a programme financed by a mining company.'

'Few things appal me more,' said the Doctor, 'than when warmongers and big business climb into the same bed. I assume the mining company wanted cheap labour?'

'As always. The Interplanetary Mining Corporation – formerly the Issigri Mining Corporation – spent millions of credits on high-tech solutions to mining problems. But sometimes only muscle gets the job done.'

'Hold on a minute,' said the Doctor. 'Did you say the Issigri Mining Corporation? Dom and Madeleine are decent people –'

'Businesses change, evolve . . . Degenerate.' The Dugraq sniffed. 'By the time of this civilization the IMC was a company out of control, a step or two above common terrorists. Its money ensured that it stayed on the right side of the law.'

The Doctor paused for a moment in thought. 'If the Rocarbies – or at least their ancestors – are native to this planet, then I assume that you are not?'

The Dugraq sighed and was silent for some minutes. The Doctor thought that perhaps this was an area which even the Dugraqs did not speak of, but eventually the scout did answer, his voice almost a whisper. 'We haven't accessed the files that might give us an insight into our origins.'

'Can I ask why not?'

'In the interest of peace on this planet it was felt best that we do not try to leave this world of shadows for the surface and the space and planets beyond. As a race we might have the learning and the morality to cope with the treasures beyond these dark caves. The Rocarbies and the Taculbain do not.'

'It is very noble of you to sacrifice your potential future for the sake of peace.'

'It is not noble,' said the Dugraq. 'It is sensible. And, in any case, all of us – Rocarbies, Taculbain, Dugraqs – have now had contact with the world over our heads. We will need to draw up a new policy, once this situation sorts itself out.'

The Doctor smiled in the perpetual twilight. 'I assure

you that once we've sorted out "this situation", as you put it, I will do all I can to help you find your destiny.'

'Thank you, Traveller,' said the Dugraq scout. 'I knew you had a trustworthy face.'

'Which you could recognize even whilst upside down in a Taculbain cocoon? That is remarkable!'

The power station was now fully in view, a large block of grey stone with glass tubes containing lifts and stairways connected to the outside walls. As light shone from the various windows the building resembled a crude gem in need of further polishing.

'It's very poor form to leave the lights on like that,' remarked the Doctor. 'Although I am grateful. I've not had as long as you to adjust to the dark.'

'I wonder if we will ever adjust to the harsh light of the world above us,' said the Dugraq, passing a hand over a sensor to trigger the main gate. 'I am used to a solid, unmoving sky that seems almost within reach. A sky full of – what are they called . . .? A sky full of clouds, a sky that seems without end . . . These things terrify me, Traveller.'

They began to walk down the driveway, past the skeletons of parked automobiles and personal transports. There was a fountain, dust idling where once water flowed, at the front of the main entrance to the building. It was in the same style as the building, and the Doctor couldn't help but grimace.

'And the Taculbain?' he asked. 'Where did they fit into the scheme of things?'

'Scientific curiosities,' said the scout. 'A small hive of specimens was kept. I believe that research was being carried out into their collective mentality.'

'You are very well informed,' said the Doctor as they approached the door.

'The Taculbain share knowledge and thought through their biology and under the guidance of their Queen,' said the Dugraq. 'We share through education. All Dugraqs have much the same knowledge. Our leaders are chosen because of their great wisdom.'

'Yours is indeed a wise culture,' remarked the Doctor. 'Now, this building. It's difficult to establish from the exterior what generating principles it uses. Its proximity to the residential areas is probably due to nothing more than the restrictions of space.'

'The old files have illustrations of the wall that once went around this entire establishment. Everything had to be self-contained and able to resist attack.'

'Let's go in,' said the Doctor.

Another sensor was triggered and the huge door hissed open.

Commander Zaitabor, acting Grand Knight of Kuabris, strode boldly down the corridor. Even now he was not quite sure exactly what circumstances had changed, exactly which event had encouraged him to strike. But the time was right. That knowledge alone was enough.

The red robes of the Brotherhood of Rexulon flowed above his Kuabris armour. Many knights stared at him uncomprehendingly, but said nothing. They would get their explanation soon enough.

He'd enjoyed killing Argaabil. He had felt a grim satisfaction as the sword penetrated skin, fat, and muscle in a single movement. For a moment the man appeared to hold his stomach together before collapsing on to the floor. All who cavort with science and superstition would die like this, as would all knights that had lost sight of the true way. The brotherhood was a corrective grouping, no more: a remnant of the Higher that was now poised to seize all power in its own right.

This acquired power would be but a brief candle. Then there would come the final phase of the Higher's retribution. And that would be glorious to behold.

And Zaitabor knew that he could now rely on Araboam to perform his duties well. The young man's life was hanging by a thread over the ice-cold moving mountains of Hell. He would not wander from the truth again, Higher be praised.

One detail needed attending to before the final meeting of the brotherhood. Zaitabor strode into his private rooms, dismissing the adviser who was waiting there. Then he walked to the window. He pushed it open, gasping in the sharp white air of the early morning. From here, high in one of the Kuabris towers, Zaitabor could see the smoking remains of the Furnace. How satisfying – and unexpected to all but the Higher – it had been to see a man of legend destroy the work of the men of science.

Zaitabor's strong hands gripped the window frame as he breathed deeply, his eyes closed. Then he raised the glass window and leant out over the sill, peering down the tower.

Just below his room hung one of the moth-men, shivering at the prospect of dawn. Its bejewelled eyes stared up at him. Its mouth opened, mandibles and probes crossing and clutching to produce the sounds. 'All has happened as you said it should.'

'Good.'

'One food supply was rescued.'

'A shortish man with dark hair? That does not matter now. Your reward awaits.'

'But the light –'

'Assemble all your people. The brotherhood meets at dawn. The early morning light will not harm you.'

The creature said something in its own tongue, and then launched itself off the tower, its huge wings a blur. The dark figure receded from view in some low-lying cloud.

Zaitabor closed the window and smiled.

* * *

'Oh dear,' said the Doctor almost the moment they stepped into the underground power station. 'I think this could be a fusion reactor after all. It might be highly unstable by now. I know these things are built to last, but there's long-wearing and there's long-wearing. If hundreds or thousands of years have passed then I dread to think what's gone wrong.'

'I have never been inside this building before,' said the Dugraq as they walked down a well carpeted corridor. 'I am afraid I have no information for you.'

'Don't worry,' said the Doctor. 'They're usually based around similar principles. We're looking for the control centre. Come on!' After their leisurely walk across the city the Doctor suddenly sprinted, the Dugraq puffing and panting as he tried to keep up.

'Why do you not use the lifts?' asked the creature as the Doctor thundered down another set of stairs.

'Don't trust them!' exclaimed the Doctor. 'We don't know who's pulling the pulley.'

The long metal corridor they were in was covered with symbols and warnings. At the end was a huge glass door. It opened easily. As before, whoever had got the station up and running again was more interested in ease of access than security.

'The control room,' said the Doctor grandly.

The area beyond was huge and white and seemed, like much of the building, to have been hermetically sealed. Rows of screens had been activated, each showing fast-scrolling data and graphical representations of output and danger thresholds. A keyboard stood neatly before each monitor, precisely aligned as if a cleaner had just gone round and tidied the place up ready for the next day's work.

There was a large metal shutter towards the far end of the room, and a blank screen in one corner. In front of it was a small raised dais, topped by plastileather-bound chairs with built-in executive terminals. The pot plant had died, leaving an ornate bowl full of mouldy earth.

The Doctor sat at one of the consoles in the main part of the room, pushing a headphone to one side. He began tapping furiously at the keyboard, nodding and tutting as the system presented more and more information. It was clear even to the Dugraq that a number of the graphs were swinging over into the red.

'Right,' said the Doctor. 'We've got to execute a type two emergency close-down procedure. I'll need your help on another console and then perhaps we can –'

'Stop,' sighed a huge voice. The Doctor and the Dugraq scout turned as an enormous humanoid stepped into the room. The crudely formed creature was the colour of clay and soil. A pendant covered with esoteric symbols hung from its neck but seemed to merge into its oily skin. 'You must not tamper with the instruments.'

'Listen to me,' said the Doctor urgently. 'I need to talk to your master. We're all in danger.'

The creature stopped a few yards from the Doctor, inclining its head slightly.

'You must contact Defrabax,' continued the Doctor. 'Tell him that this whole power station is unstable. I realize you've only got this running at less than a tenth of its full potential but –'

'My instructions are now to bring the station fully on-line,' explained the figure. It walked to the closest console and began stabbing in authorization codes with its blunt fingers. 'Do not attempt to interfere. I have assessed that I am much stronger than both of you. If either or both of you attempt to stop me performing my duties I will have to restrain you. And your bones and organs are very weak.'

'Don't bring the station on-line!' exclaimed the Doctor.

'Why?' asked the creature, although its fingers still tapped at the keyboard.

'Because if you do, you'll cause this entire plant to explode. In an instant you'll not only destroy this city, but the new world built over it.'

Thirteen

As the creature lunged, Zoe dived to the floor. Its arms swept over her, rough skin tearing into her back. She sprang to her feet and ran towards the open furnace door, still hoping desperately that her ideas about the animal might prove correct.

Zoe turned to face the creature, her bruised back to the furnace's licking flames. The beast swung its head in her direction, its body swaying from side to side, but it did not see her. It seemed to know that she should be there, but could see nothing but the great heat.

There was a shout and both Zoe and the creature turned their heads towards the source. The twins were frantically screaming and jumping up and down. The creature looked back in Zoe's direction for the last time, perhaps deciding that the heat it saw was not that of an animal, and then trotted towards Raitak and Reisaz. It had a new target in its sight.

The twins darted towards the protective metal wall around the central turbine and kicked open a small gate. The creature followed them through, into the narrow maintenance area that ran around the entirety of the enormous hissing, clanking machine. Cogs and dynamos hummed, safety valves let off steam, and in the centre a huge wheel turned.

The creature's pursuit of the twins was halted by a sudden stinging spray of hot water. Zoe noticed that as Reisaz and Raitak ran they released valves and emergency cutouts, causing jets of steam to fly over the body of their pursuer. The creature showed little pain, and continued its relentless, teasing search, peering through the broiling haze.

The turbine pounded a metallic beat, oblivious to the figures that moved around it. The twins were about halfway around the machine now, but the creature was gaining ground all the time. It made a deep hissing noise and then leapt at them, a lithe grey figure made dim by the steam. An outstretched claw caught the twins' right leg, and they tumbled to the ground.

As Zoe instinctively moved forward to try to help them Diseaeda dropped down on to the back of the creature from his hiding place on the turbine housing. He'd removed a huge greasy chain from somewhere and, as he pulled one arm as tightly as he could around the creature's neck, with the other he lashed out at the creature's face and snout. His first strike was a good one. There was a sharp splitting sound and something dark and viscous began to seep from under the bony plate that covered whatever passed for its eyes.

The twins scrambled to their feet and hobbled towards Zoe. She struggled to help them over the metal fence, grabbing a fistful of clothing in each hand and simply tugging until they were over. She glanced at Diseaeda and the creature, marvelling at the man's adrenaline-fuelled strength. He clung to the back of the bucking creature and lashed out with the chain, the monster's arms not having enough flexibility to reach behind it.

An overall-clad man, roused by the noise, came running from the far end of the chamber. He was shouting something and rubbing the sleep from his eyes. But there was no time to talk.

Zoe reached for a pile of thick metal rods stacked against one wall and gripped one in her hands. She didn't really know what to do with it, but she had to try something. She ran back to the writhing figures, hoping to use her forward momentum to spear the creature.

It side-stepped quickly, Zoe's hand jarring painfully as the metal impacted against the solid side of the machine. The twins were swinging a similar pole at the creature but it stayed resolutely out of reach.

Diseaeda couldn't hold on forever and a harsh twist from the beast sent him spinning off. There was a dull thud as his shoulders hit the metal wall, his head snapping backwards, and then he slumped to the ground.

Ignoring the motionless figure the creature leapt over the fence, flicking the twins' metal bar away, and then bowled into them with an animal lust. A foot thudded into their stomach, pinning them to the floor, and it bent down to finish them with its jaws, its teeth grinding inches from their screaming faces.

A flaming blast enveloped the monster's head and it jerked backwards. The man in the overalls had found some sort of huge blow-torch and aimed it unswervingly at the creature as the twins rolled away once more. In moments the animal was a humanoid cloud of flame. Then it leapt through the air at the man, knocking the device to the floor. There was no finesse this time, no delicious savouring of fear. A claw burst into the man's rib-cage.

Much of the creature's head and shoulders had been blackened by the attack but it turned gracefully to study Zoe and the twins, flexing its huge bloody claws delicately as if to prove that it was unharmed.

'What do we do now?' asked Reisaz, her face blistered by the heat and stained with sweat and soot. Raitak's eyes were half-closed and she was breathing heavily, a huge gash across her forehead.

Zoe shook her head and said nothing. They began to shuffle back across the expansive floor of the generating plant, staring always at the creature coming towards them. As they waited for the final attacking leap Zoe wondered what it would feel like as the claws snapped over bone and muscle or as the staring face of death swept down on hers.

The ancient android's fingers hovered over the keypad, and then cancelled the entry process. It walked over to the Doctor. 'Show me the relevant data,' it said.

'Well, I can't, not as such,' blustered the Doctor. 'You see, the readings that would absolutely prove what I am saying can only be accessed from the reactor core test room.'

The android made as if to begin keying in the codes again.

'But,' said the Doctor, 'let's find out, shall we?'

'Defrabax has not been able to access the test room,' stated the android. 'He lost the key.'

'How unfortunate,' said the Doctor. 'Show me where this room is.'

The motionless android weighed up the situation.

'Please hurry,' said the Doctor. 'You can't afford to take that risk. Not even a military android would wantonly destroy so much life, including its own.'

'Defrabax plans to bring peace and prosperity to the city,' said the android blandly.

'Exactly,' said the Doctor. 'Defrabax will be very angry if he finds that you've brought the entire power station on-line without making all the relevant checks.'

The android walked towards the thick metal door at the far end of the room. The Dugraq trotted behind them, deep in thought.

'This is the test room door,' said the android. He pointed to the rectangular slot where the key was supposed to fit.

'Let's see what we can do with this lock,' said the Doctor. He made the android stretch out its broad hands and emptied into them the contents of his many pockets.

The Dugraq's whiskers bristled with inquisitive interest. 'What are these things?'

'Sweets,' said the Doctor. 'Some prize marbles – no, please don't ask for an explanation now, we haven't the time. Compass. Tea bag – Darjeeling, perhaps? Pencil. Paper clip. Stray marble. Another pencil. Eight-track cassette – still looking for something to play it on. Screwdriver. A shopping list – the handwriting looks like Robert Burns'. I wonder if he's still waiting for his freedom and whisky?'

'Hurry, Doctor,' said the Dugraq, interest giving way to impatience.

'Aha!' exclaimed the Doctor. He withdrew a small bulb-like device with a silver thread attached. 'Found this on the floor of the TARDIS some time ago. I don't think it's essential, but it should help me open this door.'

'I used the medical emergency over-ride codes to open all the other doors,' explained the android. 'Without the key I have been unable to open this one.'

'No matter,' said the Doctor. He reached into the slot, prized off the cover plate and gently tugged out what looked like a coiled stretch of white human hair. Then with the little device he'd found in his pockets he touched a number of wires experimentally. Occasionally the bulb would light up and the Doctor would smile. After some minutes of this delicate work the Doctor began to mumble to himself darkly.

'Oh, I could stand here all day trying to do it this way,' he said eventually. 'Let's try brute force.' And with that he took a pencil from the android's palm and shoved it into the thin wires, touching as many as possible.

There was a loud flash and the Doctor was hurled across the room. The Dugraq ran to his side, and shook him by the shoulders.

After what seemed like an age the Doctor's eyes flicked

open. 'Oh, good gracious me,' he said. 'That gave me quite a turn.'

There was a further loud bang from the lock and the door slowly elevated into the ceiling. Beyond was a small room dominated by a huge glass window looking down towards the reactor core.

The computer systems were up and running and the Doctor began to tap doubtfully at a small keyboard. 'No, that's not right. I wanted . . . Ah, here we are.' The top half of the screen was split into two alternating real-time video camera sequences, showing the state of the reactor. Even the Dugraq could tell that things were in a pretty bad way. The bottom half presented a number of simple graphs. Each had a large splash of red encroaching over the screen. 'Oh my giddy aunt,' said the Doctor. 'We've got less time than I thought.'

'I can only contact Defrabax in an emergency,' said the implacable android.

'Well, I think this counts as an emergency, don't you?' said the Doctor.

Zoe and the twins edged around the walls towards the still-open door of the furnace. The creature was tracking them from a distance, but for the moment had not come any closer. Perhaps it had been injured by Diseaeda's attack – or by the station worker's torch – but Zoe felt that their luck could not last much longer.

Just as they were almost within reach of the huge metal shutters the creature sprang into the air. The twins threw themselves to one side but a fist of razor-sharp talons clamped around Zoe's thigh and twisted her savagely to the ground. As her head thumped against the floor she saw sparks and splashes of colour, and then the monster raising a claw into the air, preparing to smash it downwards.

She heard the awful sound of muscle and bone rupturing, but it was not her own. She looked up, her vision still blurred, and saw the unmistakable form of Diseaeda.

He had recovered consciousness and was brandishing one of the metal bars. He was very pale, seeming to have lost a lot of blood from somewhere, but his sudden strength was like that of ten men. He took a few steps away from the creature and then gripped the bar firmly, angling it forwards like a spear. Then he charged forwards.

Whatever the intention of his attack the results were clear enough: the huge bar sank into the creature's neck, just under its skull.

The beast turned, the bar clanging into the wall and then falling to the ground. Zoe noticed a deep wound in the creature's neck, a round slot big enough to accommodate a fist. Blood gushed over its shoulders and down its spine.

The animal was now standing a few feet away from Zoe. Pressing her hands tight over her leg wound and gritting her teeth against the pain she began crawling along the base of the wall. Even through the agony of her wound she could see the circus master standing erect in front of the creature. The twins stood at his side, shaking with fear. They had run to the worker's corpse to pick up the welding torch, but Raitak held it uneasily in her hand. The twins did not know what to do.

Diseaeda did. 'I've had enough of this,' he said, and reached for the torch. 'I'm much too old for this sort of thing.'

With that, he twisted the controls of the device and casually dropped it to the floor. A wide fan of flame shot upwards like a screen between him and the monster. Zoe could barely see through the burning, shimmering air, and presumed that the creature could not either. But why had Diseaeda discarded perhaps the only weapon to have had an effect on the beast?

The creature could no longer see Diseaeda and the twins through the haze. It half-turned, searching for Zoe.

In that instant Diseaeda jumped through the wall of fire and hurled himself at the creature with every ounce of his remaining strength. His hair was burning, his clothing smouldering, but his eyes were glazed over with a single purpose. His large body thudded into the creature, catching it off-balance. In Zoe's mind it seemed that the two humanoid figures hung in the air for a moment, two opposing forces smashed together. She saw the creature's blank face, half-twisted away as if in disgust for being surprised by the same man once more. She saw Diseaeda, the flames licking away his age to reveal a young man, and then a frightened boy.

They arced through the air, merging long before the flames of the furnace reached out to them, four arms wrapped tightly around the man but unable to prevent the momentum carrying them backwards. The creature's head and shoulders, already damaged by fire, crumpled first, and then the red spears of heat stabbed into the circus master's chest and legs.

There was a small, glimmering explosion, deep in the inferno of the furnace.

The Doctor followed the android as it walked unhurriedly into the main room and stood before the large screen, tapping a few controls in the arm of one of the chairs on the dais.

The screen glowed for a moment with phantom images, and then showed a solid wall of static. The android removed the clay pendant from around its neck and chipped away at it with its massive hands. A few moments later a small silver wand was revealed, which it placed into a slot by the screen.

The image stabilized to reveal the logo of an ancient piece of communications software. A few seconds later the screen showed a balding grey-haired man, a damp felt hat pulled down over his alert but disgruntled eyes. The image swayed unsteadily, and the man seemed to peer down at the Doctor and the others. Clearly Defrabax – if that was he – was holding some sort of small communications unit in his hand. 'What is it? You should have powered-up by now. And what are those people doing –'

'There is an emergency, master,' said the android.

'This is what is called a secure channel,' snapped the magician. 'And I'm halfway up a very lonely hillside, watching the city. You can stop pretending to be my homunculus for a moment. No one's going to hear you.'

'The reactor is dangerously unstable, Defrabax. It must be closed down. Even at its present output it will explode in less than five minutes, causing an explosion equivalent to 790,000 kilos of plastic AK.'

'But you said that the figures were acceptable.'

'The figures accessible from the main control room indicated that the reactor was just running within the manufacturer's parameters. The test room shows that the reactor core is running over 25 per cent above recommended tolerances.'

'But how did you get into the core testing room? I thought you said that there was only one key, the key that –'

'This man opened the door for me.'

The Doctor stepped forward to the android's side and doffed an imaginary hat. 'Good evening – or is it morning up there? It's so difficult to tell. It's very dark down here, you see. I'm the Doctor, by the way, and if we don't shut this thing down soon I shall never get to meet you. It's Defrabax, isn't it?'

The old man nodded. 'That's right. And what business do you have down there?'

'The knights forced me to join an expedition in search of the Menagerie of Ukkazaal.'

'Then you're responsible for this?'

'No,' said the Doctor. 'I'm no friend of the knights. I'm here purely to avert a catastrophe.'

'I don't believe you. I'm not going to stop now. Not after these long months of preparation.'

'Ask your android,' said the Doctor.'You know he'll speak the truth.'

'The Doctor is correct in what he says,' stated the android.

Defrabax appeared to be on the verge of tears. 'But I'm so close to success . . .'

'What are you trying to do?' asked the Doctor gently.

'I want to use that technology for the good of all our people.'

'And do you understand every aspect of what you believe to be down here? Do you have any idea of the centuries of learning that gave rise to this little microcosm of human civilization?'

'Of course not,' said Defrabax. 'The android has outlined certain principles. I have found it difficult to work only from the surface, to not actually be able to go down to the old city and see things for myself.' The man sighed. 'And, in any case, how much could I learn? I am but one man. A man of strong ideas but, it seems, little ability to back them up.'

'Now, I wouldn't say that,' said the Doctor. 'But the point is –'

'Where does your knowledge come from?' asked the mage. 'I can't believe that there is any region on our world as advanced as the old city.'

'I am from far beyond your world,' said the Doctor. 'But let's talk about such matters later. The important thing is that we shut down the reactor now.'

Defrabax sniffed. 'Very well. Android?'

'Sir?'

'I see that the Dugraqs have discovered my . . .

selfishness. Perhaps I have abused the trust of those that gave you to me. Change your command programming to obey the Doctor. Do everything he says.'

'Very well,' said the android, turning to the Doctor for instructions.

'I want you to know that I am not unsympathetic to your aims,' the Doctor told Defrabax. 'Once we've closed this plant down we'll meet you on the surface.'

'Very well,' said Defrabax. He reached down to switch off the device and the large screen again filled with the white and blue logo.

The Doctor smiled at the towering form of the disguised android. 'Now, I want you to undo everything Defrabax has instructed you to do. Shut this place down, obeying all safety protocols. How long will that take?'

'Approximately fifteen minutes to shut down major systems. Peripheral work will take a further six to seven hours and –'

'That can wait. Just make this place safe.'

The android nodded stiffly and moved off.

The Dugraq turned to the Doctor. 'Defrabax's heart is full of good intentions.'

'I'm sure of that,' said the Doctor. 'But he needs to realize that it takes time to develop technology like this. His society isn't ready for this level of sophistication – in fact, few ever are. In the world over our heads gunpowder is unknown. The people go as far as their legs or horses can carry them. They have largely managed to avoid polluting the rivers or destroying entire ecosystems by intensive logging. It would be a brave man to say that they're more primitive than their ancestors.'

'What do we do now?' asked the scout.

'I will ensure that no one else can operate this machinery. And then we'll go back up to the surface, preferably avoiding the sewers this time. I need to find Jamie and Zoe, and I want to find out who arranged the

Taculbain ambush.' The Doctor smiled sadly. 'A number of people have died already. I don't propose that there should be any more before I leave this planet.'

Zoe stood next to the twins. 'I'm very sorry,' she said.

'He shouldn't have done that,' said Raitak.

Reisaz nodded. 'He's saved our lives twice now. Once should have been enough.'

Zoe pulled a makeshift tourniquet tighter around her leg. The bleeding seemed to have stopped now. She would need a few stitches but other than that she'd be all right. But there was no sense of victory in her mind. Diseaeda had sacrificed himself in order to destroy a lethal and uncontrollable creature let loose into a civilization that had no real defence against it.

They closed the metal doors over the furnace and then slumped down to the floor, too exhausted and shocked to speak. After a period of contemplation the twins found a herbal lotion in one of their pockets which they dabbed around Zoe's wound and on their own blisters.

And then the twins started crying, great whooping, choking screams of uninhibited grief.

Zoe stared ahead, stoically.

Some minutes later Raitak blew her nose on her sleeve. 'It'll be dawn soon,' she said through sobs.

'What will you do?' asked Reisaz, rubbing her eyes as she looked at Zoe. 'Under our law you're free to go now, of course.'

'I'll go back to the city, find the Doctor and Jamie,' replied Zoe. 'When I tell the Doctor what's happened I'm sure he'll make sure that the other creatures stay in suspended animation.'

'We'll come with you, said Raitak. 'The circus can wait.'

'You'll be going back to the freak show?' asked an incredulous Zoe.

'On Diseaeda's death not only are all his servants and helpers liberated,' said Raitak, 'but we become its new owners.'

'It will be good to see you safely reunited with your friends,' said Reisaz.

'But most importantly of all,' said Raitak. 'We must ensure that there are no more creatures like that thing we have just destroyed.'

Fourteen

The silver globe of the sun rose slowly through the early morning mist. Woods and farmhouses were rendered as dim grey shapes in the distance. Only the road ahead was straight and true.

Zoe turned to look at the twins. They had returned to the circus to retrieve Diseaeda's favourite horse and to find a suitable creature for Zoe to ride. She was grateful for the comparative comfort of her return journey, but was shocked by the grey faces of the circus workers and townsfolk as they cleared away the bodies. The twins had been numbed by Diseaeda's death, and conversation had been difficult. Zoe had seen many deaths since beginning her travels with the Doctor and, although her faith in him was absolute, that never meant that coping was any easier. And her grief was always second-hand, like sobbing at a motiveless murder reported by the telepress. What were those affected actually going through?

Such strength of emotion was alien to Zoe. Despite the Doctor's playful cynicism she still felt that logic was a vital part of any civilized person's mentality. But did she feel this simply because she was lucky enough not to have experienced the death of someone very close to her?

The trouble with the long journey – and the twins' taciturnity – was that it gave Zoe a lot of time to think. She wasn't sure if she welcomed the prospect.

'Tell us again about your friends,' said Raitak suddenly. Reisaz jumped as if waking up from a deep sleep.

Zoe reached down to pat the horse, not sure who was the most apprehensive. 'The Doctor is a traveller from . . . Well, I'm not quite sure where, actually, but I think it's somewhere very far away. Very advanced. I don't think he likes his own people much. He prefers to explore and put things right where he sees evil at work. He's very good at that. He bumbles around until things become clear to him. It can be frustrating sometimes. But I've missed not having him around the past couple of days.'

'And the boy you spoke of? I think you said he came from your world.'

Zoe nodded, remembering an earlier conversation. 'He comes from my past. The Doctor travels in time, you see.'

'Really?' said Raitak. 'If the knights were to discover that . . . '

'If the Doctor has any sense he won't tell the knights too much about the nature of his travels,' said Reisaz.

'Why not?' asked Zoe.

The twins tried to spur their horse to quicken its pace. Raitak turned to look at Zoe. 'One of the mental attitudes that the knights promulgate is a concentration on the present moment as if unconnected to past or future. It's a fantasy, of course. The moment someone talks to you of the preceding day or how much money you have for food tomorrow the whole thing comes tumbling down.'

'And even the knights need to plan: to build buildings or to recruit new members,' said Reisaz.

'But if you could live just for the moment,' said Zoe, struggling with the concept, 'you'd be entirely isolated from pain and suffering.'

'A coward's way out,' said Raitak. 'You need to confront pain and suffering and strive to defeat them. Your obligation is to make sensible plans for the future and to learn from the past. That's why the knights are so cold and inhuman: they have no inclination to establish deep relationships. These things can only happen over a period of time.'

'They certainly don't like people enjoying themselves,' said Zoe. 'I was arrested for no good reason at all.'

'They're a mirthless bunch,' agreed Reisaz.

'It must have been very frightening for you,' said Raitak with an unusual tenderness. 'Coming to somewhere new and then suddenly finding yourself cast into a dungeon.'

Zoe smiled, the memories already beginning to recede. 'Even when travelling with the Doctor things don't always go well.'

'That's everyday life,' observed Raitak.

'I'm curious,' said Zoe. 'Why did you ask about the Doctor and Jamie?'

'We might have to fight those monsters together. If your life depends on someone it's good to know a little bit about them.'

'You're convinced that there will be more of those things?'

'I just have this feeling,' said Raitak solemnly.

The Dugraq scout knew of a secondary system of caves and tunnels that lead on to the surface, entirely bypassing the poisonous sewers. The Doctor and the disguised android followed close behind the little creature. The android scanned their surroundings for movement, alert for wandering Taculbain or Rocarbies.

The subterranean world was quiet, and darker now the power station was off-line. The android had found a couple of battery-operated torches before they left the building and the Doctor took these. He alone needed them.

The little circle of white light illuminated collapsed

brickwork, faded plaster and finally the damp walls of natural caves. When the Doctor heard what sounded like a waterfall to their left the torch's beam proved too feeble to illuminate it.

For a long time the Doctor shadowed the dim figure of the Dugraq exactly. At one point he followed the skipping creature over a narrow ridge of rock. It was only when he safely reached the end that the Doctor wondered how deep the drop on either side had been.

They emerged from a narrow tunnel into a cave that was dappled with light. Even the Doctor could now see the way forward, a huge opening of yellowish brightness.

'You get a fine view of the city from here,' said the Dugraq conversationally as they emerged from the tunnel. 'At least, when it isn't raining.'

'Fresh air, with no matter how much rain, will suit me down to the ground,' said the Doctor.

Soon they stood blinking on a chalky hillside where long-tailed sheep nibbled at grey grass. There was a strong breeze on the Doctor's face, and the closest part of the city to them, at the base of the hill, contained the Furnace. Its unfiltered fumes would have explained the dusty state of the grass.

However, it was clear even from this distance that the Furnace had been so badly damaged as to be beyond repair. An entire brick chimney had crumbled along the full length of the building. Another had split and twisted. The majority of the walls of the building itself had been destroyed but inside was a tangle of metal and brick.

Although the sun was still hidden by one side of the valley, the early morning light softened some of the city's ugliness. The grey rain-bearing clouds had receded, at least for the moment.

'Meteorologically speaking,' announced the Doctor, 'it could be a nice day.'

The android's keen senses picked something up, and it slowly scanned the sky. 'Look there,' it said, pointing.

The Doctor squinted and saw dark figures climbing into the sky. Soon there was a hazy strip of them, extending from the opposite hillside and towards the castle. 'Taculbain?' he asked.

The Dugraq nodded. 'I've never heard of them coming out into the light before. I suppose it is possible for them to function but it must require great concentration.'

'Then whatever they're doing is very important,' said the Doctor. 'We haven't got much time. Let's find Defrabax and go to the castle. I don't like the look of this at all.'

Defrabax could feel the city's panic. The mental openness that genuinely elevated him above most men allowed him to experience the emotions and images remotely. Mothers pulled children indoors from yards and bolted doors behind them. Working men dropped their tools and cowered under roofs in fear. The sky was black with the humming wings of the moth-creatures. The cry quickly went round: 'More creatures from the menagerie! We are doomed!'

Where normally his mind was full of human strivings and plans now Defrabax saw with sudden crystal clarity the first of the Taculbain alighting at the base of the castle. The moth-creatures landed and gently folded back their great wings. They filed slowly into a cave at the castle's base. They chirruped loudly to one another when the excitement became too great. Defrabax did not understand their clicking language, but he felt the meaning in the depth of the great cry: 'Soon our Queen shall be restored to us!'

The images faded.

Defrabax stood watching the approaching figures as resolute as a statue despite the wind that tugged at his hair and the fog that danced around his feet. He leant against a large staff, as colourful a figure as the city could tolerate.

The man he had seen on the communications device came and stood next to him. They both silently observed the city from the lower hillside.

'I want you to know that my intentions were honourable,' said Defrabax.

'I know,' said the man who called himself the Doctor. 'We've both managed to distract the other from the true business at hand.'

'And that is?'

'The Taculbain,' said the Doctor. 'Or, rather, the things they've done to have their Queen returned to them.'

'Only one man knows what they have been ordered to do,' said the magician, 'and that is the knight who used Kuabris robes much as you did to penetrate the menagerie. And yet I sense that the Taculbain have completed their mission.' He lifted a finger and traced it along the line of the moth-men as they flew towards the castle. 'I think that they are about to receive back their Queen.'

'We must go to the castle,' said the Doctor.

Defrabax nodded, deep in thought. 'At this moment all paths lead to the castle.'

Jamie and Kaquaan had investigated the long tapestry-covered corridor, searching for the secret door that led down to the Rexulon chamber. Jamie was disgusted when he found that he had been so simply tricked: two of the great tapestries had been swapped. The door, closed this time but not locked, now lay behind a bizarre family portrait of tiny stitches.

'I should have known,' Jamie had said, disappointed at himself.

Kaquaan had gently reassured him, steering him towards the door. They had descended quickly and, although a number of brothers were already assembling in the main chamber, had found themselves alone in the changing room. Disguised with Araboam's robes as best they could, they then donned the red cloaks and hoods of the Brotherhood of Rexulon.

Now they stood in the midst of the brothers, waiting for the ceremony to begin.

Jamie's memories of the first meeting were flowing back like an unstoppable spring tide. He remembered seeing Kaquaan on the altar, the smashed machinery, the man with the insect mask, everything. He blinked and gritted his teeth and forced himself back into the present.

This time the leader – Zaitabor – was nowhere to be seen. Jamie wondered how long a locked door and a bashed head would keep Araboam out of action. He hoped that it would be just long enough to allow him to disrupt another ceremony.

He noticed a tunnel in the cave wall towards the far side of the room. He was sure he hadn't seen it on the previous day, so perhaps the oily torch that burnt just above it was a recent addition. The flickering light caught the first of a multitude of moth-creatures who walked slowly into the chamber, standing in rows much like the brothers. Jamie stifled a cry of surprise and heard Kaquaan do the same. The brothers, their own ranks swelling by the moment, were too preoccupied to notice. Some had already started chanting and swaying.

Jamie stared at the altar and hoped that the ceremony would start soon. He had given Kaquaan the sword. His own hand rested on the blade he trusted most. This time things would be different.

The streets were deserted and silent but for the sound of crying children, muffled in back rooms and soothed in tiny cribs. The Doctor and the others moved unhindered through the streets and towards the castle, although the

Doctor felt sure that the terrifying appearance of the android would have been enough to ensure their safe passage.

As they neared the base of the castle the last of the moth-men alighted and strode into a dark passageway set into the rock on which the castle sat. The tunnel was so obvious that the Doctor concluded that this secondary exit was normally hidden in some way.

'Let's hope we find some answers,' the Doctor said, 'wherever the Taculbain are going.'

The Taculbain had no need for artificial light but the Doctor switched on his torch as he stepped inside the entrance. The marks of the tunnel's construction were clearly visible, and the ascent was gentle. The moth-creatures were already well out of sight.

A few moments later the Doctor noticed that the tunnel was becoming brighter and switched off his torch. He crept forward slowly. He knew that he could rely on the android and the Dugraq to proceed silently but was much less sure of the old man's dexterity.

At length the Doctor began to hear muffled voices. The tunnel was beginning to widen, and moments later rounded out into a large chamber, lit by flickering torchlight.

The Doctor and the others stepped quietly into the cave and surveyed the scene.

In front of them were rows and rows of Taculbain, stretching into the darkness at the edge of the room. The Doctor knew that, having lived in the caves for so long, the creatures' senses would be very acute, but so far he and his companions had gone undetected. The lines of carefully folded wings remained motionless.

The chamber inclined down slightly from the Taculbain and towards a flat central area dominated by an altar. On its surface was strapped a struggling young man the Doctor did not recognize.

On the opposite side of the altar was a large gathering of red-robed figures, variously chanting and shaking. Similar garments were worn by the tall man at the head of the altar. He wore a golden mask of an insect's face and the well polished armour of one of the noblest Knights of Kuabris. He held aloft a huge weapon resembling a war hammer and an attentive hush fell across the chamber.

'Brothers and helpers, we are here to celebrate a turning point. The Brotherhood of Rexulon now has the power to overthrow the men of evil and let the light of the Higher shine across our land!'

The Doctor thought that he recognized the voice as being Zaitabor's, although there was a puzzling stiffness in the man's movements.

'Our friends are here to receive back their Queen,' continued the leader of the brotherhood. 'They have faithfully followed their orders, though they did not know what they were doing, and they shall receive their reward.'

The Doctor noticed that even the impassive Taculbain were beginning to fidget with excitement. The man turned directly to the red-robed brotherhood. 'As for you, my brothers, you have much to celebrate now. I tell you truthfully, we shall not meet in this manner again! My elevation to the position of Grand Knight will ensure that the Kuabris never stray from the true and shining path of the Higher. We shall feast well when we burn Himesor's heretical writings!'

The leader's comments had made the Doctor certain that Zaitabor was behind the mask. The knight turned and raised his hands heavenwards. 'Oh Higher, we praise you for using the false magician to begin your destruction of all things that reek of science.' The Doctor could hear Defrabax grunting in displeasure at this description but the Taculbain closest to them appeared not to hear. 'Help us this very moment,' continued the leader of the brotherhood, 'to serve you always and do what must be done.'

There was a commotion among the Taculbain as a huge creature, bound with ropes and chains, was brought into the chamber. It resembled the humanoid Taculbain only in as much as it had recognizable limbs and head. Lacking wings and pulling a bloated body behind her, the Taculbain Queen crawled painfully into the brotherhood's chamber.

A number of Taculbain rushed forward, incensed at the sight of their leader in such humiliation. She quelled them the moment she spoke. 'No, be patient!' Her voice was deep and rich, echoing with many tongues. 'A little longer and we shall all be free. But . . . What have we done to ensure our liberation from the dungeons of this place?'

The Rexulon leader was becoming more frenzied by the moment, his voice shrieking loudly over the disquieted chirrup of the Taculbain. 'Nothing matters now! You can attack us or we attack you and whatever the outcome we shall all be swallowed up. The steam engines in every city on this world shall soon be silenced as the Higher welcomes us all through the gateway of death.' At this even the brothers sounded a little concerned, and some began to mutter to their companions.

'The Menagerie of Ukkazaal exists, my brothers! And there are dark creatures within it!'

Despite her chains, the Queen twisted to look at the Taculbain. There was a crushed sadness in her voice. 'Oh our people, what have we done?'

'They are called Mecrim,' continued the man as the Doctor's heart pounded. 'I myself have examined and destroyed texts that refer to the Mecrim, to the grim destroyers of old. They will swarm across our planet like flies and pick clean the corpse of our corrupted world. We all share in the sins of the scientists and the false leaders, and therefore we all must die!'

A number of the brothers were shouting in outrage. The Doctor was quickly assessing the situation to see what could be done.

Suddenly two brothers broke ranks and ran towards the altar. Through the flapping red robes the Doctor recognized Jamie's unmistakable garb, and he smiled proudly.

Jamie moved to the altar to release the young man whilst the other figure – a girl – ran towards the leader of the brotherhood. The Doctor could see the fear-fuelled anger that coursed through her. She had a huge sword in her hands. 'This must end!' she screamed. 'I don't know what you have done, but you must be stopped!'

The figure in red laughed.

The girl swiped clumsily with the sword but it bit keenly into the man's neck . . . and swept effortlessly through to the other side. The masked head tumbled to the floor, landing at the girl's feet.

The Brotherhood of Rexulon gasped, but there was no blood. Still the man laughed, the headless body gesticulating wildly.

The Doctor pushed his way through the uncomprehending Taculbain and joined Jamie at the girl's side. 'Doctor!' exclaimed Jamie happily.

The Doctor beamed. 'Hello, Jamie. Now, what have we here . . ?' He bent down to examine the severed head, and prised off the golden mask to reveal the blank visage of a plaster face.

The arms of the body twitched into life once again, raising hands towards the heavens. The Doctor gritted his teeth and yanked hard at the shoulder joint. The arm came away in his hands. Inside the body he could see gears, cogs, coiled springs. 'Nothing more than glorified clockwork,' he said, incredulous, turning to Jamie.

'Clockwork?' said Jamie. 'But that's so basic.'

'As far as this planet is concerned, this is state-of-the-art!' said the Doctor. 'And this man is supposed to hate technology.'

'You foolish young man,' came the voice from somewhere in the chamber. It echoed and flowed around the rough stone walls. 'I lured you here when I needed time, and you attacked like a blind beast. Did you expect to be any more successful today?'

The Doctor pointed to a gallery high above their heads where Zaitabor stood, triumphant. He stared down at Jamie malevolently. 'I've been playing games with you and your friend the Doctor ever since you came to this world. And it is on this world that you will die.'

'Listen to me!' shouted the Doctor. 'You don't know what you're doing. The Mecrim creatures must not be freed!'

'It's too late, Doctor,' said Zaitabor. 'You have been running after that wizard when you should have paid attention to me!' He nodded curtly in the direction of the moth-creatures. 'Deep in the Menagerie of Ukkazaal the Taculbain followed my orders without hesitation. The Mecrim have already been released.'

Fifteen

Oiquaquil, Captain of the City Guard, marched into the brotherhood's chamber at the head of his men with as much dignity as he could muster. He strode through the unresisting ranks of moth-men and towards the altar. Facing the Brotherhood of Rexulon, Oiquaquil drew his sword. For the first time in his life he was seizing an opportunity.

'With the authority vested in me I arrest you all for high treason,' Oiquaquil announced as loudly as possible. All eyes turned to him, but his voice remained strong. 'I hope that you will not exacerbate your cowardice by fighting. I know that many of you think that we guards are a joke. But what little respect you have will evaporate if you turn upon the City Guard.'

One of the brothers walked towards the guards, his eyes flicking all the time to the twitching clockwork figure by the altar. The guards behind Oiquaquil reached for their weapons uneasily.

'Captain,' said the man, pulling the red robes of Rexulon from his shoulders to reveal the bright armour of a knight. 'I do not know if I speak for all the Knights of Kuabris involved with the brotherhood but . . . We had no idea that our leader was working with creatures from the menagerie.' His voice began to falter, his face showing simple bewilderment at events. 'We certainly did not know that our leader was so . . . tainted by science himself.'

Oiquaquil sighed. 'It seems that Commander Zaitabor deceived many of us with his pious proclamations of devotion,' he said.

'Then I humbly ask, Captain,' continued the knight, 'that you allow us to help defend all that we hold true. The brotherhood exists only to restore the Knights of Kuabris to the true way. We want no part in the wholesale destruction that Zaitabor talked about.'

'There is some sense in what you say,' said Oiquaquil. 'We must dedicate ourselves to defending our city from the evil this man has planned. However, mark my words, when the time is right I shall sift you all like grain. I believe the brotherhood to be guilty of kidnapping and murder. The prime movers in this shall not escape justice.'

'Very well, Captain,' said the knight.

'Until that investigation is over,' announced Oiquaquil more loudly, 'all knights shall answer directly to me. We have no idea as to the depth of this subversion.' With that Oiquaquil turned and walked towards the altar, leaving the knights to discuss matters amongst themselves.

A little man dressed in tattered gold and white armour turned to him. 'Well done, my dear Captain,' he said, clapping him soundly on the back.

'I don't mind admitting,' said Oiquaquil in a whisper, 'that my hands are still shaking. This doesn't come naturally to me, you know.'

'It does to few of us,' said the man.

Oiquaquil nodded slowly, thinking. Then he stared at the man. 'And who are you, anyway?'

'I'm the Doctor. You mean you don't remember? I've been making some enquiries of my own.'

The Captain sighed. After a brief period of decisiveness he again felt like a man drowning in his own inadequacies.

'Then perhaps you can tell me what is going on,' he said.

* * *

When Zoe and the twins arrived at the city they found the gatehouse unmanned and the streets and alleyways deserted. The clip-clop of their mounts' hooves was the only sound to break the tense silence. Even the birds that normally darted between the eaves were nowhere to be seen.

'Perhaps they have all been punished,' said Reisaz.

'Don't be so silly,' said Raitak. She turned to Zoe. 'And how do you propose that we find this Doctor fellow of yours? I was thinking that we might be better off meeting some of Diseaeda's contacts and enquiring about the casket.'

Zoe shook her head. 'We need the Doctor's help. And I don't think we'll have any trouble finding him. Whatever's going on, that's where he'll be. Right in the thick of it.'

'Then perhaps we want the Castle of the Knights of Kuabris,' observed Reisaz. She pointed up the main street and towards the craggy rocks that supported the terrible grey construction. A number of people were emerging from their houses and walking hesitantly in that direction.

With a sudden wave of sound creatures began to pour out of some sort of cave and up into the air. Although the people immediately dived for cover it seemed that the moth-like creatures had no designs on the city folk.

Zoe looked straight up, the air now dark with flying creatures. She noticed slim but powerful limbs, ornate wings, and inhuman faces that somehow showed ecstasy and sadness.

An even darker shadow passed overhead, a huge creature supported by the wings of others. Then it too passed. Soon all the moth-men had gone.

'What were they?' asked Zoe.

'I don't know,' said Raitak. She pointed towards the castle. 'The knights are usually full of answers to all life's mysteries.'

'Then let's go there,' said Zoe.

* * *

'I managed to assemble a few brave guards,' said Captain Oiquaquil. 'I followed the moth-creatures here, listened to what Zaitabor was saying, and decided it was time to do something.'

'I think the knights in general and the brothers in particular are utterly bemused by events,' said the Doctor. 'Their mythical reputation lies in tatters.' He let cogs and springs fall through his hand and on to the upturned plaster head like funeral dust.

'Where did he go?' said Jamie, looking up at the now deserted gallery.

'Back down into the old city, I expect,' said the Doctor. 'It seems there are a number of tunnels between there and here. Once Zaitabor had penetrated the fabled menagerie with the help of one of the Kuabris robes he was able to establish a simpler return route – to this chamber, right underneath the castle,'

'Then we'd better get after him,' said Jamie. 'He could be –'

'Don't worry, Jamie,' said the Doctor. ' I sent an android after him with a very specific set of instructions.'

Oiquaquil looked at the almost empty ceremonial chamber. 'What role did those moth-creatures play in this?'

'They were Zaitabor's unwilling slaves,' said the Doctor. 'They would do anything to get their Queen back. I can only assume that the Taculbain spend a certain portion of the year in hibernation. Zaitabor must have stumbled upon their lair at just such a time.'

'Then how did he get that great beastie back up here?' asked Jamie.

'With help, I expect,' said the Doctor. 'But that's all in the past. If my friends the Dugraqs are right, we should be worrying about these Mecrim creatures.'

'The swords of the knights and the City Guard will surely be enough to save our city from any attack – even from the Menagerie of Ukkazaal,' said Oiquaquil.

A confident female voice echoed from the rear of the cavern. 'I'm not so certain.'

The Doctor turned to see Zoe walking towards him. He clapped his hands together joyfully. 'I can't tell you how pleased I am to see you,' he said, giving the young woman an embarrassed hug.

'It's lovely to be back,' said Zoe. 'Hello, Jamie.'

Defrabax tutted impatiently. 'We were talking about these Mecrim creatures.'

'If I'm right,' said Zoe, 'you'll need more than swords to defeat these monsters. My friends and I encountered the most vicious beast I've ever seen.' Two figures, joined at the waist, followed Zoe out of the shadows. 'The monster killed hundreds of people in minutes. We were very lucky to survive.'

The Doctor politely shook the hands of the twins as they came forward. 'Delighted to meet you.'

'Jamie,' hissed Zoe. 'Stop staring.'

'What? Oh, aye, right.' Jamie scratched his head. 'Er, hello.'

'Hello, Jamie,' said one of the twins, smiling. 'We've heard all about you.'

'Aye,' said Jamie. 'Aye, I suppose you have.'

'I'm Reisaz,' continued the twin. 'My unusually quiet sister is Raitak.'

Defrabax sighed. 'Can the introductions not wait? What do you know of these monsters?'

'The creature we saw was a tremendously powerful four-armed humanoid,' said Zoe. 'It was very aggressive, and seemed to feel little pain.'

'That could be a Mecrim,' squeaked the Dugraq. 'However, we are aware of them only by reputation. Leave well alone is the rule where Mecrim are concerned.'

'How did you encounter one of these things?' asked the Doctor.

'I ended up at a circus, where I met Raitak and Reisaz,' said Zoe. 'The owner had just purchased a creature in a self-contained cryogenic casket.'

'The creatures we're worried about,' said the Doctor, 'exist deep within an advanced city underneath this one. How do you think the casket got from there to a circus?'

'Diseaeda was a well known collector,' said Raitak. 'However the casket came up to the surface it was almost certain to find its way into the freak show eventually.'

'How would you rate the cryogenic technology?' the Doctor asked Zoe.

'Quite highly. The casket was very old, but still in working order. However, I could see that its power was running low.'

The Doctor's next question was interrupted by a series of shrill chimes from the communication device Defrabax had given him. He withdrew the unit and stabbed at a few buttons uncertainly until a picture of the android formed. The Doctor recognized the underground power station's main control room.

'Er, report, please,' said the Doctor.

'Your instructions have been carried out,' said the android. 'However, Zaitabor has eluded me. I cannot ascertain if he is still in the city or if he has returned to the surface.'

'Any sign of the Mecrim?' asked the Doctor.

'No. However, the Taculbain have now returned to their nest.'

'Very well,' said the Doctor. 'Proceed with your orders.' He pressed a button on the device and then turned to face Oiquaquil. 'I suggest that you and your men prepare to fight any creatures that might emerge from the menagerie. And keep an eye open for Zaitabor and any known associates.'

'Doctor,' said Jamie suddenly. 'Kaquaan and I knocked out Araboam, Zaitabor's second-in-command. We locked him in a cupboard.'

The Doctor nodded and glanced at the wizard's ward and the young woman. 'Do you think you could check if he's still there? I suppose he will have escaped by now, but it'll be nice to know.'

'Of course,' said Cosmae, still rubbing his sore head. He turned to the girl, staring at the clockwork torso. 'If you'll show me the way . . . '

'Yes, my love,' she said with a sudden smile like the parting clouds. She put an arm around his shoulders as they walked towards the stairs that led up to the castle. 'You can rely on me to look after you.'

'And what will the rest of you do?' asked Captain Oiquaquil.

'We'll try to ensure that you don't have to deal with these Mecrim creatures,' said the Doctor. 'Zoe, Raitak, Reisaz. I realize this will be very hard for you all, but you're the only people here with any experience of fighting the Mecrim. I'd like you to accompany me to the underground city's military bunker to see if we can find a way of stopping these creatures.'

'We are quite happy to go with you, Doctor,' said Reisaz, sounding more brave than she expected.

'Thank you,' said the Doctor. 'Now, Defrabax, Jamie and my little friend the scout. I want you to warn the Dugraqs and the Rocarbies about the Mecrim. If we don't succeed, the underground races will be attacked first.'

'Our people have feared the worst for some time,' said the Dugraq. 'We are prepared. Let us hope we can be as successful in battle as we have always endeavoured to be in peace.'

'I'm not sure that the Rocarbies will listen to me now,' said Defrabax, blowing his nose on a handkerchief. 'But I will try.' He stared at the Doctor levelly. 'Just don't damage my homunculus.'

'Your homunculus is in safe hands,' said the Doctor. 'Now, I think Zaitabor's little tunnel will serve us all well.'

He pointed towards the gallery over their heads. 'No need for all that tedious messing about with Kuabris suits.' The others followed the Doctor to the foot of the wall, staring up the rockface for ways of scaling it.

Oiquaquil turned to his men and called out some orders. Some ran to the remaining knights, huddled in one corner, and then escorted them up the stairs and back into the castle. Another group of guards marched back down the little tunnel and towards the city itself.

Oiquaquil shouted across the cavern at the Doctor's group. 'Doctor?'

'Yes, Captain?'

'Good luck.'

Deep in the nest of the Taculbain the people sat down before their Queen like children before a teacher. Her body ached from her lengthy imprisonment but that was as nothing to the sadness she felt. As she looked at them disappointment welled up within her like blood from a wound.

'Did we not realize that the surface-dweller's intentions were evil?' she asked at last. 'One cunning enough to imprison us should not have been trusted.'

'We wanted to be reunited, our Queen,' said one of the Taculbain towards the front, his eyes averted in reverence. 'The thought of us in chains was more than we could bear!'

The Queen's mandibles champed with fury. 'But to release such creatures from their justifiable imprisonment!'

'We had no thought as to the result of our actions,' chirruped the creature. 'The man merely said that he would be missed if absent from the castle for too long. He told us what to do, we obeyed!'

The Queen flexed her aching limbs, trying to find a comfortable position. 'But we are old! Although pleased to be back with us, our body is weary. Did we not realize that the transformation will soon be upon us? That one of us might be the next Queen?'

'We could not take that risk,' said the minion. 'Without our eggs our numbers will dwindle and –'

'What have we always said about our status in this place? We fear the massive numbers of the Rocarbies, and are thankful that they consider us immortal gods. We knew that one day they would discover that we are simple creatures, just as they, and that we had to prepare for the conflict by increasing our own numbers. We do see the logic in what we have done – but it seems we have raised to life creatures who are an infinitely greater threat than the Rocarbies!'

'We are preparing to defend our nest,' said another Taculbain. 'Soldier food is being distributed. The dead surface-dwellers will play their part in our defence.'

The Queen raised an arm tenderly towards the speaker. 'Yes, we know. We have done well, given the circumstances. And let us never forget that this is what happens when we meddle with surface-dwellers or allow ourselves to be compromised. We must protect ourselves better during the next sleeping. We who guard over us while we rest will not be forgotten. Our sacrifice will be honoured in future times.'

'It is good to hear you talk of the future,' said one of the moth-creatures.

'It is important that we have confidence in our own abilities,' she replied. She turned slightly as she heard approaching voices. A huge Taculbain entered, flanked by two others. It had been one of the first to respond to the special food, and was now almost completely transformed into a soldier. The mandibles had become huge attacking jaws, counter-balanced by a bony ridge extending from the back of the head. The wings were covered by a hard carapace like that of a beetle. It bowed stiffly and the accompanying Taculbain returned to their other duties.

'Well?' asked the Queen.

'As we requested, we returned to the building that contains the machinery that we were asked to destroy,' reported the soldier. 'There seems to be no way to undo our damage.'

'Did we see these Mecrim creatures?'

'In the room of metal cocoons some were still cold to the touch, others were as warm as the bright light of the surface world. Fluid was draining away. Some creatures were crumbling to dust. Inside others we could see the beasts, these Mecrim.'

'Did they seem strong?'

'If seeing is true then yes, they did.'

'Did we see any of the creatures emerge from their cocoons?' asked the Queen.

'As we left we heard a huge rushing sound, a splash of fluid followed by the jangle of metal and glass falling to the floor.

'We glanced back and saw a creature, slow but looking straight at us. A ruined casket lay overturned beside it. We saw other hands and heads moving. They began to pull themselves free and stand, dripping, on the floor. Hissing. Preparing. Ready to hunt and kill.

'The Mecrim are free, our Queen.'

'The man was found in the hills beyond the city walls. By all accounts his cries could be heard from within the gatehouse. He was agitated and unkempt. When the knights first spoke to him he seemed easily distracted and for many hours I thought he would say nothing that did not smack of rambling insanity.

'Enquiries within the city showed that he was a traveller, only recently arrived. According to the inn-keeper he had seemed quiet but secretive when asked about his business here. He did not socialize, spending long periods away from the inn. When he returned he stayed in his room and food was sent to him.

'My men investigated his room, the inn-keeper being quite willing to provide a key. The first thing they noticed was a silver pendulum hanging from the ceiling. Various marks and lines had been noted on the wooden floorboards beneath it in chalk. Some lines described the possible motion of the pendulum, other marks appeared to be calculations. Although the knights at first suspected some foreign religious sect even a cursory examination of these writings showed the man to be a scientist.

'The rest of the room was unremarkable, as he had brought little with him. There were a few maps of the countryside around the city, over which he had drawn lines and made numerous annotations. In addition on sheets of parchment he had sketched maps of what appeared to be a series of caves, although they matched none known to us. All such documents carried thin layers of dirt as if they had been taken with the man on his forays into the hillside.

'We had more than enough evidence to convict him of involvement in heretical science. I simply could not understand what such a man was doing in our midst when I am still given to believe that our reputation is well known right across our world.

'I began to question him myself. This was a day or so after his initial apprehension. He seemed calmer now, and, sifting his words for the taint of madness brought on by his abominable studies, I was able to make some sense of what he had to say.

'I was interested to hear that when he spoke of the mysteries of the pendulum he spoke as often of mystical as scientific secrets. He

had chosen the room carefully out of all those available to him in the various inns. If correctly sited he claimed that the pendulum gave him insights into the world beneath the ground on which we walk. He had come to our city across the continents and oceans that separate us from his home in search of what he called "the old ones". He was not forthcoming on their nature or status, preferring instead to regale me with vaguer stories of his investigations. However, it did strike me that although he had not heard of the legendary menagerie there were some parallels in what he told me. It was interesting to note that in the legends he had heard men were not so much turned into beasts as destroyed by the work of their own hands. He told me of the slavery that he had seen in some of our neighbouring cities and I wondered what parallels he was trying to draw.

'As he spoke it was as if he was gradually going through recent events in his mind and sorting them. I found it impossible to ask him why he had been found wandering the hillsides, and had instead to gently encourage him through his recollections of the past few days. He had been charting the caves. In particular he had been – the phrase is his, if memory serves – experimenting on the glowing matter found in some of the caves. He had scraped these "mineral deposits" from the cave walls. He was clearly referring to the contents of a number of glass tubes that we found. He claimed to have a device that allows one to examine the very fabric of any created thing. I almost had to clap my hands over my ears to block out the blasphemy.

'I remained, however, eager to establish what had happened. I knew that the trial would begin in mere hours, but his story was almost finished. He spoke finally of a tunnel he had discovered. It had descended steeply and quickly, ending abruptly with a wall of rock. Some of these rocks, he claimed, had melted through intense heat. It was as if a furnace had been constructed beneath them and the rocks had started to melt like icicles before a fire.

'He postulated that these rocks had been affected by some sort of explosion. Eventually he was able to penetrate the wall of rock, for in some places the heat had made the stone brittle.

'Beyond was a chamber of unimaginable vastness. Before he could even begin to explore it further he was attacked by small creatures. He could not describe them, and spoke only of falling unconscious and waking in another tunnel.

'There he saw further signs of fire and deep marks in the rock like those made by a strong blade. He searched for a way back to the surface world, his head throbbing, his mind, he said, feeling unstable. Memories and images he had not seen floated in his vision. He was very unclear at this point, describing nothing with sufficient clarity for me to record here.

'The only thing he remembers is stumbling across a golden casket, leaning against a cave wall as if thrown there by a giant. He peered inside, through a glass covering, expecting to see mummified remains or the dust of death.

'There was a creature inside. And it was moving.

'It was at that point, I believe, that his sanity left him. He was just coherent enough to show us the tunnel where he had come up again on to the surface, but of the casket there was no sight. A few hundred paces into the tunnel and the way was entirely blocked by a rock fall. Of the other tunnel, the one he had initially discovered, we could find no trace. I can only assume that this is one of many details embellished and tainted by madness.

'Commander Zaitabor spoke of the dark destroyers he had seen mentioned in an ancient heretical text, and wondered if there were any connection between the menagerie, the destroyers and the creature the scientist had seen. I said that such talk was dangerous, and my Commander soon saw the error of his ways. He began to put together what evidence there was for the man's innocence, while I worked on the facts that condemned him.

'I think we both knew, however, that the man's life was forfeit long before the trial commenced.'

Extract from *Trial of the Pendulum Scientist* by Grand Knight Himesor.

Sixteen

Cosmae and Kaquaan walked slowly through the castle, marvelling at how quickly the authority of the knights had turned to dust. There seemed to be as many guards patrolling the corridors and hallways as followers of Kuabris. The knights had given up without a fight, many of them perhaps having sensed for a long time that something was profoundly wrong. Zaitabor's name was whispered in banqueting halls and servants' quarters, but no one even challenged the couple as they approached Araboam's room.

Kaquaan had told her tale of recent events with great vigour, embellishing a little, making jokes at Jamie's expense, nudging Cosmae in the ribs every time she mentioned his recent predicament. Cosmae's story on the other hand had been short and muted, as there was little to say and his head hurt. He had been taken by the knights to a set of cells far beneath the castle. He instinctively knew that he was in the hands of the Brotherhood of Rexulon. There was no guard outside his strong cell door, and only very occasionally did a knight bring him food. He had been told that he could shout for as long as he liked, but he would never be heard. He believed this to be quite true.

From further down the corridor there had come an intermittent sound that reminded him of grasshoppers on a summer's day. This he now knew to be the native language of the Taculbain Queen, and the dismal brotherhood cells had been her sad abode for a number of years.

Cosmae continued his recollections. 'I was given some sort of herb to eat,' he said. 'The leaves were bright yellow. I was determined not to eat the stuff, so I chewed and pretended to swallow. When no one was looking I spat it out again.'

'Perhaps that's what I was given,' said Kaquaan. 'Perhaps that's what made me sleep, ready for the sacrifice.' She shivered.

'How much further is it?' ask Cosmae.

'Not far,' she said.

'Well, I think . . .' Cosmae stopped walking, and rubbed his head. 'I'm really not feeling too well,' he explained.

Kaquaan placed her hands on his cheeks and stared into his eyes. 'You look poorly,' she said. 'You'd better go home. I'll meet you there when I've checked up on our friend with the wandering hands.'

'But I can't leave you – just in case he's still in there.'

'Do not worry,' said Kaquaan, resting a finger on his lips. 'I've still got his sword. And I'm sure the City Guard will help, if it comes to that.' She raised the blade to the light. 'You know,' she smiled, 'I am quite enjoying this.'

'Very well,' said Cosmae. He turned to leave. 'A few days ago I could think of few things worse than being rescued by a woman. But it's different with you.'

Kaquaan smiled. 'I know. I'll catch you up before you're even home. You'll see.'

She watched the young man walk back down the corridor and past a pair of chattering guards, staring in awe at the rich designs patterned along the ceiling. Then she moved away in search of Araboam's quarters.

'I wouldn't have thought it possible,' said Jamie, 'but this place is worse than the city. At least there I can see where I'm going.'

'If you have always lived somewhere you get used to it,'

said the Dugraq scout. 'It takes me a long time to adjust to the bright light on the surface.'

Defrabax followed behind at a distance, his eyes wide to capture every element of what he saw. Before him, and beneath an oppressive solid sky of rock, sat the old city he had seen previously only in his dreams. Even in the dim light he found the place magical and tantalising. 'Magnificent,' he said at last. 'The men that produced such a place must have walked amongst the gods.'

The Dugraq snorted. 'From what we know of the people here they probably came from the other place.'

'To finally be able to see what before I could only imagine,' continued Defrabax. 'To be able to walk the streets I thought that only my homunculus would ever walk.'

'Our worker,' corrected the Dugraq.

The man threw his arms into the air. 'Oh, this is wondrous!'

'It's dark and unpleasant,' said Jamie. 'And the sooner we can get away from here, the better. How much further is it?'

'Not far,' replied the scout. 'No, not very far.'

'You know,' said Jamie, swinging a boot at some litter, frozen solid by the years, 'the Doctor said he'd explain what the brotherhood did to my memories, but he didn't.'

'He seemed very preoccupied on the way down,' commented Defrabax. 'His mind was elsewhere. But there is one thing we can be sure of: Zaitabor knew a lot more about science than he ever let on to his fellow knights.'

'So you think he used some sort of mind-control device?' asked Jamie.

Defrabax seemed to weigh up the options, disguising the fact that he had no idea what Jamie was talking about. 'It's possible, I suppose.'

'More likely,' said the Dugraq, 'that he used some of the plants grown down here by the Taculbain.'

'Plants?' said Jamie. 'Here? I thought plants needed light to photosomething.'

'I believe the word is photosynthesize,' said the Dugraq. 'You're right, but some plants can survive in the dimmest of light. The Taculbain are great herbalists. They rely on particular leaves to trigger bodily transformations. If they want more soldiers, they feed certain of their number a particular type of dried leaf. There's a plant to change gender, another precipitates the transformation into a Queen in the rarest of individuals. It's a very useful system. I would imagine that these herbs would have very unusual effects on humans. Perhaps, centuries ago, such drugs were another area of research in this city. Who knows?'

'I'll not turn into one of those moth-creatures, will I?' said Jamie.

The Dugraq laughed. 'I don't think so. But if you start sprouting wings, I'll be the first to tell you.'

'How do you know where we're going?' asked Zoe, as they came to a halt before yet another fence topped with razor wire.

The Doctor passed a torch to the twins and asked them to hold it in position. He pulled out a pin and began to stab experimentally at the padlock that held shut a small gate. The thing was red with rust and Zoe rated the Doctor's chances of success at less than zero.

'It's very simple, Zoe,' he said through gritted teeth. 'We're looking for the main military bunker, the place where they conducted the nastiest and most dangerous experiments. You know what the military mind is like. The place is bound to be right at the heart of their best-protected area.' He waved his arms around him. 'This place is smack bang in the middle of the city. When everything was working it was better protected than Fort Knox.'

'Fort what?' asked Reisaz.

The Doctor pointed at the grey building just visible

through the lines of fence and wire. 'I think that looks like the place, don't you?'

'I wouldn't dare to speculate, Doctor.'

The Doctor threw the pin to the floor in exasperation. 'Oh, dash it! The lock's rusted solid.'

'I could have told you that,' said Zoe.

'Sometimes,' said the Doctor, grasping his lapels in a most uncharacteristic action, 'I wonder why I bother . . .' He looked along the length of the fence in both directions. 'Wire cutters would do the trick, I'm sure, but we'll have to make do with what we've got. Now, our friend the Dugraq seemed to indicate that they occasionally come to this place to seek out information. And I dare say that this is the android's "home" as well. So there must be some way in. Perhaps there's a hole in the fence somewhere.' With that, the Doctor strode off in the direction of the nearest lookout tower.

'And scree beasts might levitate,' said Raitak contemptuously.

Kaquaan crept up to the door that led to Araboam's quarters, although it was clear that the young knight had long since departed. The door had been kicked open from within with such force that the lock had sheared away from the wood. The floor was covered with splinters and dust, scuffed into patterns by footsteps.

She stepped inside, noting that the huge wardrobe in which they had locked Araboam had received similar treatment. The door had come away from the hinges and lay on the floor. Kaquaan stepped over it and towards a mound of paperwork that Araboam seemed to have thrown to the floor in disgust. She recognized some of the sketches as being Cosmae's. A number had been slashed with a blade.

The symbolism was obvious enough. She ran from the room.

* * *

'This is the realm of the Rocarbies,' announced the Dugraq as they descended a large metal stairway.

'I feel like I'm being watched,' said Jamie, looking around in the darkness nervously.

'You almost certainly are,' said the Dugraq. 'The Rocarbies are very territorial creatures. They've probably been tracking us since we crossed the main thoroughfare.'

'I can't say I'm looking forward to this meeting,' admitted Defrabax, at the rear of the party.

They stepped off the stairs and into a small tunnel which led to a long, gently curved slab of concrete. One side ran to the curved walls, the other touched only shadows.

The Dugraq paused in the centre of the expanse, staring mournfully at the redundant video screens that lined the far wall. 'Doubtless they once encouraged the purchasing of products,' said the little creature quietly. 'Products to take away the fear of death and disguise age beneath layers of rubbish. And where are those people now? Where are the items that once promised everything short of immortality?'

'You're very philosophical,' muttered Defrabax sourly. 'Perhaps we should apply our intellects to the –'

'Such scorn makes you almost indiscernible from the Rocarbies,' retorted the Dugraq. 'No wonder you got on so well.'

'This is not the time for arguments,' said Jamie.

'No?' said Defrabax. 'Tell me when it is, and I'll give that little rat a clip around the nose.'

'You *human*!' shouted the Dugraq, his lips curling around the insulting word. 'There is no beauty in your mind!'

Defrabax's intended reply was cut short as the wide tunnel resounded to the sound of creatures roaring. Jamie glanced quickly both ways and saw ape-like creatures coming towards them, heads thrown back, teeth bared. Large numbers of the creatures were pulling themselves on to the platform from the darkness with their huge arms. As the first group approached them on all fours Jamie realized that escape was futile. 'I presume these are the creatures we're here to see?' he asked.

The Dugraq nodded.

'Then we won't need to run away?'

'Let's hope not,' said Defrabax.

They allowed themselves to be surrounded by a ring of chattering apes. After a few moments an enormous grizzled creature pushed its way through the crowd and made straight for Defrabax. Its stare was fixed on the old man.

'You have come down to us,' it stated as the other creatures became quiet.

'I have,' said Defrabax. 'Things did not go well on the surface.'

'We know,' replied the Rocarby leader. 'You have come to explain. There will be no explanations now. We shall go up. Take the light that we want.'

'No,' said Defrabax. 'You mustn't. You must –'

'You tell us nothing now,' said the creature. 'Rocarbies take their share of the light!' The creatures behind the leader began to jump up and down, whooping in delight.

'That's not why we came down here,' said the Dugraq. The leader turned to examine Jamie and the scout for the first time.

'You are with this bad man.'

The Dugraq realized that the Rocarby was asking a question. 'We're here to help you,' he replied.

'Defrabax was here to help us,' said the Rocarby bitterly.

'You don't understand,' said Jamie. 'There are some creatures down here that have been . . . brought back to life. They will kill you.'

'They can try,' said the Rocarby. 'We not concerned.'

'But you must listen to us,' said Jamie. 'Your lives are in danger.'

The Rocarby ignored the protestation. 'What we do now. Go up to the light. And Defrabax. Came down to the dark. He stay here forever. Rocarbies not happy. Cheated.'

'But I didn't cheat you!' shouted Defrabax. 'My intentions towards you were entirely reasonable.'

The Rocarby leader shook its head in a strangely human way. 'We will kill you. Keep you here forever.'

'Please, sit down,' said Araboam, holding a blade at Cosmae's throat. 'Treat this house as your own.'

Cosmae sat in an armchair, the young knight a shadowy presence behind him. 'What are you doing here?' he asked.

'My lord and I decided that after the final meeting of the Brotherhood of Rexulon we would come here. We want to ensure that Defrabax's homunculus will be powerless against the Mecrim.'

'And you're happy with what Zaitabor has done? That he's released these creatures simply to cause carnage and punish the world?'

Araboam walked around the room, his fingers clenching nervously around the hilt of the small sword he was carrying. Cosmae could see that there was unease in his movements, whatever he said with his lips. 'There are always things that we do not understand. I must trust my lord.'

'And what has he done to secure this trust?'

'He is Grand Knight and leader of the brotherhood. Under him our entire world will be restored to true observance of the decrees of the Higher.'

'What decrees? The knights believe nothing, elevate meaninglessness to an art-form!'

Araboam grabbed Cosmae's throat and held the point of the sword against his lips. 'Such casual blasphemy will not go unpunished.'

'Maybe so,' said Cosmae quietly when the knight pulled the blade back. 'But do you think you will escape what Zaitabor has planned? Perhaps these creatures will destroy everything.'

'Perhaps,' nodded Araboam. 'But perhaps the Higher has something better to take our place.'

'Then you're as mad as he,' said Cosmae. 'Insanity has eaten into you like a disease. People have said that you were once a gentle and kind child. You've been corrupted!'

'Refined would be a better word,' said a voice from the doorway. Zaitabor stepped into the room, his red Rexulon robes hanging over his Kuabris armour and blue Commander's cloak. His face was as calm and pale as the plaster mask that had covered the automaton. 'What you call madness, I call insight. It depends on where you are looking from. In the light of the Higher, what seems to be insanity is perfect sense. Without the guidance of Kuabris and Rexulon, all actions are base and reprehensible.'

Araboam straightened up, and bowed before Zaitabor. 'My lord, I had hoped that you would come here as planned.'

'I am pleased that you alone remain faithful to me,' said Zaitabor. 'That rabble should not have acquiesced so quickly. And to the City Guard! Mere brutes with no knowledge of the ways of Kuabris.'

'No one really fell under your spell,' said Cosmae.

Zaitabor walked up to the young man and smashed him in the face with one armour-clad arm. Cosmae felt his nose give and suddenly his lips were salty and wet.

'Magic spells have nothing to do with it,' said Zaitabor, wiping his armour on a scroll from the table. 'And the homunculus of your master is no clay golem. What know you of the creature?'

'I know nothing of it,' said Cosmae, blinking back tears. 'Only that it obeys my master and him alone.'

'And yet now that has changed. It was the Doctor who sent the creature after me.'

'Why is the homunculus important to you?' asked Cosmae.

'It is strong enough to cause problems,' said Zaitabor. 'I was only just able to lose it in the dark city before coming here.' Zaitabor threw the parchment back onto the table and idly flicked through the books and papers there. 'You see, the Taculbain reports on your master's plans were most thorough. But it does seem that he had an unexpected change of heart. He planned to replace our own despised Furnace with something from beneath the surface. Why did he not do so? I believe everything was in place. And why now allow the Doctor to control the creature?'

'He would seem to have lost faith in his own judgement,' commented Araboam.

'That arrogant old man? It would seem impossible, and yet you are right. What other explanation is there? The charlatan must have been exposed. And I can only conclude that there was some danger in what he had planned.' Zaitabor smiled. 'If this is true then perhaps we should complete his work. The Higher might well have yet more destruction planned for this place.'

Zoe's fingers ran over the door sensor pad. 'I know you're normally good at locks, Doctor,' she smiled, 'but I think that I can sort out this one soon enough.'

The Doctor sat next to the twins on the ramp that led up to the bunker's main doorway, sucking his burnt fingers. He stared at the hole in the fence through which they had come. 'I was sure that was going to work,' he complained bitterly. 'It worked in the power station.'

'This is a bit more fool-proof,' said Zoe, choosing her words carefully. She made a final couple of adjustments, and then replaced the plastiglass panel. 'That should do it,' she said, running her hand over the sensors.

The huge door grated open. Only a slight whine hinted at the great age of the place.

'It's incredible,' said Reisaz. 'This still works after so long.'

'Unlike civilian equipment,' said the Doctor, 'military hardware is built to last.'

They stepped into a dark reception area, a ceiling with mock skylights yards above their heads. Various doors and corridors led off in turn. Zoe walked to the main desk, and sat behind a small console. 'I think I can bring the lighting and heating on from here,' she said. 'There's not been much power loss in the backup batteries.'

'We probably have Defrabax's experimentation to thank for that,' said the Doctor. 'The Dugraqs were clearly interested in preserving the status of the Mecrim, too. Anyway, just concentrate on bringing the computer systems and lighting on line.' The Doctor strolled up and down. 'I was going to suggest that you only instigate dim lighting, but as these Mecrim creatures can see in the dark . . .'

The lights flared around the building. Even the Doctor and Zoe were forced to shield their eyes for a few moments. 'Now, we need to find the cryogenic control area. We must undo whatever it is the Taculbain have done.'

'Doctor,' said Raitak, 'how did they get past those doors?'

'I can only assume that the Dugraqs have some entrance of their own that the Taculbain also used. I really should have asked the scout before he went haring off. Anyway, we're in now.'

Zoe was tapping at the console. 'I've got a map of the installation. The cryogenic control centre is almost exactly beneath us, two storeys down.'

The Doctor ran for the stairs, Zoe and the twins following. 'I would have suggested the lift,' said the Doctor, 'but there are limits to my trust of old technology.'

The stairway was crudely constructed and very dusty. Even when the building was in use it must have been no more than an emergency backup. The Doctor went down the steps two at a time with amazing speed. Soon he was at the bottom, waiting for the others to catch up.

'It's this way,' said Zoe, leading them down the corridor. She paused for a moment at the door sensor, but this one proved much easier to open. 'The digits I input manually,' she explained to a bemused Raitak and Reisaz, 'correspond to the palm print of a service engineer.' The twins nodded to cover their ignorance.

The door hissed open and they walked inside. The room was large but the walls and much of the floor space was taken up with computer equipment. The far wall was a huge window that looked down upon some sort of hangar. Strip lights flickered, illuminating the metal corpses of tanks and attack craft. 'A mere side show,' announced the Doctor. 'The cryogenic areas themselves are some levels below us.'

He sat at a console and brought it on-line. He asked Zoe to do the same with an adjoining one. The computer system was in some sort of sleep mode, but both screens soon glowed with menus. As the Dugraqs had indicated, the wisdom of centuries was just waiting to be tapped.

The twins sat in a chair and watched the Doctor and Zoe work. 'Try to find the cryogenic diagnostic program,' said the Doctor. 'I'm going to see if I can access the security cameras from here. We might be able to . . . Ah, there we are.' The software on the Doctor's screen vanished to be replaced by a sequence of small squares. A number were blank or showed nothing but static, but most contained grainy video images of empty rooms or featureless corridors. The Doctor moved a cursor into position and a single frame expanded to fill the entire screen. The image was very blurred, but it did show a bare room that contained about fifty metal caskets.

Zoe glanced at the image. 'Yes, that's the right room. The units exactly match the one I saw in the freak show.'

'Good,' said the Doctor. He pressed a few keys and the image began to expand, showing more detail of one particular casket. Many of the electrodes had been ripped from the side of the machine, and a huge hole had appeared in the plastiglass covering. A severed tube poured white fluid on to the floor. 'Well,' said the Doctor, 'I'm not sure whether that's good news or not. The Taculbain were clearly instructed to attack the machinery rather than switch the whole lot off. I'm not sure that even with the large number of backup systems built into cryogenic units we can do much from this end.'

'I'm boosting input and output to maximum,' said Zoe. 'In some cases the field generated might be enough to encapsulate even a broken unit.'

'Good,' said the Doctor. 'If we can avoid going to the units in person then I'm –'

There was a sudden rending sound from the doorway. The Doctor and the others turned to see the impression of a claw moving down the closed metal shutter. The material warped and bent and finally gave way to admit a huge four-pronged claw. In a blur a viciously hooked arm came through. The creature was straining against the door.

'Oh dear,' said the Doctor, his voice barely carrying above the animal cries from the corridor. His face was gaunt in the harsh neon light. 'The Mecrim know we're here.'

Seventeen

A small number of the ape-like Rocarbies could hold back their frustration no longer. Enraged, they rushed at Defrabax, knocking him to the floor. They began to pummel his head and chest with their fists.

Jamie ran forward to help, but was pushed aside. The massed Rocarbies were beginning to scream and shake their heads in delight.

An unexpected voice from the direction of the stairs cut through even the hollering of the apes. 'Stop!' The Rocarbies turned to see three of the moth-creatures stepping on to the concrete expanse, their wings unfolded, their hands outstretched. Jamie noticed that the head of one of the creatures was armoured, terminating in huge jaws like a man-trap. Perhaps this was one of the soldiers that the Dugraq had mentioned.

'Stop,' said the leading Taculbain again. 'This is not the way forward.'

The Rocarbies threw themselves to the ground and averted their gaze. 'It is the gods-among-us,' whispered one. 'They have a message for us.'

The Taculbain stepped through the crowd, brushing past Jamie, the Dugraq and the semi-conscious Defrabax. They came to a halt before the Rocarby leader, who risked a quick upward glance. 'Do not punish us,' he said. 'We have never heard your words before. We will do anything that you want.'

'We have been sent by our Queen,' said the Taculbain.

'We need your help. There is an enemy, a race of destroyers, that will soon move across our world. These creatures will kill all our peoples. Only if we unite will we stand a chance.'

'Of course,' said the Rocarby. 'What we have is yours. But this human . . .'

'For the moment he is of no consequence. Such matters can wait. These are the orders of our Queen.' The Taculbain turned to address the little Dugraq, who bowed respectfully. 'Your plan was to warn your people also?'

The scout nodded. 'That is correct.'

'Then we are of one mind. We will leave the soldier here to help organize defences against the Mecrim. We will accompany you.'

'Your help would be gratefully received,' said the Dugraq.

'And the man?'

'Oh, I think he'll survive,' said the scout, bending down to examine Defrabax's wounds. The mage smiled at the little creature weakly.

'Then let us go,' said the Taculbain. 'There is only small time before the beasts attack us.'

The Doctor, Zoe and the twins ran across the room to the only door that they could see. It hissed open with little prompting, revealing a small square chamber full of filing cabinets.

'Any ideas?' asked Zoe as they heard the creature smash its way into the cryogenic control room.

'Yes,' said the Doctor. 'We need a stronger door.'

'There's a weapons-testing room on this level,' she said, remembering with perfect clarity the map she had seen.

'Splendid,' said the Doctor, opening the only other door in the room.

As they ran into a short corridor the walls began to shake as filing cabinets were hurled aside in the small room. They didn't have much time. Zoe led the way down the passageways. The twins brought up the rear, occasionally looking back at their pursuer. It had emerged from the room and was beginning to gain ground, although it was not yet running at full speed. 'I'd forgotten how ugly it was,' muttered Reisaz.

They came to a halt before a huge studded door of dull grey alloy. Zoe passed a hand hopefully over the sensor but wasn't surprised when it didn't open. 'I'll need a high-level clearance,' she said, setting to work.

'Do hurry, Zoe,' said the Doctor. The creature turned the corner, grunting with delight.

'Trust me, Doctor,' said the young woman. 'Computers always recognize a kindred spirit. Isn't that what you said the other day?'

'Just get the door open, there's a good girl.' The Doctor began to mop his brow with a large handkerchief. 'You can remind me of my less sensitive aphorisms at some other time.'

The doors hissed open, and they ran through. A hinged arm flicked into the space between the closing doors and they began to slide open again. The creature impatiently pushed its bulk into the gap.

'Manual override!' shouted the Doctor, but Zoe was already at work. With a sigh of pneumatics the doors trapped the creature's shoulder. Zoe boosted the door's power intake to maximum, but the machinery groaned and was unable to fully close the doors.

With a roar the creature began to insinuate itself into the gap.

'Very well,' said Zoe quietly, mere inches from the snapping claw as she bent down to the emergency control panel once more. 'Let's try this.' She pressed a few controls.

A huge metal shutter began to grind inexorably down from the roof, moving into position just in front of the doorway.

'It's not going to close in time!' exclaimed Raitak, transfixed by the scene.

The creature seemed to be aware of the descending shutter and began to push downwards and into the outer door, its arm resting on the ground. Its head turned in their direction as it began to pull itself through the metal doorway.

With a sudden squeal the shutter ground through the creature's arm and touched the floor. The severed claw flexed for a moment and then stopped. The machinery was silent.

'Well done, Zoe,' said the Doctor.

'How long will that keep the creature out?' asked Raitak.

'Just long enough for us to think of something,' said the Doctor, turning to examine the room for the first time. The shutter began to vibrate as the Mecrim slammed into it in frustration.

Half of the room was dominated by computer and testing equipment, the other was a glorified firing range. A selection of weapons and ammunition was locked in cases along the walls. The Doctor inspected the armoury slowly. 'Crude,' he muttered to himself. 'Not what we're looking for anyway.' He turned to Zoe, already seated at a console. 'Find out everything you can about the Mecrim,' he said.

Within minutes the screen was filling with information. 'Some of the files are corrupted,' she announced. 'But there seems to be a complete backup copy linked to a personal directory. I'll skim through that.'

'Switch it on to audio,' said the Doctor, sitting cross-legged in the centre of the room. 'Let's hear what happened to these people.'

The synthesized voice that filled the room was a computerized memory from the dawn of time. '– isn't good enough stop I don't believe that we can wait that long stop Nikolas has done some more tests semicolon appended to this memo stop I'm sure that you now appreciate the nature of the problem that we face stop Two dead already stop new paragraph I request immediate evacuation stop end read back and send when ready.'

Kaquaan stood watching Defrabax's house, recent events fresh in her mind. She had slipped quietly through the city streets, desperate to remember the location of the old magician's house. As she had turned the corner she had seen a tall figure walking imperiously towards Defrabax's abode. She had crept into the shadows and had watched as the red-robed knight pushed open an unlocked door and walked inside.

So, Zaitabor had returned to the surface. Why? The unlocked door suggested that Cosmae was not alone inside. What did Zaitabor and his minion want with the boy?

Kaquaan had moved into a better position, watching the front door. She knew that there must be an entrance around the rear of Defrabax's house – she remembered her first encounter with the homunculus – but Zaitabor's assured manner seemed to indicate little interest in concealing his movements.

She emerged from her reverie, aware only of the slow passing of time. Her mind invented and refined countless scenarios, the most likely of which seemed to be that the knights had murdered Cosmae and departed through the back door. Only when she was about to run to the front to investigate was there some movement from within.

Zaitabor and Araboam emerged, both still wearing the robes of the brotherhood. Cosmae stood between them, his face bruised, his hands bound behind his back. A sword to his throat ensured silence.

Kaquaan took another step back into the shadows. She nudged into something that she knew wasn't a wall. A hand closed over her mouth.

The Doctor ran the words of the message over in his mind. With a chill of impossible remembrance he realized that he recognized the woman's voice from his waking deam. 'Who was that speaking?' he asked.

Zoe paused the playback. 'It's Dr Jenn Alforge, head scientist on Project Mecrim. A memo to a Ciaran Dugied at –'

'Play the whole file,' said the Doctor, staring at the marks that were beginning to appear on the metal shutter. 'I think we've got time.'

Zoe tapped some commands into the console and then the voice started again.

'Computer-based syntax, punctuation, paragraph breaks. Confidential letter from user to Dugied, insert date and time.

'Dear Ciaran,

'I'm finally settling in. Good staff here, reasonable surroundings. Less than happy about the Mecrim project itself, but then, you already know that. Nik's preliminary report appended to this.

'Is the dog still quarantined? It's a shame, I think – even though you know the good reasons behind it.

'Heard of some border skirmishes the other day – not reported on the civilian news, quelle surprise. You won't forget us, will you?

'Best wishes, Jenn.'

The voice changed from the woman's to that of the computer's own clipped sounds as it worked its way through the report.

'Genetically adjusted Mecrim creature, provisional

classification. Order: Reptiloprimate. Family: Astridae. Genus and species: Singropoda mecrimus. DNA owned and licensed by the Butler Institute.

'Height: 1.6 metres to shoulder. Weight: up to 150 kilograms. Sexual maturity: two to five years. Mating season: late spring to summer. Gestation: six months. Number of young: one to two. External gender differentiation: none. Habit: Social, lives in large groups. Diet: large mammals or equivalents, occasional carrion, sometimes supplemented by berries and bark. Lifespan: estimated to be over 20 years.

'Appearance and other factors: The Mecrim is a six-limbed bipedal humanoid. It has an internal skeleton, complete with humanoid rib-cage protecting vital organs, but its legs and primitive arms resemble those of an insect, featuring vestigial exoskeletal structures and secondary jointing. With the exception of its armoured head a Mecrim gives the appearance of having no skin, with the muscle and ligaments exposed. In actual fact, the top layer of Mecrim muscle performs this function, being incredibly tough "skin substitute".

'A Mecrim has four toes of equal length, arranged at right-angles in the shape of a cross. Its legs feature an upper knee and an extended "ankle" that functions as a secondary joint. The musculature seems to allow for a reasonable turn of speed, although by temperament and even when hunting the Mecrim could be described as being casually arrogant.

'The upper limbs consist of a pair of arms that terminate in a four-digit "hand" and a pair that feature a more primitive hooked claw. The head incorporates a complicated mouth and the eyes are partly concealed. Tests reveal that Mecrim see heat rather than light.'

Zoe paused the playback and beamed. 'So I was right!'

The Doctor nodded. 'You were. But what can we do with that piece of information?' He rose to his feet, glancing across at the shutter. Huge dents were appearing in it now. 'You said that the creature was always attracted to the largest possible "heat signature"?'

'Yes,' said Zoe. 'I speculated that this was because it would equate that with the most likely threat to its own survival.'

The Doctor nodded. 'And presumably any one Mecrim can recognize the pattern of one of its own kind and therefore not attack.'

'That would seem logical.'

'So what we need to do is throw a spanner in the works,' said the Doctor. He walked over to one of the glass cases and tapped his finger against its surface. 'Now, if we could modify the ammunition of this armour-piercing launcher . . .'

'Modify it in what way?' asked Zoe.

The Doctor rummaged around for the shells. 'We want to change these bullets so that they impact into these creatures but do not explode. Instead we want them to give off a vast amount of heat. Any other Mecrim will therefore not recognize the creature as one of its own species but as a potential threat. If we can change the heat signature of some Mecrim to that of, say, a reasonably sized elephant, then we might be able to start a civil war.'

Zoe remembered that soon after she met the Doctor he had shown her a mind-projected account of his most recent encounter with the Daleks. One 'humanized' Dalek faction had been set against another. The slaughter was colossal. 'There is a flaw with this plan,' she said. 'There's almost certain to be at least one survivor. And even to get to that stage we will have to have fired at well over half of all Mecrim.'

'That's true,' said the Doctor. 'But we'll burn that last bridge when we've crossed it.' He opened a strong metal box and began to unpack its dart-like explosives. 'See if you can find out from the computer system how many creatures we're facing.'

Zoe nodded and began to tap at the keyboard. 'You'll need to ensure that the heat emission is consistent with a living creature,' she commented. 'The Mecrim eventually recognize flames and so on as non-living heat sources.'

The twins sidled over to the Doctor's side. 'Do you know what you're doing?' asked Raitak.

'Of course,' said the Doctor, jabbing a pin into the outer casing of one of the shells. 'But one false move and this whole building will go up in smoke.'

'We'll keep very quiet,' said Reisaz, taking the hint.

There was a loud thump from the shutter, two figures now seeming to hurl themselves at the thick metal. Although designed to resist almost anything short of a thermonuclear explosion the Doctor did not believe that the metal would hold out much longer. It was buckling and a single claw had already worked through into the room.

'Also scan through the rest of the files involving the Mecrim,' said the Doctor. 'Tell me anything that refers to the demise of this miniature civilization, or any other flaw in the Mecrim that we can exploit.'

'There were twenty-seven of the creatures originally,' said Zoe, having found the information she was looking for. 'I just hope they haven't bred over the past few centuries.'

The Doctor stared at the shutter. Most of an arm had now been forced through, the claws thrashing against the metal. 'So do I,' he said.

Confidential Memorandum

From:	Dr J. Alforge Pr. Mecrim	**To:**	C. Y. Dugied Control 429
Date:	2416,2111,21:55 (WST)		
Subject:	Mecrim claw		

Dear Ciaran

The report you requested is attached. To summarize, the strength of the Mecrim claw does not depend entirely upon the composition of the talons or on the pressure exerted by the arm itself. You know I'm no physicist, but the gist of it seems to be that the Mecrim can vibrate the molecules of its claw to allow it to penetrate another substance. Imagine being able to turn your hand into a gaseous state – you could then 'merge' with some other object, and then 'reform' your hand. The results, as we have already seen, are truly horrific. The Mecrim are able to 'push' their claws through humanoid tissue with the minimum of effort.

The lab tests on the single Mecrim trapped in a lead cell make terrifying reading.

Are you seeing Marcus tomorrow? Say hi for me.

Best wishes

Jenn

Confidential Memorandum

From:	Dr J. Alforge Pr. Mecrim	**To:**	C. Y. Dugied Control 429
Date:	2417,3004,10:15 (WST)		

Dear Ciaran

Another day, another letter, disguised as a memo. How the devil are you? I'm feeling awful, if truth be told. I've had a pain in the stomach all day – feels like it's more than just nerves.

The Head Observer from our mysterious benefactors was here today. He seemed very impressed by our reports. I think he's a sadistic bastard. For God's sake don't file this with the official memos.

Hope you're well anyway.

Best wishes

Jenn

Confidential Memorandum

From: Dr J. Alforge
Pr. Mecrim

To: C. Y. Dugied
Control 429

Date: 2417,0405,11:25 (WST)

Subject: Mecrim gut microbe 23D

Dear Ciaran

Very bad news. The above-noted microbe, extracted for detailed research from Mecrim study number 09, has proved to be a highly dangerous one. Nik thinks that contact with air could prove deadly for humanoid life: I'm ordering thorough checks of our corpse disposal routine, and of our lab procedures. Nik's report will follow.

Please put some ships on stand-by in case we need to evacuate this place. I request that emergency science colony status 171 be granted until we are sure that this microbe *hasn't* escaped into the atmosphere.

Get that bastard out of my hair. He should have gone days ago.

Still feeling ill. Let's hope it's not . . . No, let's not even think about it.

Cheers

Confidential Memorandum

From:	Dr J. Alforge Pr. Mecrim	**To:**	C. Y. Dugied Control 429
Date:	2417,1106,19:50 (WST)		
Subject:	Mecrim gut microbe 23D		

Ciaran –

People are dying here. Don't you understand? We thought we could use the Mecrim, but even in suspended animation they have proved stronger than us.

My condition is deteriorating, but not as fast as most. In some people you can see the flesh being eaten away.

Just do two things for me. I don't care about the changing front line or military contraction:

One, declare this world off-limits. I reckon you've got ten days to get a ship here. After that there will be no one to rescue.

Two, declare Project Mecrim a failure. Please. For me. The Head Observer from the institute has contracted the disease, but the medical labs have used him as a guinea-pig for some rather dubious cybernetic research. Cured of the plague, it only seems to have made him more insane, more convinced that, had it not been for this 'oversight', Project Mecrim would have been a success.

Overrule him. Do whatever you have to. He's hoping to return to the institute soon, leaving the rest of us to rot.

Don't forget me.

Personal File End Marker

Downloaded from:	Control 429
@ Req. of:	BI Central
Date:	2417,0112,09:15 (WST)
Personal Status:	Dr Alforge d. 2417,1306,05:07 (WST)
Cause of Death:	Provisionally assigned to 23D
Project status:	Closed
@ Req. of:	BI Central, Control 429
Stated reason:	No report received from observers to justify continued expenditure
Colony status:	Closed
@ Req. of:	BI Central
Stated reason:	

These files authorized for Grade Four and above, eyes-only.

Any other usage is strictly illegal. Action will be taken.

FILE ENDS

Eighteen

As Kaquaan struggled against her assailant she heard a deep voice in her ear. 'Please be silent and do not move. I am following the Doctor's orders. Any noise or commotion will only draw attention to ourselves.'

Kaquaan turned to see the lumbering form of Defrabax's homunculus. This time she did not scream. In fact, now that she had the opportunity to examine the creature in the full light of day, she realized that its 'costume' was a rather feeble affair. The clay-like substance that covered much of its body was chipped and cracked around many of the joints, and what she had once thought of as parts from other creatures and esoteric symbols were mere jagged marks in its surface.

'You are now the Doctor's . . .' She struggled for the right word, and then remembered what the little shrew had said. 'You are the Doctor's worker.'

'I am programmed to obey the Doctor,' agreed the creature, staring at the three figures as they moved down the street. 'You must stay here. I can move faster and more quietly alone. I have been tracking Zaitabor for some time now.'

'What are they going to do to Cosmae?' asked Kaquaan.

'I do not know. I will try to ensure that he comes to no harm. Please stay here.'

Without waiting for her reply the homunculus strode off in silent pursuit of Zaitabor.

* * *

The Doctor stared over Zoe's shoulder, pointing at the digitized face on the screen: a bulky, sour-looking face atop a brief textual profile. 'Now that face looks familiar . . .'

'How can it? The man must have died a very long time ago.'

'I'm not so sure,' said the Doctor. 'Anyway, time to test my theories.' He held up the gun somewhat clumsily. 'It'll be just like an African safari.'

'Have you ever been on one?' asked Zoe.

'No,' said the Doctor. 'But I did once watch a Tarzan film.'

The door finally burst open and two Mecrim leapt into the room. As they came forward they seemed to examine the Doctor and the others in turn, their talons flexing.

'Here goes,' said the Doctor, aiming at the uninjured creature as they scuttled between the desks towards them.

He pulled the trigger. Nothing happened. 'Ah, I appear to have left the safety catch on,' said the Doctor, inspecting the weapon as if he had all the time in the world. 'It's here somewhere.'

'Do hurry,' snapped Raitak, edging down into the shooting gallery.

'Don't fluster me!' shouted the Doctor, fumbling with a rocker switch towards the base of the handle. He returned the gun to his shoulder and squinted through the sights. The creature seemed terribly close through the magnifying lenses. The Doctor brought the cross-hairs into position and pulled the trigger.

There was a loud crack. The creature's shoulder twitched under the impact. 'It should start cloaking the Mecrim's heat pattern with its own about now,' announced the Doctor.

The Mecrim that had lost an arm glanced at its companion. The results were almost instantaneous. It threw itself towards the other, its claws a blur. The creatures tumbled to the floor, raking each other with talons. The Mecrim the Doctor had shot pushed itself on top of the other, instinctively defending itself, and forced its head into the shoulder of the other, severing its arm.

'Quick,' said the Doctor. 'Let's go.'

'Where?' asked Reisaz.

The Doctor smiled. 'Somewhere where there are lots and lots of Mecrim,' he said.

Jamie, Defrabax and the scout stood before the Dugraq leadership. 'You are a very honourable scout,' said the grey-furred Dugraq. 'You have done well.'

'We must arm our people,' said another. 'If the Mecrim emerge they will hunt us first.'

'Yes,' said the leader. 'Arm everyone. Quickly.' He turned to Jamie. 'Will you help defend our people?'

'Of course,' said Jamie.

'And Defrabax?'

'Defrabax is a very old and silly man,' said the mage. 'I have put this entire world beneath our own in jeopardy.'

'I am sure you can help us now,' said a female Dugraq. 'We need to defend our future, not dwell on the past.'

The leader nodded at this wise pronouncement. 'And the honourable Taculbain, now reunited with their Queen?'

The two moth-creatures stepped forward. 'After a period of reflection we realized that we had no alternative but to aid in the defence of this kingdom of shadows. We too had a role to play in this disaster. We have made foolish decisions.'

The soldier Taculbain arched its wings. 'We are moving our soldiers into position on the edge of the Rocarby and Dugraq domains.' It paused, receiving communication from its fellows. 'The Mecrim are here!' it announced, taking off into the air.

'Where do you keep your weapons?' asked Jamie.

The scout pointed towards a concrete tunnel set into an artificial hill. Dugraqs were lining up in rows and being handed weapons from within. 'That's our armoury,' he announced. 'A limited collection of projectile-based weapons salvaged from a ruptured bunker.'

There were screams from the edge of the park. Near a metal framework of open boxes shots were being fired, tiny flares in the perpetual darkness. A number of Taculbain were hovering like hawks and then swooping down towards the ground.

The scout had already covered the distance between the leaders' forum and the armoury. Jamie watched him push his way towards the front of the queue and grab two guns. 'Come on, Friend of the Traveller!' he shouted, tossing a revolver towards Jamie.

Jamie caught the gun and followed the Dugraq towards the edge of the park. Five Mecrim had ripped through the railings, silver-grey figures in the darkness. They were already surrounded by tiny corpses. One Dugraq was caught in the vice-like lower arms of a Mecrim. The arm closed, and the bloody, split corpse dropped to the ground.

The much larger Taculbain flying about their heads were providing a diversion, the Mecrim jumping into the air whenever one came close. A ring of Dugraqs with guns had surrounded the beasts. Jamie joined them and let off a couple of shots at the creature closest to him.

As more Taculbain swooped into view the Mecrim seemed barely to know that the other creatures were there. The bullets dug deep but the Mecrim barely moved. They stared at the flapping moth-men over their heads.

Two Taculbain soldiers, their huge open jaws like stags' antlers, dived down at a Mecrim that had ended up away from the others. One soldier was caught by the vicious claws of the creature, allowing the other to duck down and lunge at the Mecrim's chest. The Mecrim pushed at the head of the Taculbain in its arms until the neck snapped, and then dropped the huge corpse to the ground.

The second soldier had chewed a hole in the Mecrim's chest. Thick blood was oozing out. The Mecrim lashed out at the Taculbain's shoulder, the arm and wing falling to the floor. Another Mecrim had moved into position and now jumped onto the back of the Taculbain, its mouth parts working at the unprotected neck.

Other Taculbain soldiers swooped to attack just as the second of their number fell away, its corpse sticky with green blood.

Jamie aimed a shot at the wound on the Mecrim but missed, impacting instead upon the strong rib-cage. A couple of brash Dugraqs ran forward shooting, but were thrown high into the air like rag dolls.

Jamie did not even look to see where they landed.

Cosmae had a jumble of uncoordinated memories of their descent into the underground world. He was aware of a cave mouth on the chalky hillside, a natural tunnel, a few chambers full of rushing water, and then finally the dark city, stretching out before them like a reminder of Hell. The roof of stone hung over their heads like the inside of an eggshell, glowing slightly with natural luminescence. Zaitabor had taken a handful of papers with him from Defrabax's room, and he referred to these often as they crossed the city's streets and walkways.

It was all a blur to Cosmae and, as he stared around him at what appeared to be shops and houses, he was almost thankful for the beating he had already received. It was enough just to concentrate on walking, on breathing. He was glad he would not have to expend too much energy making sense of this benighted place.

'Defrabax's power station,' announced Zaitabor eventually. Before them lay a large building that seemed to have nothing in common with the fire-belching Furnace Cosmae knew from the surface city. 'May this object of contempt bring forth destruction!' Zaitabor handed the city map to Araboam and they walked towards the entrance.

Cosmae shook his head to clear his vision. Zaitabor glanced down at a parchment, and then waved his hands over a black patch on the wall next to the door. The door magically and silently opened.

Araboam pushed Cosmae into the building. Cosmae stood on what felt like seamless animal hide. It stretched for as far as he could see down the various corridors. The walls were absolutely square, the room's proportions perfect. Cosmae had never seen something so defiantly unnatural before.

'Over here,' said Zaitabor, leading the way down the main corridor.

It must have been his injuries, but Cosmae could have sworn that they were being followed.

The cryogenic chamber had been almost completely destroyed. The individual units had been smashed and overturned, the door breached as if it had been tissue paper. The Doctor sighed. 'I wasn't too keen on my original plan,' he remarked. 'And now we'll never know.' He tapped the gun. 'Come on.'

'Where are we going?' asked Zoe.

'The domain of the Dugraqs is nearby.' The Doctor walked down the corridor, Zoe and the twins following close behind. 'Hopefully Jamie and the others will be there by now. The problem is, I expect the Mecrim will be as well.'

'Doctor,' said Zoe as they walked, 'those files we looked at. That gut microbe that almost wiped out the entire colony.'

'Yes?'

'With Mecrim on the loose, surely the plague will recur?'

'Well, the ancestors of Defrabax and the others probably still carry the immunity to the disease.'

'But I don't, and neither does Jamie.'

'I know,' said the Doctor. 'But let's deal with the Mecrim first, shall we?'

A Dugraq walked around distributing ammunition as calmly as was possible under the circumstances. Jamie took a few steps back, glancing over at the scout to see how he was reloading the gun. They avoided eye contact, for both knew that the Dugraqs were being massacred.

As Jamie pushed the bullets into the chambers he totted up the carnage. As far as he was aware getting on for fifty Dugraqs had been killed. Over ten Taculbain had died trying to defend them. Only two Mecrim had been injured, in both cases the result of gunfire being trained on a wound opened up by a Taculbain soldier. Although moving a little more slowly than the others, neither Mecrim seemed unduly hindered.

There were over ten Mecrim now. They trotted forwards, and the Dugraqs fanned away. Jamie heaved a sigh of relief as another group of Taculbain soldiers took position in the air just above the Mecrim.

This couldn't go on much longer.

Cosmae watched Zaitabor sit in front of one of the many box-like constructions. Each was covered with changing lights that formed patterns and words. The knight arranged all the papers in front of him. Then he began pressing nodules on the device in front of the box.

All the boxes showed different pictures. There was a groaning hum from somewhere, like the earth moving.

The noise began to rise in pitch. The boxes let out more and more red light.

'My lord,' said Araboam. 'How know you so much about this infernal building?'

'The Higher is most gracious!' cried Zaitabor. 'Have you no faith?'

At that Araboam lapsed into worried silence.

Cosmae watched the red lines on the metal cubes get longer and longer.

Jamie heard a sad voice at his shoulder. 'Hello, Jamie. You seem to be a natural marksman.'

Jamie turned, managing a smile in spite of the stench of death. 'I've never picked up one of these things before.'

'Try this,' said the Doctor, offering Jamie the weapon that he had carried with him. 'Fire once at every Mecrim that you can. I think most of them are here now.'

Another flight of Taculbain had been killed. The Mecrim – Jamie lost count how many there were – began to stalk forwards again.

Jamie had seen Redcoats carrying rifles and felt a little more comfortable with the weapon the Doctor had given him. He placed the stock into his shoulder, and closed his left eye. A few moments later he squeezed the trigger.

Nothing happened. The least Jamie was expecting was a small explosion like that which destroyed the Furnace.

'I was sure I hit it!' he exclaimed, turning to the Doctor.

'You did,' said the Doctor. 'Look!'

A couple of Mecrim were already attacking their companion, severing limbs like children picking legs off an insect.

'Now,' said the Doctor. 'Keep firing, one per creature.' Jamie glanced over his shoulder as the Doctor moved back to where Zoe and the twins stood, arms around each other's shoulders, faces wet with tears.

Gritting his teeth, Jamie stared back at the Mecrim that stood in front of piles of corpses. He fired the gun again. And again. And again.

The building was ablaze with light and rumbled with what sounded like thunder. 'A glorious sound!' exclaimed Zaitabor. 'The sound of destruction, the warning-note that will be heard by all who have meddled with science.'

'Stop!'

Cosmae turned towards the voice but was pulled harshly across the room to Zaitabor's side. A knife appeared at his throat. He was just able to turn his head to see the homunculus walking into the room. Araboam's mouth dropped open with surprise.

'Stop,' repeated the homunculus. 'Return all controls to their initial settings. If you bring all systems on-line then there will be a massive explosion.'

Zaitabor laughed. 'There will? Good. I thought as much.'

'I have been ordered to stop you.'

'Really? That pesky Doctor fellow still trails my shadow. And what will you do?'

'I shall use the minimum force necessary. But if you do not stop I shall use force.'

'Make me,' said Zaitabor, turning his back to the tall grey figure. The knight casually operated some controls.

Cosmae watched the homunculus walk across the room.

'Come any closer,' said Zaitabor, holding the knife to Cosmae's throat again, 'and I shall kill the boy.'

The homunculus stopped, confusion audible in its voice. 'The Doctor has ordered me not to endanger life.'

'Good,' said Zaitabor. 'Now that I have your co-operation, tell the Doctor that none of us will survive the retribution of the Higher!'

Cosmae stared at Araboam, hoping for some hint of rebellion, but his eyes were glazed.

'I shall contact the Doctor,' said the homunculus.

'I'm sorry you had to see more death and destruction,' said the Doctor.

'It's real, it happens,' said Zoe simply.

'Will it soon be over?' asked Raitak.

'I think not,' said the Doctor. 'We still have a most unusual madman on the loose.'

As if on cue there was a shrill noise from the Doctor's pocket. Defrabax sighed sadly but said nothing.

The Doctor rooted through his clothing for the communications device and switched it on. The picture cleared to show the android in the power station control room. The Doctor stared down at the little screen in the communications unit, watching Zaitabor who stood just behind the android.

'Doctor, I have failed,' reported the android. 'I have been unable to prevent the –'

'Move away, machine!' shouted Zaitabor, walking forwards, dragging Cosmae behind him and still holding a dagger to his neck. 'Greetings, Doctor.'

'Hello, Zaitabor. At least, I assume that's you and not some clockwork toy.'

'No tricks now, Doctor. It is I, Zaitabor, humble instrument of the Higher.' The little figure on the comms unit stared defiantly upwards.

'Murderer of a civilization would be a more appropriate epitaph,' snapped the Doctor.

'I would not expect one so steeped in evil to understand the mysterious ways of the Higher.'

'I suppose nothingness is rather mysterious, in an empty sort of way,' said the Doctor. 'That's what you'll usher in if you operate all the power station's systems.'

'Indeed, Doctor. I find the prospect thrilling!'

'I wonder why,' said the Doctor. 'In fact, I have many questions to ask you. For example, why do you know so much about science? Few people could switch a nuclear power station back on, even if they were following Defrabax's instructions. And how did you create the clockwork version of yourself?'

'To defeat an enemy you must know your enemy.'

'Then perhaps you can answer this simple question. Who are you?'

'I am Zaitabor, acting Grand Knight, faithful follower of the ways of Kuabris and Rexulon.'

'Really? Then who are your parents?'

Zaitabor looked puzzled. 'I . . . I don't remember my parents.'

'Why?'

'I don't . . . I'm not sure.'

'For a man claiming to be tapped into a divine power, you don't know a great deal,' said the Doctor. 'Shall I tell you who you are?'

'No, I must destroy this –'

'Listen to me!' The Doctor's voice carried great conviction, even over the flickering comm link. 'Many, many years ago a Mecrim gut microbe was accidentally released into the atmosphere, resulting in a virtual plague. Almost the entire civilization was wiped out. However, some humans survived, developed resistance to the disease, and over the centuries their descendants spread out over the entire world. It's not surprising that the city that formed over the top of the older, more advanced one would be so afraid of science. A deep fear of what had happened was passed down from generation to generation. Whoever Kuabris and Rexulon were – if indeed they existed – they were certainly aware of the fear that technology engendered in them.'

'Your casual blasphemy will be –'

'But you, Zaitabor,' said the Doctor, his voice quelling

even the knight's outrage. 'You are not one of those descendents.'

'Then who do you say that I am?'

'You arrived on this planet a very long time ago. Your job was to report on the research that was being carried out here. You overstayed your welcome and contracted the disease. Desperate to survive, you abused your position. You made sure that you would survive, even if everyone else died. The surgeons literally hacked out the infected tissue and stuck in cybernetic parts. All your sytems, including your brain, were given electronic backups in case of further degeneration. Then you tried to flee in a shuttle craft, taking with you a single Mecrim specimen in a cryogenic casket. For some reason there was an explosion. The cybernetic and computer systems ensured your survival, but only by causing a shut-down that lasted for centuries. Over time the automatic systems replaced damaged parts and rid you of every hint of infection. You were a guinea-pig in an advanced self-replicating cybernetic experiment, and you outlived the scientists who operated on you by hundreds of years.'

'This is ridiculous!'

'There was, however, a problem,' continued the Doctor with scarcely a breath. 'I can only guess that the software to control the brain was almost entirely wiped by the explosion. The microprocessors were built to learn, to adapt – but the only thing they remembered was that technology and science were, in some indefinable way, *evil*.

'You awoke in mental darkness and confusion, and sought meaning and identity in the nearest inhabited place. You insinuated yourself into society, and took on the role that most suited you – that of a Knight of Kuabris. You doubtless learnt quickly, rising through the ranks, but never speaking of your past – because you haven't got one.

'I can only guess what happened next, but no doubt you found yourself being drawn to those few Kuabris texts that remained from the previous Grand Knight. Before Himesor was made Grand Knight you had already stolen one of the holy robes. Some semi-dormant computerized memory told you that the suit would offer protection against the deadly gases of the sewer. Over a period of time you – and others – discovered various entrances to this submerged city that avoided the sewers. The irony is you needn't have bothered.'

The Doctor paused, aware for a moment of the sounds of the Mecrim fighting each other. For the first time he could see the lights of the power station somewhere in the distance.

'You see, Zaitabor,' said the Doctor, staring down at the unit in his palm, 'you aren't human.'

Nineteen

'Your words are meaningless,' said Zaitabor, 'You speak the unintelligible sounds of science and expect me to –'

The Doctor stared at the small image of the man in the palm of his hand. 'Really? Are you sure that you do not understand me? Tell me, what are your earliest memories?'

There was a faraway look in Zaitabor's eyes, his words stumbling. 'Nothingness . . . Then the ability to grapple with the void, giving it definition, knowing that by being able to assign a word to my condition I must be alive . . . Then a rush of input, raw data, so much I could not put words to. Darkness again, and then a gradual letting-in of information. Surroundings, distinct from me, distinct from the receding darkness at the core of my being. Realizing that there were things beyond me, that I was a unit in a sea of data . . . Seeking definition from surroundings, from other units. Understanding life.' Zaitabor's face hardened in an instant. 'I remember nothing of my childhood. My first memory is offering myself to the Higher and the wisdom of the way of Kuabris.'

'You had no childhood!' said the Doctor. 'At least, not in this life.'

'I am a man!'

'You can fool yourself, but you cannot fool your own augmented biology. Have you ever been ill? Have you ever felt tired? How much of your humanity is a clever, randomized program, with hungers, desires and dreams put on for show, disguising the emptiness of your soul?'

'This is a mere distraction,' said Zaitabor, turning away. 'You are trying to confuse me, to thwart the Higher's great plans.'

'I've seen the image of the man you once were. You look a little better for the weight you've lost, but you have the same diseased mind.'

'I shall initiate the final sequence,' said Zaitabor. 'The core will overload.'

'Where did you learn such words?'

'I am not justifying anything to you!' screamed Zaitabor. 'This dark city will be destroyed!'

The Doctor sighed. 'I had hoped to reason with you, but it seems that you find this particular human concept alien. Still, one way or another, I shall stop you,' he affirmed.

'Any attempt to stop me will result in the boy's death,' said Zaitabor, pulling Cosmae back into the picture.

'Who will die when that reactor goes up anyway,' said the Doctor.

Zaitabor pressed the knife hard into the young man's throat. 'You want to see him die now?'

'No,' said the Doctor. 'I promise that the android will make no moves against you.'

'And yourself?'

'I never make promises I can't keep,' said the Doctor, flicking off the comm unit. He turned to Jamie, Zoe and the others. 'I've got one chance to get rid of the remaining Mecrim,' he said, 'and stop the power station exploding. But I'll need something that can get me to the power station fast.'

'I've seen lots of old fliers and hover vehicles around the city,' said Zoe. 'I'll try to restart one of those.'

'Good,' said the Doctor. 'Do you think you could

bring one back in, say, five minutes? Take Jamie with you.' He pointed towards the far end of the park. 'I'd suggest going in that direction. It looks like the Mecrim will stay here for a while.'

'We'll be back as soon as we can,' said Jamie, following Zoe.

'And what are you going to do?' asked Defrabax.

The Doctor glanced in the direction of the Mecrim. There were about fifteen of the creatures still standing, and they tore into each other with unquenched aggression. Heads were crudely hacked off, legs snapped, rib-cages shattered. The edge of the park was a grisly blur of movement, watched by shocked Dugraqs and hovering Taculbain.

'The Mecrim are attracted to large animals, as the twins found out,' he said, nodding in their direction. He pointed to his gun. 'With this we were able to fool a number of Mecrim into attacking their own kind. Now, I'm going to reprogram the entire gun and the last cartridges it contains. I want it to give off the heat signature of a boiling blue whale. And then I'm going to lead the last Mecrim to their doom.'

'We have a legend of such a man, who mesmerized verminous beasts and led them to the sea,' said Defrabax. He caught the Doctor's eye. 'But now is probably not the time to recount it,' he added hurriedly.

Zoe and Jamie ran across the muddy plain that was once the park's playing fields. 'There's one,' said Zoe, pointing to a flat area of concrete. It still bore the faint lines of parking spaces, although in the semi-darkness they resembled strange geometric shapes unearthed by an archeological dig. A single metallic-blue object sat in one of the bays.

'And you're expecting to get one going after all this time?'

'If they were well designed, there's no reason why not,' said Zoe. 'Whatever geological or other processes covered this city seem to have preserved its contents reasonably well.'

Zoe ran up to the machine and within moments had lifted the covers from the engine housing.

'Where are the wheels?' asked Jamie.

'There aren't any,' said Zoe. 'It floats over the ground.'

'Oh,' said Jamie. 'I see.' He ran his hands over the windscreen and the faded seats, then opened a door to look at the cockpit controls. 'Do you want me to press anything?' he asked hopefully, eyeing the switches and dials.

'Not yet,' mumbled Zoe, holding a number of rubber-coated wires in her teeth.

'Well, I'll get in, just in case,' said Jamie, slipping in behind the steering wheel. 'I've always fancied driving one of these things.'

'One of what things?'

'One of these. Whatever it is. Does it work like the jeeps we saw when we battled the Cybermen?'

'This is much more sophisticated,' said Zoe proudly, replacing the engine coverings. 'Quite long-lasting, too.' She jumped into the seat next to Jamie's. 'Not bad for a soft-top family model.'

'Aye,' said Jamie knowingly. 'Not bad.'

'I've had to by-pass all non-essential circuitry – lights, electric windows, that sort of thing.'

'Right.'

'And there's about ten minutes' power left in the emergency cells.'

'Ten minutes. That's good. Now, which button do I press?'

'That one.'

The vehicle began to lift off from the ground, Jamie grinning brightly the whole time.

'Now,' said Zoe. 'Press that to disengage the parking lock, and this to go forwards.'

'You sure?'

'I think so,' said Zoe. 'I've never actually seen this model before.'

The hover vehicle shunted backwards slightly, bumping into something. Zoe turned to look behind. 'I don't remember there being a wall –'

A Mecrim stood behind them, its claws already deep into the plastileather back seats.

Zoe screamed and Jamie thumped the controls until the craft shot forwards. The rear end scraped along the rushing ground as the Mecrim struggled to climb in.

'Faster,' said Zoe. 'Faster!'

'I'm trying,' said Jamie.

The hover vehicle shot over the park like a dart through the air. Jamie was thankful that he hadn't yet been called upon to steer or stop. He pressed another switch, hoping to increase speed still further, and succeeded only in causing the left side to tilt towards the ground.

'Turn that off!' snapped Zoe.

The Mecrim's long arms were reaching out towards them, scrabbling at the back of their seats. Jamie felt a claw rake down his back and bit his tongue against the sudden stinging pain, edging forwards in his seat. 'There's a gun in my belt,' he said, swerving the flier around a tree.

Zoe grabbed at the revolver and turned in her seat, her hands shaking with unfamiliarity and fear. She pointed the business end in the rough direction of the creature and pulled the trigger.

There was a loud crack. She estimated that she'd missed the Mecrim by several metres.

She tried again, gritting her teeth and narrowing her eyes. This time she had the satisfaction of seeing the bullet thud into the beast's chest, but it seemed to make no difference.

'Hang on,' said Jamie. 'Let's try something else.' He began to rotate the wheel from side to side. A couple of times the pitching vehicle hit the dried mud beneath them, gouging furrows in the earth and threatening to topple over.

Still the creature clung on, its long legs seeking to push it further into the machine.

Jamie scanned the controls in front of him, trying to make sense of the pictograms and symbols. 'This looks interesting,' he said, pushing another switch.

There was a whining sound from the rear of the vehicle, metal arms and clear plastic rising into position. As the roof tried to swing upwards it pushed at the Mecrim, which started to lock its primitive arms around the frame.

Jamie pulled down hard on the steering wheel and the roof mechanism shrieked. There was a thump and the Mecrim was gone, tumbling along the ground.

Zoe turned back and slumped in the seat, breathing heavily. They were approaching the Dugraqs and the main battle site.

'I didn't disconnect the roof,' she said, as it grated into position around them, 'because I didn't think anyone would be stupid enough to want to use it.'

Jamie grinned.

'Thank you, anyway,' said Zoe.

Jamie began to angle the hover vehicle towards the very recognizable form of the Doctor.

'Oh, and Jamie?'

'Yes?'

'You do know how to stop this thing, don't you?'

Defrabax and the twins walked around the parked vehicle. 'That's quite something, isn't it?' said the mage.

'It would make a fascinating exhibit,' said Raitak.

The Doctor bustled back towards the vehicle, Jamie and Zoe in tow. 'Now, I suggest you all get well away from here. When I activate this gun the Mecrim will think that a huge creature has just hoved into view. They'll stop attacking each other and, with any luck, follow me all the way to the power station.'

'You must let us come with you,' said Jamie.

'No, it's much too dangerous. There have been enough deaths already, and frankly I'm worried enough about Cosmae. You two stay here with the Dugraqs. You've provided me with all that I need.'

'You know how to drive it?' asked Zoe.

'I taught Jamie everything he knows!' said the Doctor proudly. He jumped in behind the steering wheel. 'I've heard the 603 is quite something. Stand back!'

With that he operated the vehicle's hover mechanism, and then pulled the trigger on the gun. A heat-haze immediately surrounded him in the cockpit.

The Mecrim turned from their personalized massacre and looked up. As one they charged towards the Doctor's flier, tumbling over each other in the excitement. Zoe had never seen them move so fast.

The Doctor rotated the vehicle on the spot, and then sped off into the distance. The Mecrim ran right past the Dugraqs, Taculbain and humans, and were soon lost from sight in the streets of the old colony.

The Doctor glanced between the rear vehicle sensor array, showing multiple blips of pursuing Mecrim, and the computerized bar graph that showed his diminishing speed and power. 'Not far to go,' he said, staring at the approaching power station. 'Just don't let me down now.'

He looked behind just in time to catch a Mecrim making an optimistic leap towards the back of the vehicle. Its claws fell well short, and it collapsed beneath the charging feet of its companions. Moments later it was back in the pack, running at full speed.

A large metal gateway appeared before the Doctor. Had he come this way before? The Doctor never found out if there was a sensor in the gate to facilitate opening as the flier smashed straight into it and careered towards the main reactor building.

Clutching the gun to his chest the Doctor slowed the hover vehicle and then jumped out of the door. He was aware only of the hardness of the ground as he hit it, and the wave of heat that crashed over him as he rolled.

He staggered to his feet, one shoulder feeling very bruised. The Mecrim had come to a halt some yards away from where the hover vehicle had hit a wall. They were confused, but it wouldn't last long. Soon they'd discover that the flames weren't a living creature.

The Doctor ran towards a doorway into the building. It slid open as he approached, the noise making the Mecrim turn. He had to ignore them now, just trust his luck and his judgement.

He ran towards the control room, still holding the gun to his chest. The metal was beginning to blister under the immense heat that was being discharged. The Mecrim were grunting behind him, their feet hammering on the floor – but above even this the ominous groaning of the generators could be heard.

The corridor seemed to stretch for ever, the pursuing Mecrim sounding ever-louder behind him, but the Doctor knew that his emotionally heightened perceptions were not to be trusted. In a rush the control room appeared before him.

The door opened. The Doctor took in the scene in an instant, the android motionless in the corner of the room, Araboam standing behind a shivering Cosmae, glancing nervously towards his lord, and Zaitabor himself sitting at a terminal. His hands were flickering over the keyboard, the screen a mass of red warning signals. He turned at the expected intrusion. 'Too late, Doctor.'

With no time for words or thought, the Doctor flung the red-hot rifle at Zaitabor and hurled himself to the floor. He felt the rush of the Mecrim as they dived over him and arced through the air, claws and mouths snapping, thrusting their brothers to one side as they fought to attack the huge, mysterious creature first. The silver-grey Mecrim hit Zaitabor just as he stabbed the last button.

The room exploded in an enveloping, shattering red heat.

Twenty

Jamie and Zoe were still some distance from the power station when they felt the explosion and saw the flames stab through the windows. Without a word they started running.

Zoe knew that somehow the Doctor had done enough to prevent the explosion of the entire power plant: the fact that they were alive was proof enough. But what had happened?

After what seemed like an age they found themselves running along the corridor towards the control room. Part of the ceiling had collapsed, and Jamie had to help Zoe over the rubble. Beyond that a huge metal beam had fallen against the control room entrance, but Jamie was in no mood to be stopped. He heaved at the post until the door was cleared, and then dropped to his knees to move the debris away from the door. The opening mechanism alternately groaned and sighed, Zoe tugging at the door until it finally started to move.

They darted through the gap and saw two storeys of rubble covering the room, the computers and chairs lost beneath a new landscape of stone and pipework.

In the corner an arm protruded from a pile of small grey bricks. Jamie ran to it and tugged it free from the rubble. Nothing was attached to it, the stump terminating in wires and hydraulic tubes. Jamie kicked more of the bricks away with his boots until the smashed face of the android was revealed, a mock-human visage visible beneath a feeble mask. A voice crackled from somewhere in the android's throat, but the lips had stopped moving. The eyes were closed, as if in sleep. 'Thank God for that. I thought that –'

The android didn't speak again.

'Jamie, over here,' called Zoe. She was knee-deep in loose rubble, throwing great chunks into the air with her hands. Jamie ran to her side, pulling free the half-covered body. It was Cosmae, white with dust, a huge gash across his face. He looked feverish, his eyes darting from side to side.

'Stay with him,' said Jamie. 'I'll look for the Doctor.' He began picking his way more carefully over the debris.

Someone was coughing to Jamie's right. He ran to the spot, and saw a small figure emerging from a tangled mess of table legs and computer parts.

'Doctor!' exclaimed Jamie. 'You're all right.'

'Yes, thank you, Jamie,' he said, wiping his hands on a large blue handkerchief. 'I think I'll survive.'

'And Zaitabor?'

'He and the Mecrim took the full force of the blast.' The Doctor pointed towards the largest pile of blackened stonework. 'I'll explain later. Are you and Zoe all right?'

'Aye, we're fine. I think Cosmae's been badly injured, though.'

'Let's have a look at him, then,' said the Doctor, nimbly moving over the jagged concrete blocks.

Zoe was sitting at the young man's side, holding his pale hand. Cosmae's eyes were now half-closed. The Doctor put a hand to his forehead, and then felt for a pulse. 'His heartbeat is very weak,' he whispered.

'You're safe now, Cosmae,' said Jamie. 'Just don't give up.'

They watched over the boy for some time. Zoe knew his legs or even his back could be broken, but it was impossible to tell and she had no desire to aggravate his injuries. Occasionally he cried out, and the Doctor and Jamie held him as firmly as they could to prevent him from hurting himself on the rocks. But it was clear that the light of life was fading from his eyes.

A few minutes later the Doctor stood up and breathed heavily. Zoe sat and stared at the boy's face, her mind numb. 'The Taculbain and Dugraqs will be here soon,' she said quietly. 'The old man will doubtless arrange the funeral.'

Jamie stood up, his teeth clenched.

'I'm . . . sorry.' The voice came from the far side of the room, the speaker stumbling over the inadequacy of the words.

Jamie turned and saw the bruised form of Araboam stumbling towards them over the shifting debris. His armour was dented and scratched, and blood was trickling from a wound in his side.

Jamie ran towards him and grabbed his arms. 'You're *what*?' he shouted.

'I must have been mad,' said Araboam. 'I've fallen so far from what once I believed.'

Jamie shook the knight like a rag doll. 'You were involved in all this! So you should have died, not Cosmae!'

Araboam began to say something, but for the second time that day Jamie clubbed him to the ground. He fell on to the unresisting body, still punching feebly at the man's head. 'It should have been you,' he said, as the tears finally came. 'You're the one who should have died.'

The Doctor and Defrabax were talking outside the ruined power station. They were the calm centre in a storm of activity as Dugraqs rushed to and fro, clearing the control room of rubble to ensure that all the Mecrim were dead.

'So what happened?' asked Defrabax.

'When I asked the android to pursue Zaitabor I also wanted to make sure that no one would tamper with the power station. Some explosives were installed that would trip in just before the main generating system went critical.' The Doctor looked slightly apologetic. 'I meant to warn everyone about their existence, but it seemed to me that only a madman would try to use the power plant again.'

'And that's what happened.'

'Yes. When I realized that Zaitabor was going to use the power station to destroy the entire city I hoped that perhaps the smaller explosives would take care of the remaining Mecrim too. I was very lucky, and it worked.'

'What danger were we in from the Mecrim creatures?'

'It's difficult to say,' said the Doctor. 'If they were to become established in an area and begin to breed then your entire world might have been in serious trouble. In any event a lot would have depended upon the co-operation of the various societies on the surface.'

'Our world is very fractured, very insular,' said Defrabax. 'I hope that one day we shall all mature.'

'The other danger was the plague,' said the Doctor. 'I'll run some tests to make sure that you're not in any danger. And I'll check up on Jamie and Zoe when we return to the TARDIS.'

'TARDIS?'

'My vehicle,' said the Doctor.

'Then you'll be leaving us soon?'

'Yes,' said the Doctor. 'There's always work to do somewhere else.'

Defrabax looked around him at the city of miracles again, still scarcely believing his eyes. 'I can guarantee that for weeks to come I will dream of nothing but the other lands and worlds that you have seen.'

The Doctor clapped Defrabax about the shoulders. 'Never lose your dreams,' he said. 'But in future try to dream in patience, there's a good fellow.'

'Wise words. If I had been more patient perhaps Cosmae would still be alive.'

'You don't know that for sure.'

'No. But I feel that I contributed to the lad's death. His mother will sleep less soundly in her grave tonight.'

'I sent Jamie up to explain things to Kaquaan,' said the Doctor. 'Told him that'd be more constructive than beating Araboam to a pulp.'

Defrabax nodded. 'I gave him directions to my house. If she isn't there now, she will be soon. Although she hardly knew him a couple of days ago, terrible events do draw people together. I hope she'll get over the shock and the sadness.'

'Victory is often laced with tragedy and grief,' said the Doctor. 'The sadness of triumph is a feeling that I know only too well.'

'It sounds to me as if you need a holiday,' said Defrabax.

The Doctor smiled. 'They rarely work out as planned.'

'Then perhaps you've been travelling too long. It's time to journey home.'

'No,' said the Doctor firmly. 'That at least is out of the question.'

Defrabax turned towards the power station. 'I must attend to Cosmae's body,' said Defrabax. 'Please excuse me.'

The Doctor nodded and thrust his hands into his pockets. He stood alone, staring at the dark canvas of the city's shadows.

Jamie pushed open the front door of the house and saw the young woman sitting at the bottom of the stairs, her head in her hands. She glanced up, smiled in recognition – and then saw the look on Jamie's face. 'What's happened?'

'It's all over,' said Jamie. 'Zaitabor is dead, and your city is safe.'

'And Cosmae?'

Jamie sat down next to Kaquaan and placed an arm around her shoulder. 'He died in the explosion. I'm sorry.'

Kaquaan blinked back the tears. 'I . . . I wasn't able to rescue him again.'

'Zaitabor threatened to kill Cosmae to stop the android attacking him. But his death wasn't in vain.'

'Oh, Jamie, but it was. So futile! I hardly knew him, but he charged after me all the same.'

'I think Defrabax asked him to –'

Kaquaan wasn't listening. 'I've coped with too many deaths in my life! When will it end?'

'It ends now,' said Jamie, knowing that he was saying the first thing that came into his head. 'You'll see.'

'Everything sunny from here on? I don't believe it. I just don't believe it any more . . .' She started crying, and buried her head in Jamie's shoulder, turning Cosmae's name over and over on her lips like an evocation.

Jamie patted her back awkwardly. 'It's all right, my wee lassie. Things'll be better now. You'll see.'

A sort of silence drifted over the old man's house, and for a long time Jamie just stared into space, struggling with his own feelings of anger and sadness and not knowing how best to comfort the young woman.

'Stay with me for a few days,' mumbled Kaquaan through the tears. 'Please.'

'Well, I expect the Doctor will be keen to go. He usually –'

'Please.'

'Aye, well, the Doctor said he wants to do some tests, make sure I've not caught the disease. I suppose we could stay, just for a day or two.' He stroked the woman's hair. 'Aye, of course we'll stay.'

'I'd nurse you if you were ill,' said Kaquaan, forcing a smile. 'You too were very valiant in coming to my rescue.'

'Ah, well, I often rescue damsels in distress,' said Jamie.

Kaquaan ran a hand through her hair. 'Most have long, flowing locks, I'm sure.'

'Maybe. But Cosmae thought the world of you. And I think he was right to.'

Kaquaan blew her nose on the sleeve of her blouse. 'Things seemed so very different when I first came into this house. So much has changed – and so much that might have happened has been snuffed out.'

'Aye. Well, I'd better be getting back to the Doctor. There's a lot of things to –'

Kaquaan grabbed Jamie's face and kissed him on the lips. 'I don't care how embarrassed you are,' she said, noting his flushed cheeks. 'You'll stay with me for a while.'

Her tone of voice indicated that further argument would not be tolerated.

Epilogue

'This is it?' said Defrabax, pointing to the tall blue box in the alleyway. A broken gutter was dripping water on to its roof, and some street urchins had left a pile of scavenged bricks against its side. 'You travel to the stars in this?'

'Never trust appearances,' said the Doctor. 'You of all men should know that.'

'The next few days will seem very quiet,' said Defrabax.

'That's no bad thing,' said the Doctor. 'You must use your new influence wisely. Captain Oiquaquil will need all the help he can get if he is to negotiate successfully with the Rocarbies and the Dugraqs.'

'Rest assured we will do all we can to accommodate the creatures from the menagerie who wish to emerge into the light,' said Defrabax. 'That has always been my intention. And those who wish to stay below ground – like the Taculbain – we shall strive to protect.'

'And the people of your city?'

'We will I am sure improve things – but the impetus, the desire to change, the technology will be ours.'

'A tutor of mine once said that sometimes it is more important to strive than to achieve. Dull chap, full of clichés. But perhaps he spoke the truth.'

'We shall see. Will you ever revisit us?'

'Ah,' said the Doctor, rubbing his chin. 'That's beyond my control. But if we ever come here again . . . I'll know which public houses to avoid.' He turned to look down the street. 'Where are those two?'

'Dawdling with the freedom that only youth allows,' said Defrabax. 'I sense that you, Doctor, are far older than you seem.'

'When one passes the big three-oh-oh one doesn't discuss such things,' replied the Doctor sniffily.

Jamie and Zoe walked towards the TARDIS, followed by Kaquaan, the twins and the Dugraq scout.

'Have the days really passed so quickly?' said Reisaz.

The Doctor smiled. 'The calm after the storm. Anyway, I expect Raitak is itching to get back and sort out the circus.'

'The thought has crossed my mind,' said Raitak. 'Real life beckons. But I shall miss you, Madam Zoe.'

'The Freak Show will never be the same again,' said Reisaz with a broad grin.

'Goodbye,' said the Doctor, shaking their hands. 'It sounds like Diseaeda was, in his own way, a fine man. I'm sure you'll keep his principles alive.'

The Dugraq bowed before the Doctor. 'Thank you, Traveller. You have done good things for our world.'

The Doctor reached down to pat the creature on the head. 'I was given a good deal of selfless help.' He turned to Kaquaan. 'I'm sorry to have to take Jamie away from you, but the time has come to continue our journey.'

Kaquaan smiled. 'I know.' She turned to Jamie, hugging him. 'Just think of me when you rescue all those other women.'

Jamie emerged red-faced from the embrace, studiously avoiding Zoe's amused look. 'Aye, well . . .'

Zoe shook hands with the twins and stepped into the TARDIS. 'Goodbye,' she said.

The Doctor followed her in, trying to prevent Defrabax from seeing too much of the TARDIS interior. 'Goodbye all. Do come along, Jamie.'

Jamie waved from the doorway, and then the little door closed.

Defrabax walked up to the box and ran an inquisitive hand over its surface. He could hear the voices within above a low, resonant hum.

'So, Jamie, what have you been doing for the last three days?'

'You can refuse to answer her questions if you wish.'

'Och, now you're both laughing at me.'

'I'm sure it was all perfectly innocent. Doctor, that's the wrong control.'

'Is it? Oh yes, you're right. I was just thinking about the spirit of trans-racial cooperation that Defrabax and the others have shown. I wonder how long it'll last.'

Zoe's reply was lost as the machine began to groan and shake. Defrabax immediately darted away from the craft. As he did so it faded from his eyes with a grating sibilance. The flashing light on top of the box left a slight imprint on his eyes, but soon that too disappeared from view.

Defrabax blinked in surprise. Still, this wasn't the strangest thing he'd seen recently and, in any case, he had his reputation to think of. He turned, finding himself alone with the twins and Kaquaan. He extended broad arms around their shoulders. 'Now then, ladies. I've not frequented the taverns of this part of the city for many a fine year, but fidelity to the wishes of my beloved Cosmae requires us to have a quiet drink of contemplation and celebration.' He steered them gently along the street. 'I think I know just the place . . .'

Available in the *Doctor Who – New Adventures* series:

TIMEWYRM: GENESYS by John Peel
TIMEWYRM: EXODUS by Terrance Dicks
TIMEWYRM: APOCALYPSE by Nigel Robinson
TIMEWYRM: REVELATION by Paul Cornell
CAT'S CRADLE: TIME'S CRUCIBLE by Marc Platt
CAT'S CRADLE: WARHEAD by Andrew Cartmel
CAT'S CRADLE: WITCH MARK by Andrew Hunt
NIGHTSHADE by Mark Gatiss
LOVE AND WAR by Paul Cornell
TRANSIT by Ben Aaronovitch
THE HIGHEST SCIENCE by Gareth Roberts
THE PIT by Neil Penswick
DECEIT by Peter Darvill-Evans
LUCIFER RISING by Jim Mortimore and Andy Lane
WHITE DARKNESS by David A. McIntee
SHADOWMIND by Christopher Bulis
BIRTHRIGHT by Nigel Robinson
ICEBERG by David Banks
BLOOD HEAT by Jim Mortimore
THE DIMENSION RIDERS by Daniel Blythe
THE LEFT-HANDED HUMMINGBIRD by Kate Orman
CONUNDRUM by Steve Lyons
NO FUTURE by Paul Cornell
TRAGEDY DAY by Gareth Roberts
LEGACY by Gary Russell
THEATRE OF WAR by Justin Richards
ALL-CONSUMING FIRE by Andy Lane
BLOOD HARVEST by Terrance Dicks
STRANGE ENGLAND by Simon Messingham
FIRST FRONTIER by David A. McIntee
ST ANTHONY'S FIRE by Mark Gatiss
FALLS THE SHADOW by Daniel O'Mahony
PARASITE by Jim Mortimore
WARLOCK by Andrew Cartmel
SET PIECE by Kate Orman
INFINITE REQUIEM by Daniel Blythe
SANCTUARY by David A. McIntee
HUMAN NATURE by Paul Cornell

The next Missing Adventure is *System Shock* by Justin Richards, featuring the fourth Doctor, Sarah and Harry.